THE WING THIEF

SAMANTHA ATKINS

SMASH BEAR
-PUBLISHING-

SmashBear Publishing

Office 48276

PO Box 6945

London

W1A 6US

www.smashbearpublishing.com

Or Email:

info@smashbearpublishing.com

To Dylan and Efa, my favourite people. Never lose your imagination

Let me ask you a question. It's a pretty straight forward question, but one that you shouldn't rush to answer. Do you believe in magic?

PROLOGUE

He pushed his way forward through the darkness, trying to ignore the pain in his feet and the ache in his legs.

It'll all be worth it, he thought.

His heels cut against the sharp rocks and the cold bit into his cheeks, but still he kept moving. His hand wrapped tightly around the prize he'd fought so hard to get. Calloused fingers twisted over its edge as he gripped harder, briefly allowing his gaze to drift behind him, hoping to make out their shape as he dragged them through the dark.

It was surprising how many winged creatures there were. It had never been more than a fleeting thought until the day came that he'd needed wings. He knew the truth, though he would never admit it to himself. He knew the types of wings he needed to enact his curse were impossible for him to get. They remained somewhere he could not go.

This pesky ingredient made his revenge so much more difficult. In desperation, he'd decided to compromise. *Perhaps different wings could work?*

With the precision of a maddening mind, he considered every creature with the gift of flight. Picturing all those wings made his insides churn, hatred burning his throat. If he could, he'd destroy them all. He clicked his fingers and bright, red sparks shot out of the tips. He pictured the wings with every click, thought of how it would feel to finally hold them, to finally win.

He had stolen so many wings over time, it became impossible to count. Some had been harder to obtain than others. His favourites were the ones taken while they were sleeping. He'd simply creep in and, with the help of a little magic, whip them off with a swish of his fingers. Others had not been so fortunate. There had been a creature or two that, no matter how persuasive he'd tried to be, would not part with their precious wings. He'd had to get rather firm in those cases. Birds in particular had always been a pain – there was one type that had jewelled feathers all over its body and had been incredibly stubborn. That had been a fight he didn't care to dwell on. As he thought of that time, his fingers briefly touched his right arm, feeling for the scar beneath his clothes.

It seemed a shame - not that he felt much shame - but deep down he'd known with every wing he stole that it wouldn't work.

It had to be a fairy.

But he kept on trying, refusing to admit defeat. Revenge was the only thing that kept him going these days.

A dip in the path brought him back to reality as he stumbled and tripped, all the while trying to protect the wings in his wretched hand.

'Ahhh!' he cried as he fell. 'Can't you give me a little *help?*' he screamed to the trees.

'You know they won't help you,' he spoke out loud to himself and spat on a trunk in response, absentmindedly waving his free hand over his face to rid it of the buzzing critters.

'I've always hated trees,' he snarled, loud enough to ensure that every tree around him heard.

Looking ahead, he was relieved to see he was nearly there. He didn't want to take the wings back to his home, he was always worried an angry creature might follow him and he couldn't have word getting out about where he lived. There were just too many important things kept there.

No, instead he hid what he needed for the test nearby, buried in a small ditch. As he approached, recognising the shapes through the dark, he carefully placed the wings against a nearby rock and then clicked his fingers, allowing light to form between them.

He kneeled cautiously down on the ground, darting his eyes in every direction to ensure he was completely alone. Warily, he pulled his hood tighter over his horrid face and began to claw through the dirt like an animal. Feeling for his things, his hand curled around a small vial and pulled it out of the earth, showing more tenderness towards it than he had for any living creature.

He looked upon the vial and smiled, displaying a mouth full of yellowed teeth – the vial was full and he merely needed to place it against the wings to know whether it would work.

He turned to face the wings, 'time to shine!' he smiled, trying to hide his desperation – deep down he already knew how this would go.

Carefully opening the vial, he placed it next to the wings and allowed their scent to mix with the fumes. Magic can always recognise itself, and wings in particular have a certain magical smell.

Fairies probably smell like vomit, he grimaced.

Nothing happened for a moment. He crouched there with the vial and the wings and waited. He let out a frustrated groan as the fumes leaving the vial changed from transparent to white.

'ARGH!' he screamed, the sound making the trees shake. 'You're supposed to be *red!* Why aren't you *red?*'

Holding his calm long enough to place the lid back on the vial, he stood up. Pocketing it, he stared at the wings, thinking them the most hideous things he had ever seen.

'You're *pathetic,*' he spat at them, 'you can't even do this right, what's the matter with you?'

Head spinning, he began to pace, angrily glaring at the wings balancing innocently against the rock.

Another failure. Maybe it won't ever work.

He shook his head to rid it of his doubts. He reminded himself that it would work - it had to work. If he didn't have his revenge, he had nothing.

Hatred oozed through him - hatred at the wings for wasting his time, at the forest for making things so difficult, and at himself for failing again.

'I NEED A FAIRY!' he hollered, loud enough to rouse every sleeping creature.

He lunged forwards, grabbing at the wings. His fingers tore through them, ripping each feather off one by one. He plucked and pulled, twisting them until they were unrecognisable. Stopping for a moment, he stared at his work – scattered feathers lay everywhere. As he lit up the scene with his fingers, he mused over how depressing they now looked – such vivid shades of blues and purples nestled against the muddy floor.

He glanced towards his pocket that held the vial, 'You think this is bad, just you wait. Just wait and see what happens when I get hold of the fairies.' He brushed his filthy hands against his trousers and patted his pocket. Whistling a tune, trying to ignore the anger inside, he turned from the wings and walked home, not once glancing back over the carnage he'd caused.

1

The Home Tree

There is a land, much like our own, that houses a particularly varied amount of magical and mysterious creatures. These creatures have stayed safe and secret all this time for one very good reason: the land has willed it so. Despite being within the human world, it is so guarded that no mortal could ever accidentally stumble upon it without first seeking it out. Since no human would ever know what they were looking for, its secrets have remained hidden to outsiders for longer than most could care to remember. This land is known as Letherea.

Of all the Letherean creatures, none are quite so proud of their home as a gnome called Grecko and a young fairy named Vista.

When it comes to gnomes, please don't be fooled and imagine them looking the way you have been brought up to think they look. As with everything, fairytales have turned these creatures into something very different indeed. Now, gnomes are not known for their beauty, that much is certainly true. But they are also not known for wearing pointy hats and having long beards.

A true gnome would be difficult to miss, as they are much taller than the majority of Letherean creatures. In the human world their size would be similar to a very tall adult man – this may not seem overly large but, in comparison to fairies and other small creatures, it is very tall indeed. Their limbs tend to be fairly out of proportion with the rest of their body and their arms are likely to drag along the ground as they walk. When matching this with a pair of overly large feet, they can have some problems when it comes to running at any reasonable speed.

Yet a gnome's face, whilst it may not be considered handsome in any way, is a kind and gentle one. They have eyes that can make any creature feel completely safe and secure, and their softly spoken voices are perfect for soothing lost or lonely souls. They have, on many occasions, been described as carers of the forest - looking after whatever needs it most.

Fairies, on the other hand, look very similar to the way humans imagine them to be. They are indeed small (about the size of a child's hand) and exclusively female, with glittering wings that carry them from place to place. This doesn't mean to say that fairies can't walk - they can - it's just that flying is their preferred means of travel. The main difference between true fairies and the fairies that humans typically envision is that true fairies do not possess any real magic of their own. They have magic in their wings that enables them to fly, of course - but that is where their magic ends.

A fairy is also not born possessing wings. They need a few months after entering the world, to develop the strength and courage they need to take that first leap from the Home Tree. A typical fairy is only about the size of a child's hand when her flying day arrives, so as you can imagine, it must be quite a nerve-wracking experience. When the day came for Vista to take her jump she was just four months old.

I should point out that fairies do not age the same way as humans do and at four months Vista was now considered a young adult in her own right.

On the morning of her flight, Vista awoke much earlier than usual. Gingerly, she propped herself up into a seated position, careful not to wake the sleeping fairies around her. She cast her eyes over the room, feeling the urge to take in her surroundings for what felt like the very first time. The Home Tree housed enough beds to hold up to twenty fairies; each bed was carved into the walls, creating small grooves in which they could sleep. The centre of the room was large and spacious, the floor and walls shining a beautiful golden brown. Vista reached out a slender hand and gently stroked one of the many grooves that made up her bed.

For her comfort she had a small, fluffed up pillow and blanket made from the feathers of a wishing bird, so-called due to its rather marvellous knack of granting wishes. These birds are decorated with every colour imaginable so that when they fly across the sky they twinkle with all the colours of the rainbow. Legend tells that if someone were lucky enough to have one perch upon their shoulder, then it had deemed them worthy and would bestow upon them one wish. Vista often dreamed of how this would feel - to be chosen, the fact that her shoulders were much too small for any creature to perch upon hadn't even occurred to her.

She lifted her arms and stretched, her mind a flurry of questions. Vista had always dreamed of the day she would take flight and finally get her wings. She wanted to know everything: how it would feel when the wings were attached, if she would still be able to sleep comfortably, if they would be as magical as she'd always dreamt they would be. She wriggled her back against the blanket, soaking in the feeling of a bare back – after this morning, she'd never know that feeling again.

Smiling to herself, she quietly rose and tiptoed away to the sound of blissful snores.

As she walked towards the kitchen, it was dawning on Vista how she'd spent so long waiting to leave the Home Tree that she had never stopped to fully appreciate the beauty within it. The golden glow of the walls continued as Vista moved away from the bedroom. Each wall shone as though it had just been polished with the finest flower pollen - which it probably had been. It was never surprising to see one or two fairy younglings miserably polishing away after getting into trouble for one reason or another. To the side of the kitchen was the living area, again it was spacious and was the most commonly used room within the Home Tree (fairies taking their lessons and generally congregating within it).

The room had perches carved into the side of it and the floor, rather than being bare like the bedroom, was decorated with a rug made entirely of petals – each petal selected from a different fairy flower. Their entire world existed inside the large tree.

The Home Tree had been around for as long as the forest itself. Its trunk was stronger and more powerful than any other tree to exist – although that could simply be a popular fairy opinion, of course. It belonged to the fairies and existed solely to protect them until they were ready to take flight. Providing them with shelter, warmth and security.

It was a known fact that once a fairy takes her first flight, she does not return regularly to the Home Tree. Fairies are expected to remain nearby, in small communities, and never venture out of their part of the forest; the reason for this is unknown to most, but a fairy knew well to follow the rules and never question the reasons – a trait that Vista seemed to be lacking. She shook her head slightly, not wanting to spend her morning fretting.

The kitchen was empty as she entered, just as she'd expected it to be this early in the morning, but the warm, sweet smell it carried was there. Vista closed her eyes and inhaled deeply, grateful for a rare moment of peace and quiet. Breezing her way over to the hand-crafted shelves she selected what was, in her opinion, the finest looking apple and honeysuckle scone she could find.

Excited by the thought of eating her scone without nineteen other excitable fairies around her, she settled herself down quietly into one of the large perches and stared dreamily out of the window into the forest.

From her position in the Home Tree (it being one of the tallest in the forest) she could see acres of large trees spread out before her, some almost appearing to touch the clouds. They left Vista wondering if it might be possible to climb and touch, or maybe even collect a piece of cloud for her very own. Of course, in Letherea anything was possible.

The trees before her shone a mixture of rich greens and vivid yellows. Fragments of colour came and went, swerving through the leaves – evidence of passing birds gliding through the branches, flurries of colour speckling their every movement. The sun bounced off the treetops but, unlike in the human world, it left behind a trace of glitter – decorating the scenery with flecks of golden dust. A gentle breeze drifted upwards, sending wafts of heavenly flowery scents in Vista's direction, a teasing taste of the beauty that lay beneath her.

The ground of the forest was also something of intrigue; it wasn't like the ground an outsider from our world would understand, solid and unwavering. No, the ground of Letherea seemed almost to have a mind of its own. For example, if you were someone whose intentions were good and true, someone on a quest of some sort perhaps, then the ground would have the ability to assist you on your travels. Now obviously it wouldn't do the travelling for you, but it would do its part to aid you in your walking. Whether that was by making the path easier to find or offering up sweet flower nectar for you to drink - any way it could think of to help ease your tired and weary legs.

However, if you were the type of person whose intentions were not so good (or even downright bad), then you could indeed have a very difficult road ahead of you. The path could seem to stretch until it was all you could see. You could become blinded to everything except your own sorrow, and the weariness of endless walking could be enough to end the journey for some of even the most determined creatures.

A loud thud startled Vista and, with slight disappointment, she realised that her quiet, relaxing morning was over with the arrival of another fairy in the kitchen. Not one to forget her manners, Vista turned to face her company with a smile.

She was greeted by Mila, an overly keen, yet clumsy fairy who was also flying today. The thud Vista had heard had been a pan Mila knocked over during her attempt to sneak in.

Mila was a tiny little thing, the smallest of all the fairies in the tree. Her bed was situated just above Vista's; this in itself seemed like a bit of a design flaw – to have a fairy as clumsy as Mila sleeping on a bed that wasn't directly attached to the ground.

She was probably what humans would describe as the 'typical fairy'. Her skin was pale and her hair was yellow - not blonde as most would assume – but yellow, as if it had been painted. She had a small, dainty frame and wore a dress made from the petals of a luck flower; each fairy wore an outfit made from a certain type of flower. Vista had always envied Mila's luck flower dress, it was so bright, full of vibrant reds and greens, she could be spotted from a mile away. This would no doubt come in handy when she was finally up in the air!

Privately, Vista dreaded the thought of Mila flying; the poor thing could barely walk without tripping over something, so just imagine what it would be like with her up in the sky. There would be branches to avoid and rogue birds to dodge (usually birds made quite good flying companions for fairies, but a fairy with Mila's clumsiness could have a difficult time avoiding their feathery wings). Another worry would be all the fairies at risk of a bump or two if Mila were close by.

Vista's dress was a bit plainer than Mila's. It was more of a sea-blue colour; made from the petals of a water flower, and although it did have a nice way of twinkling and catching certain lights when she moved, she had always secretly wished for something a little brighter. It did, however, compliment her hair quite nicely. She had dark hair, the colour of tree bark. This made her feel like a proper nature fairy, as if the trees themselves had created her.

'Oh gosh Vista, I'm so sorry, I was trying my best to be quiet. Heaven knows how I'll manage to fly today if I can't even walk properly!' Mila squeaked. You didn't have to be a genius to spot that Mila was looking for some reassurance that she wasn't going to fall straight from the tree and splat onto the ground when taking her first flight that morning. Vista felt an obligation to offer some sort of hope - even if that hope might be false.

'Don't worry, flying surely must be more straightforward to us than walking,' Vista offered a reassuring smile.

'Are you nervous about today?' Mila asked, sitting down next to her.

'A little I suppose,' Vista admitted, 'but I've been waiting for this day for so long, I just can't wait to get started.'

Mila considered her answer for a moment. 'What do you think it's like out there? I can't really imagine anything outside the Home Tree,' she wondered as her eyes glazed and drifted towards the window.

Vista smiled briefly, and with only a slight hesitation, indulged Mila with her fantasies about life outside.

'You know, I've heard whispers of just how vast Letherea actually is, but I can't wait to find out for myself. I don't have much intention of finding a home just yet. My plan is to get out of this tree and see as much as I possibly can,' she paused trying to suss out Mila's reaction, which wasn't giving much away. 'I've heard there are rivers filled with fish that not only swim under the water, but can actually fly above it just like us! There are witches and trolls and *real* magic! One thing I know for sure is that the forest is so much bigger than just our Home Tree. I can't wait to get out there and finally be a part of it!' Vista's pulse quickened, the way it often did when she dreamt of adventure. Her grin threatened to split her face in two and she bit down on her lip in a conscious effort to calm herself.

Focusing on Mila again, Vista was slightly surprised to find that Mila wasn't sharing in her excitement at all. Her face looked puzzled and she'd scrunched up her forehead as though trying to figure out the most confusing riddle.

'Surely you can't really mean all that? We mustn't leave our part of the forest, you know that. That's the way it's always been, we're safer here.'

'But *why* has it always been that way? Just because fairies don't break the rules? We're not trapped in this part of the forest, you know. This may be our home, but it should be our choice whether to stay or go.' Vista crossed her arms defiantly, angered by the doubt in her plan.

Why is Mila telling me what to do? She has no right!

Vista's heartbeat thumped in her ears and she willed it away, the feeling of betrayal oozing through her. All Mila had done was make Vista even more determined to do things her way and prove everyone wrong - starting with getting far away from the Home Tree. She was determined to show them all just how far a fairy could go if she just believed in herself.

After some long, awkward moments of silence and uncomfortable looks, the kitchen began to fill with chattering, excitable fairies all eager and ready for the day ahead. Her disappointing conversation with Mila, however, made Vista decide not to indulge anyone else with her plans for after the flight. For that matter, neither did Mila.

As the others hugged and gave their best wishes, Vista returned to pondering the world outside the window, trying to distract herself from her restless legs.

2

New Wings

An hour or so had passed before the bells finally started to chime; it was the fairies' notice that the time for flights was approaching. It's also important to note at this point, that time doesn't work the same way in Letherea – a few hours in the forest would be more like a few minutes to a human. This is why the trees and plants seem to grow at such a speed, and why the fairies and other creatures age so much quicker than the outside world does. Luckily for them, this doesn't shorten their lives in any way as the majority of Letherean creatures tend to live for hundreds of years.

A calm fell over the kitchen as the chatter and giggles subsided. One of the fairies' teachers made her way into the room. Her name was Lilleth, and she was considered to be one of the wisest and most beautiful of all the fairies. Her hair was stunningly white, like fresh snow and sat like a halo above her dark skin. She wore a dress made from the petals of many different types of flowers - it's said the reason for this was due to her being around so long, but no fairy could ever agree upon her exact age. The petals had the charming effect of leaving a perfumed smell in their wake. Whenever Lilleth walked by, the flowery fragrance would follow her.

Lilleth was thought of as mother to the fairies and as such, commanded attention and awe effortlessly the moment she entered a room. She was closely followed by Starla and Greeta, fellow teachers who assisted Lilleth in her tasks and who were never far behind her. Both were equally beautiful, although neither quite as captivating as Lilleth.

'Good morning, my children. I'm glad you're all awake and ready for another momentous day.' Lilleth smiled, greeting the entire room. 'Today, four more of you will take your first flight and set forth to find your new homes within the safety of our forest.' Lilleth turned her attention towards Vista, Mila, and two other fairies due to fly that morning. The other two, Bess and Lorella, were both looking equally nervous and, as with most of the fairies, slightly in awe whilst standing in Lilleth's presence.

'After your flights today you will be on your way to becoming great fairies. Starla, Greeta and I all know how much you are capable of and how well you will flourish within our community. Everything begins with this flight; all you have to do is believe in the power of our family, and believe that whilst alone we may be small, together we are strong. Remembering this is how we remain connected. It's what will help you gain control of your new wings.'

It was interesting to Vista that Lilleth always referred to them as 'her children'. There were rumours that Lilleth had once had a child of her own. A child who, if the rumours were to be believed, had taken a dark path and was not to be spoken of when in her presence. Vista assumed (as most fairies did), that this was just idle gossip.

As Lilleth continued to speak, she presented each of them with a brand-new set of wings ready for their transition into official flying fairies. As Vista's fingers gently reached out to stroke hers, she shivered. They were made of the most magnificent silk known to Letherea, so fine that parts of them appeared almost invisible to the naked eye – even a fairy eye, which is particularly good at spotting the finest details. They were similar in style to the wings of a butterfly, with edges that curved like waves. Their length would stretch over Vista's back and extend outwards from between her shoulder blades, meaning Vista would be able to admire the tops of her wings whenever she liked. The intricacies on their surface enthralled her, calling to her fairy appreciation of beauty. Standing before them, she noted the delicate markings, admired the slight silver sheen that glowed through every swirl and imagined how they might look catching the sun's rays as she flew across the sky.

Wings this beautiful deserve to be seen.

With a shaking hand, she took hold of them and turned her gaze towards Lilleth, waiting for guidance as to how she would attach them to her body.

Lilleth smiled, used to these looks of self-doubt. 'Don't worry, they know what to do.'

Seeming to hear this, the four sets of wings slowly began to rise out of each fairy's hands and float briefly in the air in front of them. They moved with magnificent grace to the backs of each fairy and waited in position.

'Now, the important thing to remember is to relax and let the wings become one with you. They are a part of you and always have been. They will know what to do,' Lilleth reminded them.

A slight warming sensation crept from the base of Vista's spine up towards her neck. Excitement raced through her, and she sternly reminded herself to keep still. She thought back over all the nights spent imagining this moment - wondering what it might feel like, worrying over whether it would hurt. It tickled Vista to picture herself fretting on her bed, seeing now it had all been just wasted energy. There was no discomfort at all. Her nerves left her as she embraced the feeling. Vista's new wings moulded themselves against her, leaving her skin tingling. Within a moment it was done, and the wings and Vista had become one.

'Your wings are a part of you now; as much so as your arm or your leg. Treat them well and they will always look after you.' Lilleth made her way towards each fairy individually, wrapping her arms around them in celebration.

Vista stood, trying to keep from fidgeting. The others stood easily, enjoying the envious looks from the other fairies and welcoming Lilleth's words.

Should I be able to feel them on my back?

Vista wasn't sure how she was supposed to feel at this moment, but she'd always assumed she'd feel... something. She looked over her shoulder at her wings, slightly reassured by the sight of them.

They're attached, stop worrying.

But it wasn't easy. Vista couldn't help but notice that the other fairies wings had begun fluttering slightly as they walked around the room, so why weren't hers?

Maybe they're fluttering but I just can't see it?

She briefly considered asking Lilleth but worried about sounding paranoid. Ultimately, she decided that her wings must be fluttering, they just didn't feel quite like she'd imagined they would.

It must be the nerves.

Turning her attention back to the room, she smiled at the fairies gathering around her.

'We'll find you after our flight!'

'We'll miss you!'

'Don't forget to visit!'

After what felt like an age , it was time for the first fairy to take her flight.

'Bess,' silence fell upon the room as Lilleth spoke, 'you will be our first flight today.'

Blushing with nerves, Bess stepped forward, her wings flexing as she moved.

Spying an opportunity to practise whilst everyone else was distracted, Vista tried flexing her own wings. She wasn't entirely sure how to do it - she'd always assumed it would come naturally, but now she found herself struggling. Scrunching up her fists, Vista thought 'flying' thoughts but her wings didn't move.

They'll move when it's my turn, she tried to reassure herself.

Bess slowly made her way out of the crowd and towards the Home Tree's entrance which was made up of a small circle carved into the side of the trunk. There was no door, simply because there had never been any need for one - the Home Tree was always open to all fairies.

The circle had deep grooves carved into it, creating a pattern of swirls throughout the wood. It led out onto a thick branch. The bark of the branch was dark, as was the outside trunk of the entire tree and rich in colour, smooth and welcoming. During a first-flight day, the branch was surrounded by fairies - all coming to watch the big event. A fairy's first flight was considered a very special day indeed. Fortunately, despite the amount of fairies, the branch was extremely wide. It was so large that even the most nervous of fairies would never need worry that their wobbly legs might send them tumbling off the edge before their time.

Bess placed her right foot firmly onto the branch. Following a brief pause, no doubt testing the strength of the branch, she followed with her left foot.

'Now, Bess, don't forget what we've taught you. Believe in us and believe that we are all connected, and you will be fine.'

Taking one nervous glance back towards the others, Bess's eyes briefly met Vista's. Before she could think of anything to say or do to offer some reassurance, Bess had turned around, stepped away from the branch, and was gone.

Vista's heart leapt into her throat, feeling certain that Bess had failed and was currently plummeting towards the ground. As quickly as she had thought it, her fears were squashed as with incredible ease, Bess emerged before them, the silver swirls in her wings beaming proudly in the early morning sun. Bess was shining, every inch the fairy she was always meant to be.

Cheers and applause erupted from the fairies and Vista held her breath, awed by what she had just witnessed. It had worked! Bess's wings had done exactly what they were supposed to do and so effortlessly, it seemed as if she'd been flying her entire life.

'Well done, Bess! Now, you know what comes next; go forth and find yourself a new home. Be kind, and gentle, and always look out for your fellow fairies. We are always close by should you need us.'

Lilleth was almost shouting this last bit over her fellow fairies' shrieks of delight. Despite her need to shout, the pride in her voice was clear: they really were her children.

Bess's face flushed and she smiled so widely her face seemed unable to contain it. Her goodbyes were brief and before they knew it she was gone, flying away to a chorus of applause and laughter that echoed throughout the Home Tree.

Next up was Lorella. Vista barely blinked as she watched Lorella jump, her new wings carrying her away amongst the clouds. Vista's eyes stung, holding back tears. Two down.

The time had come for Mila's flight. She wasn't sure if she had imagined this part, but Vista was quite certain that the second Mila stepped out onto the branch, the entire colony took a united inward breath.

Mila's eyes moved backwards and forwards, unsure of where to look. Her gaze briefly rested on Vista, and Mila gave the briefest and most anxious looking smile that Vista had ever seen. In return, Vista tried her best 'you can do this' face. There was no question she and Mila had different views on how life should be lived outside the Home Tree, but there had always been something about Mila. Maybe it was her pure innocence that made it impossible to stay upset with her for too long.

Lilleth gave the same encouraging speech that she had given Bess and Lorella; this time, however, with a little more emphasis to ensure that Mila understood. With an uneasy stride, Mila made her way towards the edge of the branch and prepared for her jump. As you can imagine, the nervous energy mixed with the silence that fell amongst the crowd made for an eerie atmosphere. Before anyone knew it, it happened. Mila jumped, and by some miracle her wings proved their worth and lifted her high above the heads of thrilled and relieved onlookers. Applause could be heard for miles around, and even Mila herself had a look of shock on her face with the realisation it had worked. She was now officially a flying fairy!

A calm stillness washed over Vista, and her confidence rose after watching Mila's successful flight.

If she can do it, I can do it, Vista thought.

Vista's freedom hung in front of her like a beautiful temptress as Lilleth gestured to her to come and take her place on the branch.

She tried another wing flutter. *Still nothing.* Walking forward, she focused on trying to keep her smile steady. *They'll work when I need them.*

A realisation crept in that she may never see these fairies again and her smile faltered briefly before she quickly fixed it.

Focus on your freedom, Vista thought to herself. *Think of your adventures.* Exhaling, she concentrated on getting onto the branch without slipping. *One step at a time,* she thought, carefully placing one foot forward. Instantly, Vista was taken aback by how smooth the bark felt beneath her feet. When picturing this moment, the branch had always been rough - but perhaps years of fairies striding across it had caused the path to soften. Despite its worn down smoothness, it felt strong. The Home Tree branch was solid, seeming capable of holding a creature fifty times her size. Lifting her head, she gazed around her. Vista faced the forest, suddenly awed by its beauty. The breeze from the wind brushed lightly against her cheek, carrying with it the scent of flowers from the ground below. Vista inhaled deeply, the air tasted sweet on her tongue.

To her left, she noted half a dozen fairy elders all perched along the branch and acknowledged them with a gracious smile. To think how many times they must have sat and watched these first flights – the number must be astounding. Despite this, they held their smiles and patiently observed Vista as she took in the sights.

To Vista's right, she saw hundreds of different flowers, the sweet scent of each one filling her nostrils. The blue, glistening river was just visible through the mass of trees, and there came a quiet, yet distinct rustling noise from the ground below as Letherea's magical inhabitants went about their daily business. Everything on this branch spelled out one thing for Vista: freedom.

She glanced back, wishing she could feel her wings' reassuring presence and wondered if the others had felt this way before their flight.

The sound of her own name pulled her back to reality with a jolt. 'Vista, you are the final flight of the day. I have no doubt you will do us proud.' Vista struggled to maintain eye contact with Lilleth, knowing just how far away from her family she was actually planning to go. She couldn't bear the thought of Lilleth somehow reading her mind (not an actual fairy ability, more a paranoid fairy's worries). After all, no one likes to let down their mother.

The branch beneath Vista's feet felt sturdy. Never had she appreciated the feeling of a surface more than the moment before she was about to jump off it. The forest floor suddenly seemed very far away. She risked a peek down. She could see the ground, could see the masses of shrubbery surrounding the tree, but it certainly looked much smaller from her height. Nausea swirled in her stomach and her knees trembled slightly.

One last glance towards her well-wishers, and it was clear it was time for her to make her move. Each fairy looked so encouraging and confident that it was nearly enough - just nearly - to convince her that she could do this.

I can do this, I can do this, I can do this.

Vista prayed these words would somehow stick, like a mantra in her brain. With one cautious foot teetering away from the branch, Vista closed her eyes. Taking a deep breath, and without giving herself another second to hesitate, she threw herself forward and leapt into the unknown.

3

***

A Helping Hand

An immense rush of freedom flooded over her the instant her feet left the branch. Unfortunately for Vista, this feeling was fleeting. Within seconds of jumping, it became obvious that her wings - her brand new, beautiful wings - were not quite so trustworthy after all. She screwed her eyes shut and willed them to work; she'd assumed they would connect the moment she jumped. Vista began to panic, bile rising in her throat. She scrunched up her fists and threw her arms in front of her - completely helpless. Her wings were supposed to know what to do.

Work, wings! Why aren't you working? Fly! Fly!

Air caught in Vista's throat and a gargled scream escaped her as she acknowledged the horrifying fact that she wasn't flying, but falling. Falling at an alarming speed. Her chest heaved deep, rasping breaths, and she desperately flailed her arms and legs, trying to climb her way back up through the air to no avail. Above her, the panicked cries of fairies filled the sky, their eyes desperately searching to see where she might land.

She screamed, but only incomprehensible sounds came out as her eyes screwed tightly shut again. Her body fell quickly, clearing the full length of the trunk and crashing roughly through bushes and debris until, with a rather undignified thud, she hit the ground.

What followed, for mere seconds, although in Vista's mind could have stretched out for an eternity, was the kind of stunned silence that tends to follow such a shock. Nothing appeared to move. Nothing made a noise. All Vista could hear was the sound of her own ragged breaths escaping her lips, whilst her heart beat so violently it threatened to burst out of her chest.

Now you must understand that this flight had been all Vista had dreamt about since she first knew how to dream. To fall was, as far as Vista was aware, unheard of within the fairy community. The cold spread through her limbs as she tried to make sense of what had happened. Tears filled her eyes and her body shook as she bit down on her lip, pressing a hand to her mouth to try and stifle her sobs. With great difficulty, she managed to mask the noise from the fairy elders above who were now screaming her name and desperately trying to locate her amongst the bushes. Despite the shock, she was acutely aware that if she were found, she would be taken back to the Home Tree. A fairy who couldn't fly had no fun in life - Vista knew that for a fact.

There had only ever been one other fairy who couldn't fly. It was quite a long time ago and Vista had never actually known her, although from how often she was whispered about she felt as though she had. The situation had been slightly different to Vista's as well (that fairy's wings had been taken from her before she'd even had the chance to jump). Fairies used to wonder how such a thing could have happened, but the fairy elders had kept the specific details to themselves.

Vista only knew a few details. That she had been born from a joy flower (which was ironic considering her sad life) and had stayed in the Home Tree and been taken care of, as is the fairy way, forced to watch as countless flying days came and went. Endless numbers of fairies taking their first flights to freedom, knowing that she would never be able to follow. This thought terrified Vista more than any other. Vista couldn't stand a life where she wasn't able to live free – watching others achieve her dreams of flight whilst she was discussed in hushed whispers. The idea was devastating.

Sitting on the ground debating her options, she began checking herself over for any signs of serious injury. Steadying her breath, she looked down at her hands. They had been resting in what looked a bit like the hazelnut soufflé Mila had attempted to bake that one time (emphasis on attempted), but was in fact a rather large puddle of sticky, gloopy mud. With a pained stare, she moved on and started patting herself down from head to toes until she was satisfied (or as satisfied as she could be in this situation) that there were no visible injuries and she would indeed be able to walk.

The fact that Vista had no serious injuries after a fall this big would seem miraculous for a regular human in the real world, but to a fairy in Letherea it's not all that surprising. The sheer weightlessness of a fairy does tend to work in their favour when it comes to situations like this, their lightness making it highly likely that any injuries are minimal. So as devastating as a fall like this may look, it's merely the equivalent of a feather falling from a tree.

How could this have happened? I can't believe I fell!

A thought hit Vista like a lightning bolt as she prepared to stand – *the wings!* She had forgotten to check her wings. It seemed quite obvious to Vista they were the reason she had fallen. They were clearly faulty. There was no doubt in her mind that there must be some sort of tear on them which had gone unnoticed pre-flight. Some sort of damage that had caused her to be wallowing on the ground covered in sludge, leaves, and dirt, rather than soaring through the sky, tasting freedom and dancing with the birds.

With all the adrenaline currently coursing through her body, it took a great deal of effort to keep her hands steady enough to handle something as delicate as her wings. She reached behind her and awkwardly fumbled her hands up and down over their great length.

To her dismay, the intricate patterns on the surface seemed to be intact. She curved her palms around the beautiful arches they made, and with total devastation found that her wings felt perfect - exactly as she'd always dreamt they would feel.

If my wings are intact then why did I fall? This question would come to haunt Vista's mind for quite some time.

Lost and unsure of what to do next, a sound nearby made her jump in fright. It was a strange rustling sort of noise, as if something was being dragged through the dirt towards her. Squinting, she tried to make out the figure, but it was no use; there were just too many bushes. Before she had time to find a hiding spot or even call for help, the bushes in front of her parted, giving way to a creature much larger than herself. He was so large that from Vista's position on the ground, it was a struggle to see his face properly.

"Ello there!' the figure cried, crouching down. 'Yer look like yer 'ad a mighty big fall then, yer did, are yer alright?'

The creature's voice was loud but gentle at the same time. Vista was relieved to find that, despite his size, he didn't appear to mean her any harm.

When she didn't reply straightaway the creature continued to speak undeterred, 'I reckon yer should do a bit more practising before yer get chucked out o' the tree like that.'

He craned his neck upwards, assessing the height of the fall and tutted. Turning to look down at Vista, he scratched his head with a concerned, fatherly look on his face. The sounds of the fairies desperately crying out for her whirled all around them. 'Aye, do yer want me ter go get 'em? I can tell 'em where yer at? They sound real worried 'bout yer up there.'

Vista was snapped out of her trance. The creature had begun to push himself up from his crouching position and, if he stood up, he'd surely be spotted. The bushes surrounding them were tall, but even they would likely only reach his shoulders. Just as the creature was about to step through and call for the fairies' attention, Vista cried out, pleading with him to stop.

'No please, please don't call them!' she begged in hushed tones. The creature stopped in his tracks and looked down at her. Vista was shamefully aware of what a hopeless mess she must look.

'I'm sorry, but if you call them, then they'll take me back up to the Home Tree and I can't go back there. I've spent every second dreaming about finally being in the forest and going back up there just isn't an option.' She was aware she'd started babbling and sounding a tad dramatic – the sound of her own voice, so whiny and pathetic, almost unrecognisable to her.

She gave the creature a defeated sigh, assuming he would think her mad and no doubt call for help even louder now. With one last shot, Vista looked him straight in the eyes.

'Please, I'm begging you, let me stay down here. My wings may not work but I can walk just fine. I just don't want to live up there anymore – I want to be here, in the forest...' She pushed her chin into her chest as she tried to hide her tears, wanting to maintain some shred of dignity by at least not crying in front of the stranger.

To her surprise, his expression changed from a look of concern to one of pity. He crouched down further and moved his face close to hers. 'Alright miss, I'll help yer, but it don't mean I reckon it's a good idea or nothing. Jus' can't seem ter help meself when I see someone needing help, yer know?'

Vista's relieved expression must have been enough to confirm in his mind he was doing the right thing, because the next thing she knew, she was being scooped out of the dirt by the creature's hand. The rough hand was extremely filthy, it appeared long enough to drag in the dirt as he moved. Lifting her up, he held his hand close to his chest. It swayed slightly as he slouched and walked, despite his obvious efforts to keep it still. Vista gripped his thumb for balance, wrapping both her arms around it. She put all her efforts into remaining upright and squeezed a little harder to avoid falling off. One fall was quite enough for one day.

She turned her attention towards the stranger's face. From where she sat, her main view was a stubbled chin covered in patchy, blemished skin and a protruding nose with wisps of fur-like hair hanging from the nostrils. Hygiene and appearance clearly weren't a priority for this creature. After only ever living amongst fairies who took great pride in their appearance, it was a rather unusual sight to Vista.

As the swaying motion steadied slightly, she cautiously released his thumb and curled up in a ball, bringing her knees to her chest, suddenly very tired. Closing her eyes, she breathed in the pungent, musky aroma no doubt coming from the creature's hand. Trying to move past it, she realised she could also detect other smells and tried to focus on those instead, such as the comforting scent of flowers and leaves as they brushed against her.

Opening her eyes, she watched as the creature turned back towards the magical forest, back the way he came. Vista stared at wild plants of every colour imaginable, each one taller than anything she'd ever seen before. Not too far away came the sound of flowing water.

That must be the river!

Vista made a mental note to herself to come back and search for it the first chance she got. It surprised her how different everything looked from down on the ground. The colours were beautiful – there was no denying that. Yet she was aware that she didn't feel the way she had expected to feel when finally amongst it all. Perhaps it was simply because of the situation she found herself in. She knew the first time she saw it she had expected to be viewing it from above – soaring over the flowers and dipping into the grass, breathing in its earthy smell before flying up again to take in its view from afar. *Why didn't my wings work?*

Abruptly, Vista turned her thoughts back to the beautiful colours – desperate to avoid the crushing disappointment she felt inside. Letherea was surrounding her now. For better or worse, she was leaving the Home Tree.

They continued moving further and further away from where Vista had crash-landed so awfully. Taking a deep breath, she squeezed her eyes tightly shut and tried to block out the faint, distant sounds of fairies still calling her name.

I'm free, she told herself, *this is what I wanted.*

She thought of her freedom over and over again and of the adventures she could still have, pushing any feelings of guilt or worry aside. Looking up again into the creature's face, she focused instead on where exactly he might be taking her.

4

Grecko's Hut

It was almost dark by the time Vista and her new companion finally stopped moving. A gentle nudge to her side from the creature's stub-like finger roused Vista from her troubled sleep. Embarrassed to think she may have been drooling into his hand, Vista quickly wiped at her mouth and propped herself up, stretching out all her limbs in the process.

'Reckon yer must 'av needed some sleep, eh?' he chuckled shyly. With the creature now standing still, Vista was able to study him closer. He was big, but then again there wasn't much that wasn't big in comparison to a fairy. His face was etched with lines, like an old piece of paper that had been crumpled up and then unfolded; each line held a story, a tale of some worry or hindrance that life had thrown his way. His clothes weren't much of anything special: a plain grubby top that hung well below his knees and a pair of ill-fitting trousers that seemed to have been torn at the ankles – most likely his own handy work to enable him to walk without tripping. His feet were bare, but his lack of shoes didn't seem to bother him much; his feet hardened, accustomed to the harsh forest ground. Looking up at him,

Vista noticed that when he smiled, it did wonders for his face - it softened his features. He looked just like the sort of friend a fairy could use in a place like this.

Leaning forward, she awkwardly attempted to return his smile.

'Yes, I suppose I did need some sleep. This isn't exactly how I thought my day would turn out.' Vista blinked away tears, aware of what an understatement that was.

'Aye miss, ain't no need fer tears! I'm 'ere now, I'll look after yer until yer find yer feet...' he paused, fumbling uncomfortably at his own remark, not wanting to come across as insensitive in any way. 'Or maybe it ain't yer feet, but yer wings yer wanna find.'

Hastily, Vista rushed to reassure him, 'Thank you, you're very kind. I honestly don't know what I would have done this morning if it hadn't been for you.'

Truthfully, she wasn't sure what her options would have been, had he not come along. Either she would have had to go into hiding and attempt to figure out life on the ground by herself, or she would have had to return to the Home Tree and face the humiliation of being forever known as 'the fairy who fell'.

A surge of guilt passed through her as she thought of the Home Tree. *The fairies might still be looking for me... Lilleth might still be looking.* Vista imagined how it must be there, no one knowing where she was or if she was hurt. Her eyes pricked with tears and the pain of trying not to cry caused her mouth to dry up. She blinked and told herself that they'd likely be glad she had left, now they didn't have to spend their days caring for a flightless fairy.

Why didn't my wings work? She thought again.

In a panic, she wondered how long they'd been walking, worrying his long arm had gotten sore from being positioned so awkwardly against his chest. 'Oh no, I hope your arm isn't too tired? I know it must be uncomf—' An even worse worry suddenly struck her, 'oh gosh, I'm so sorry, I just realised I don't even know your name?' The rudeness of not asking his name embarrassed Vista greatly. Her fall that morning had caused her to forget all her manners.

A smile broke out on the creature's face and he answered proudly,

'The name's Grecko, little miss, an' I'm very pleased ter meet yer!' He held out a short, stubby finger for Vista to shake; she gave a little giggle as she placed her delicate hands around it. 'An' don't be worrying 'bout me holding yer. I know me arms are a bit long, but it ain't like yer weigh a lot, is it?' he chuckled.

Vista smiled, her first genuine smile since her fall that morning. 'Well, Grecko, my name's Vista, and I'm very pleased to meet you, too.' It surprised her how quickly she felt comfortable in his company.

Glancing around, she found she still had no idea where Grecko had actually brought her. This was a lot of trust to literally place in the hand of a creature whom she had only just met.

'Grecko, where have you brought us?'

'Ha!' Grecko let out a laugh. 'Oh, forgive me, Miss Vista, where is me manners? This is me home, yer welcome ter stay 'ere with me fer as long as yer like.' he said warmly, his generosity and kindness shining through.

'You really are very kind, Grecko. I've heard stories about creatures on the ground who are as generous as you are. I hope this isn't rude to ask, but are you a gnome?'

Standing a little taller, Grecko gave a satisfied nod. 'I am indeed, Miss Vista. One very proud gnome at yer service.'

Impressed she'd figured something out without needing to be told, Vista grinned. 'Well, I'm lucky to have you here, Grecko the gnome. I've heard lots of wonderful things about your kind.' Peeking around his hand, she tried to catch a glimpse of his home.

The sun was slowly saying its farewells for the day and disappearing behind the trees, meaning all Vista could make out were bushes, more plants and, of course, the familiar scent of dirt. In fact, this looked very similar to the area that Vista had fallen into earlier that day. If she hadn't known any better, she'd have guessed they had spent the entire day walking in circles, only to end up exactly where they had started. She promptly reminded herself that Grecko knew Letherea a whole lot better than she did, and surely he would know the location of his own home.

'Um, Grecko, did you say this was your home? I'm sorry, but I think I'm missing something. All I see are more leaves and bushes?'

Clumsily, he smacked his head with a chunky palm and chuckled. 'Oh no, me home is jus' behind these plants 'ere, see...' With his free hand, he awkwardly pushed his way through the surrounding shrubbery. Incessant leaves tickled Vista's cheeks until in a slight clearing, a small hut came into view.

All words were lost to Vista as she laid eyes upon the hut that Grecko called a home. It was certainly a far cry from the Home Tree. Even looking directly at it you could almost miss it, that was how well it blended into the mud, dirt and wildlife on the forest floor. It had a roof of sorts, but not a roof as one would expect, no – it was more like a tree branch had fallen and was now being used as a barrier to protect the hut's insides from rain, bird droppings and other falling objects.

There were obviously several gaps, all ranging in sizes, that would indeed allow any of these things to fall through, but an attempt had clearly been made to fix them with long grass stems or anything else the forest could provide to be used as some sort of tether.

Appearing not to notice Vista's hesitancy, Grecko moved them towards his home. Pushing the ineffective roof that also seemed to work as a door aside, he made way for the two of them to enter.

Inside, the hut was equally bleak. There was a bed in which Grecko must sleep, but to say it looked comfortable in any way would most certainly be a lie; it didn't even look an appropriate size for a gnome. It was made up of stacks of dried leaves and branches all piled high, and once again tied together using grass stems to hold them in place. It had a quilt of soft grass and flower petals resting upon it, presumably for comfort, although Vista had a hard time imagining how much comfort this thin sheet could provide. For a pillow, Grecko had what appeared to be a bunch of old clothes bundled together and a blanket made up of what looked like old, matted fur, likely from an animal that had not been living for a very long time.

The sight of Grecko's hut made Vista's heart break. He had a small area close to where they stood in which the floor was slightly charred and blackened. This, she assumed, must be where Grecko made fires, either for warmth or cooking, or most likely for both.

There was a bucket near the bed used for washing up. It was an old, cracked bucket that, on quick observation, was much too small to effectively wash someone of Grecko's size, no doubt requiring a few trips to the nearest river. For a fairy of Vista's stature, however, the bucket could prove to be the ideal size for a warm bath should she be willing to venture into it in the first place. She pondered over how long it had been since Grecko had been able to bathe comfortably.

Silence filled the space, causing Grecko to cough self-consciously. He shuffled from foot to foot.

'I know it ain't nothing like yer Home Tree,' he paused, struggling to find the words that would best explain his living situation, all the while avoiding Vista's eyes. 'I ain't got much, I know, but I do cook a nice fish supper. Bet yer ain't eaten nothing since breakfast, 'av yer?'

While her heart broke for Grecko, appearing embarrassed by his humble surroundings whilst she had only ever known comfort, there was no denying that the mention of food sent gurgles through her empty stomach. Thinking back, the last thing Vista remembered eating was the carefully selected apple and honeysuckle scone that morning. Sitting in the Home Tree near that open window dreaming of her impending freedom felt like a lifetime ago now. In her wildest dreams she never could have imagined her first night of freedom looking anything like this.

Resentment flowed through her. *My wings don't work.* Despite her best efforts to forget, her brain just wouldn't stop remembering.

Shaking her thoughts away, she turned her attention back to Grecko. 'A fish dinner sounds lovely; is there anything I can do to help?'

————

VISTA LAY STARING AT THE CEILING OF THE HUT, LISTENING TO GRECKO'S loud snores beside her. The blanket she lay upon scratched at her skin and she moved uncomfortably from side to side, trying to find a spot slightly more comfortable than the rest. Warmth and soft amber light emanated from the slowly dimming coals as the stove cooled. Vista had never had to worry about being cold before; the Home Tree was always the perfect temperature, as if the tree itself was alive and taking care of them. Some part of her knew she still had to deal with the events of the day, but how could she? How could any fairy cope with not being able to fly? She had left the only life and family she had ever known and was now deep in an unknown part of the forest.

A shiver ran through Vista as she remembered the strange occurrence just before Grecko had gone to bed. He had crept soundlessly (which was surprising considering his gnome-sized feet) and made his way around the room, ensuring everything was away before putting out the fire. Vista had watched him pop his head out of the hut for just a moment and stand motionless. To a novice fairy like Vista, he had appeared to be listening for something, and she'd even found herself holding her breath so as not to make a sound. What he was listening for had been unclear, but watching him do this had made Vista feel the need to do the same from her bed. Tweets and chirps could be easily heard close by, but something told her the distant calls of harmless birds wasn't what Grecko had been listening for.

Whilst there was no reason for her to feel unsafe lying there watching Grecko, Vista remembered how tense she had felt, the atmosphere in the room changing. A few moments later, however, Grecko had tucked his head back into the hut, allowing Vista to breathe again.

'What were you doing just then?' The question had escaped before Vista had considered if she really wanted to know the answer.

'Me?' Vista knew he was stalling. 'Oh, I was jus' listening, that's all.' Grecko had perched himself on the edge of the bed, the sheer weight of him causing the whole bed to dip, leaving Vista holding on to the side to stop herself from rolling. She had persisted and asked him again. Looking back now, however, she wished she hadn't. 'Miss Vista... not all the creatures that live in Letherea is as kind as I am.'

he'd explained, 'Yer lucky it was me who found yer when yer fell outta that tree - reckon the forest planned it that way. Some plain dangerous folk out 'ere. Yer'd do well ter steer clear of 'em.'

In every fantasy Vista had had of the forest, it was a magical, wondrous place where she could do whatever she wanted. Now, lying restless, the reality of her situation was a hard pill to swallow. A warmth had crept over her then as she felt Grecko lightly pulling a blanket over her miniature shoulders.

'Just in case yer get cold, Miss Vista,' he'd whispered – as quietly as you could imagine a great, bulky gnome could whisper.

He'd fallen asleep then, much quicker than any fairy back in the Home Tree - he seemed to be snoring before his head even hit the pillow. Vista, wide awake and with no sign of tiredness creeping in, tried to think of anything other than what could be lurking in the darkness beyond the hut. She felt like she had gotten to know Grecko quite well over dinner and sighed comfortably as her body relaxed into a more pleasant memory. Vista's full stomach was a comfortable reminder that not everything was all that bad.

She'd been quite mesmerized by how Grecko had started the fire; she had never seen it done before.

'Who taught you how to make a fire?' Vista had asked, realising she didn't know much about Grecko's past.

After a brief hesitation, in which Grecko seemed almost reluctant to answer, he'd cleared his throat and awkwardly scratched his chin. 'Me dad taught me. He knew loads 'bout living in the forest. He was a smart gnome, he was.' While speaking, he'd stared intently at the fire, not once looking up in Vista's direction.

'I'm sorry Grecko, I didn't mean to bring up a sensitive subject.' Vista had been hoping for reassurance that he was alright; the thought of comforting someone other than herself was a bit daunting.

'Not a problem, not like it's bad ter talk 'bout him or nothing. Jus' that I never do I spose.' His voice had remained flat and sombre, very different to his previously chirpy tone. He'd kept his eyes firmly on the flames; it was obvious this was a subject best avoided.

Vista thought over the fish they had eaten for dinner - Golden Coos. It had been hard to face eating something so beautiful, with their golden spines and mirroring tufts of scarlet bristles. Grecko had told her of how they spoke to each other under the water, or rather how they cooed at each other. 'Yer know some folk say if yer ever hear a group of 'em cooing, it means they're tryna warn yer o' summit. Dunno how true that is mind. They say Golden Coos know loads o' stuff an' they is always listening.' Grecko had told her. He'd given thanks to the forest before they'd eaten as well and that had pleased Vista greatly.

She rubbed her stomach, thinking of the magical fish and their abilities. This thought gave her some comfort and finally she felt calm enough to sleep.

Fish and Berries

Vista awoke suddenly the next morning, kicking herself free from the tangled sheets. Her breath came in ragged gasps, heart pounding in her ears. A nightmare had caused her to panic but the memory of it was already disappearing despite Vista trying to cling to it; for some reason it felt important. One image was seared into her mind; the Home Tree burned and blackened. No sign of life surrounded it, as if the area had been blighted.

Looking around, trying to ground herself back in reality, Vista realised she was alone and began wondering where Grecko might be.

Waiting helplessly in the bed, she allowed her gaze to drift around the room. It was light now and everything looked different. Vista had wondered if the hut might appear slightly cosier in the day time, but found she was mistaken - if anything it looked even bleaker.

Grecko was a humble gnome, that much was clear. He had very few possessions to speak of, making the hut seem quite empty. In the daylight, the ground looked cracked and dry - Grecko had no rug or floor covering so his sparse furniture stood on the forest floor. Everything around Vista looked haggard and old. She took a deep breath and tasted the stale air within the hut, making her even more keen to get out of the bed and seek the fresh air outside.

Taking a deep breath and gritting her teeth, she gingerly peered over the edge. *It doesn't seem too far... Not as high as the Home Tree.* Ignoring the nausea stirring inside of her, she shuffled her way along the bed and warily swung her legs over the edge. Rolling onto her stomach, she fought off any panic and prayed desperately that the sheet was strong enough to hold. Clamping her hands around it, she managed to form a kind of rope – hoping it would ease her gently down. Reminding herself to keep breathing, she slowly wriggled backwards and, little by little, shimmied her way down the side of the bed. Fortunately for her, she was incredibly light and on the ground before she knew it, breathing out a sigh of relief. Conquering something so huge made her feel braver. Standing, she brushed crumbs of dried dirt off her feet and legs and looked up. Hands on her hips, she nodded triumphantly. *Today's already a better day!*

A voice speaking outside the hut made Vista jump.

'Ere we are, yer'll all feel better after this, won't yer, aye?'

Who's Grecko talking to? Does someone else live here too? Vista was certain there hadn't been anyone else around the previous night. Hesitantly, she made her way across the room and ventured outside.

'Oh wow...'

There was no denying the ground surrounding Grecko's home wasn't the healthiest looking. The mud was dried and cracked, in desperate need of some rainfall. Contradicting this, however, were the flowers - hundreds of different types - all blooming wonderfully around the hut. Each one of them seemed to sparkle, their petals rich with colour. Each flower was unique: some towered near Grecko's head whilst others sat low to the ground, some carried leaves on their stems whereas others were almost bare. One thing, however, was certain; if flowers had feelings - and Vista was certain they did - then these ones clearly felt loved.

'There yer go, plenty fer all o' yer, don't worry.'

Vista scanned through the flurries of flowers, searching for

Grecko. She spotted him, kneeling on the ground pouring water over each one individually. *This must take him all morning.*

'Morning, Miss Vista. How d'yer sleep?' His chirpiness quickly changed as he caught sight of Vista's sweat-drenched, bug-eyed appearance. 'What's happened? Yer look awful!'

'Oh, it's nothing. Just bad dreams, don't worry about it.' Her crimson face matched the surrounding petals, and she desperately tried to change the subject. 'Your flowers are amazing, Grecko.'

Eyebrows still creased, Grecko seemed unsatisfied with her answer, but all the same took the bait. 'Aye, I love 'em, I do! Water 'em every day. We don't get much rain 'ere so I gotta make sure they all 'av enough ter drink.'

'Well they're clearly thriving with you around!'

He cocked his head to the side as he looked at her, 'We all needs some looking after sometimes, Miss Vista.'

It was obvious what he was implying, but when things got too personal Vista tended to feel uncomfortable and her fingers fumbled with her skirt as she chewed on her lip.

'We'd better be on our way if we're gunna see the fish... if yer still wanting ter come o' course?'

Grateful for the change of subject, Vista smiled, 'That sounds brilliant Grecko, lead the way.'

———

IT DIDN'T TAKE LONG TO WALK FROM GRECKO'S HUT TO THE RIVER, AND Vista was thrilled. Goosebumps coated her arms, and she gave an involuntary shiver, not from cold, but from the sheer joy of finally laying her eyes upon a sight she had only ever seen in her dreams. Unlike her dreams, however, in which the water flowed in a straight line, the river before her stretched and curved out of sight. Vista looked in both directions but the end couldn't be seen. It gave the illusion of going on forever, perhaps forming a perfect circle – having neither a beginning nor an end. The sound of the water seemed softer up close; it ran smoothly along, gliding through Vista's line of vision. A sweet scent of freshness floated towards Vista's nose and she breathed it in, enjoying the cold feeling in the back of her throat.

As they stood, to Vista's delight, several fish burst out of the water, droplets spraying everywhere as they broke through the surface. The fish glided through the air and Vista let out an ecstatic squeal, squeezing Grecko's thumb as hard as she could.

'Grecko, look,' she pointed excitedly, 'the flying fish... they're real – I can't believe they're real!' Bouncing up and down on her knees, she didn't take her eyes off the magnificent creatures for a moment. Even their colours were breathtaking – they were as silver as the moon on a winter's night.

They flew above the water as easily as they swam beneath it. Back and forth they weaved, intertwining with each other and making patterns with their bodies. Vista held her breath and felt tears prick her eyes as she realised they were dancing together.

'This is the most incredible thing I've ever seen, Grecko. I could watch them all day long.'

Briefly, she looked away from the fish and glanced up towards Grecko. He wore a relaxed smile and replied, 'Me favourite animal in all o' Letherea. Each one's amazing.'

'Do you know much about them?' Vista asked hopefully.

Grecko stared out at the water and scratched at his chin with dirty, blackened fingernails.

'Well, lemme see... Flying fish is beautiful, but ain't very smart, which is a shame. They're always getting caught an' eaten by birds an' such. It's 'coz all they wanna do is come outta water every day. Now, I ain't complaining – one o' me favourite things ter do is come ter the river an' watch 'em fly – but I always wonder if they jus' stayed underwater where they belong, maybe we'd 'av more of 'em around, yer know?' He picked up a handful of pebbles and began absentmindedly tossing them into the water one by one.

'But if they keep getting caught when they fly above the water, wouldn't they have learnt to stay underneath where it's safer by now?' Silently, she prayed she wouldn't soon be seeing a hungry bird swooping down for its breakfast.

'Sometimes I wonder that meself, but then I reckon we all do things that are dumb sometimes. Reckon it's all part o' being alive. Who knows, Miss Vista... who knows.'

Grecko rubbed at his eyes with his free hand, as though trying to force himself to focus.

'We better start fishing an' picking berries, or else we'll be 'ere all day. I dunno 'bout yerself, but I'm getting pretty hungry.'

As Grecko placed Vista down onto the ground, she watched him lift a large pointed stick out of his bag.

Vista swallowed uneasily, 'Does it hurt the fish when you catch them with that?' Secretly she hoped that even if it did hurt them, Grecko would know to lie to her rather than tell her the truth.

'Nah, not the way I catch 'em. I bin doing it a long time now an' I always make sure ter be fast. If yer fast then the fish don't feel it. Promise!'

As he spoke he stared out over the river. Vista had never seen him look so serious. It was a good thing – the killing of anything should most definitely be taken seriously.

'Well, good luck.' It was a half-hearted wish, torn once again between her hungry stomach and her concern for their safety.

'No luck needed, Miss Vista, I always catch me fish!' Grecko pointed in a direction behind her. 'Now if yer go over that way, jus' a bit away from our river, yer should be able ter get plenty o' berries ter last us a day or two. Only pick the nice juicy ones, mind. Them ones that look all shrivelled up taste like old boots.' He screwed up his face in disgust, making Vista giggle, wondering how he knew what old boots even tasted like.

'Where should I put the berries after I pick them?'

Grecko tilted his head slightly, confused. 'Huh... That's a good point, that is. I tend ter jus' put 'em in me pockets, but don't reckon yer'd fit much in yer pockets now, would yer aye?' he chuckled a little and drummed his fingers against his chin, thinking.

'Aha, 'ere yer go. Yer can use this dried up leaf. It ain't too heavy so don't fret, it'll fit two or three berries in it, easy. Yer can use the leaf ter drag 'em back 'ere before going an' getting some more.' He placed the dried up leaf in front of her and smiled proudly. 'Don't worry yerself, miss, yer can't go wrong if yer jus' go where I told yer ter go. Won't be long an' we can go back an' 'av a nice breakfast, aye?'

Realising this was her cue to leave, she reluctantly took hold of her dry leaf. 'Right, see you in a little bit then.'

She began pulling the leaf with fierce determination. Never in her life had she felt so small; this so-called 'light' leaf was almost the same size as her. Imagine trying to drag something the same size as you across a stony forest floor!

It quickly became obvious that the most difficult part of dragging a leaf across the ground was the steering; there was lots of to-ing and fro-ing to be done around various bits of nature blocking the path. Nevertheless, this was Vista's first chance to prove she could actually be of some use to Grecko, and she wasn't about to mess it up.

There must be more to eat than fish and berries around here, she thought longingly.

Quicker than Vista had expected, she came across a round, lovely looking purple berry on the ground in front of her feet.

'Aha!' she cried in relief. Glancing upwards, Vista was elated at the sight of all the berries she could ever possibly need. 'Well, that was easy!' she mused, feeling rather proud of herself.

Closing her eyes, she listened to the forest. The birds were the first thing she heard. She listened to their pleasant chirps and waited... There were no other sounds. How odd it seemed, for it to be so quiet and still.

It was strange how when looking out of the Home Tree window, the forest floor had always appeared so loud and full of life. Yet within these bushes, she could easily have believed that she and the birds were the only living creatures in the whole of Letherea.

Keeping her eyes closed, she took a deep breath of forest air; it was so relaxing that Vista almost forgot she had a job to do. Wiping her sweaty forehead with her forearm, she turned back to the task at hand.

Each bush varied greatly and seemed to have its own personality and style. Some were luscious and full of greenery; these appeared to have the juiciest looking berries full of deep blues and violets. Other bushes looked beige and rather malnourished. These had berries on them as well, but they were dark, some even black in colour, and quite shrivelled. There was no doubt that these were the ones Grecko had compared to old boots down by the river.

I wonder what made him taste them in the first place? It was quite clear which ones Vista would choose when faced with both options.

Whatever his reasons were, Vista ignored the sad, beige bushes and turned her attention back to the luscious green ones. She then commenced the task of selecting what she believed to be the finest looking berries.

Taking this responsibility very seriously, she began sniffing them, weighing them; she even licked one or two, but decided not to mention that part to Grecko. Whenever she felt she'd found a particularly delicious-looking one, she would wrap both hands around its stem and pull with all her might until it detached itself from the bush with a triumphant snap. One by one, Vista built up a pile until there were twenty juicy-looking berries counted and ready to be delivered back to Grecko. Vista's pile gave her a huge sense of achievement, despite knowing how small and easy this task would appear to a creature the size of Grecko. Loading three of them into her dried-up leaf, she started on the mission of getting each one of them back to the river's edge.

When she arrived with the first three, it wasn't surprising to find that she was sweating again. If it was difficult dragging an empty leaf, then it shouldn't come as any surprise to find that dragging it back with a heavy load would be even more of a challenge. One at a time, she lifted the berries out of the leaf and heaved them into the clearing, placing each one down on the ground, ready for Grecko to find.

Vista rubbed her hands into her filthy dress – *it's already ruined*, she figured.

Gazing towards the river, she kept a keen eye out for Grecko.

He wasn't difficult to spot, maybe fifteen feet away from where Vista stood (gnome feet, not fairy feet), and looking very out of place amongst the calm, picturesque river scene. He was waiting patiently, as still as a moonbeam.

Swiftly, with a quickness you wouldn't expect from a creature so big and bulky, he plunged his stick into the water, and tutted under his breath as it came up empty.

Vista thought back to his earlier confidence and wondered how long he would have to stand there waiting until a catch finally swam his way. Not wanting to distract him from his work, she crept soundlessly to her leaf and back the way she came, bracing herself for her second load of berries.

So much easier with an empty leaf! Hauling it over small pebbles and holes in the ground suddenly felt like a breeze.

A strange sight made Vista stop in her tracks. She had made it to the pile of berries, that much she was sure of, but something wasn't right. She stared for a moment, not quite able to put her finger on what was bothering her.

The berries still lay there, in the same innocent pile she had made not that long ago, but, Vista realised, it looked slightly smaller than it had before.

Rooted to the spot, she began obsessively counting them. *One... two...* Her eyes darted between them all. *Five... ten...* Almost done... *Fourteen.*

'Fourteen,' Vista whispered, panic rising in her voice. 'Fourteen...' she repeated, this time a little louder. A scuffling noise ahead drew her attention. She grew pale and pressed her elbows sharply into her sides, subconsciously attempting to shrink herself. Her mind drifted into a memory of a tale she had been told as a young fairy. She distinctly remembered tales of intruders in Letherea - a long time ago. The story had served as a warning to fairy younglings that the unknown was not to be trusted. Vista had never been one to listen to such nonsense and despite feeling a slight nervousness, had never shied away from new things before. This was the first time that the lesson seemed to be hitting home. *Who's there?*

'H... hello?' Vista sighed, frustrated by the obvious fear in her voice. 'I... I know someone's out there. Someone took my berries.' Not wanting to sound petty she continued, 'I'm more than happy to share them...' It was then she remembered Grecko, her big and hopefully intimidating friend. 'That is *we* are happy to share them. I'm here with my friend the gnome. You can't miss him, he's extremely large. He's just over there in the water.'

She pointed in the direction of the river and looked around her for any signs of movement. When no reply came, she forced herself to think rationally.

It's just a few missing berries, it could have easily been a hungry animal passing through. If they'd meant to hurt me, they'd have come out by now.

The longer she mulled it over, the calmer she felt. *That'll teach me not to leave food on the floor...* Rolling her shoulders, she felt her body relax, certain now she wasn't in any immediate danger.

With purpose, she took a step towards the berry pile. As she did so, however, movement from the bushes ahead made her pull back.

If you've ever had the feeling that someone was watching you, then you will understand. It's an innate feeling, something that can't be brushed off. An eeriness that causes all the hairs on the back of your neck to stand on end. You can look all around you and see nothing, but still, the feeling of being watched is there.

Vista felt this as she looked into the bushes. Her knees trembled, threatening to buckle at the first chance they got. Contradicting this, though, was the adrenaline - pushing her forward; demanding that she move; needing to know exactly who was watching her.

There was a crunch as she took a step, a small twig breaking under her foot.

'I... I can see you.'

This, of course, was a lie. She could see nothing ahead except bushes and berries, but her gut told her that a creature was there. She could feel its presence. The creature's stare burned through her. Whether she imagined it or not, she could feel its hot breath on her face.

Six more steps and she was standing directly in front of the bush. Large and oppressive, it towered over her tiny frame. She was the innocent fly, about to be engulfed by the dreaded spider.

The bristles on the bush were close to her face - so close that if she tilted her head she could feel them tickle her skin. The air was heavy with trepidation, and Vista's stomach had become a lead ball weighing her down.

Not wanting to give herself time to change her mind or think it through, she reached out a shaky hand and grabbed hold of the bush. Bristle by bristle she pushed them aside. Pulling and pushing, her eyes scanned around her, trying to catch sight of whoever was lurking nearby.

Questioning her sanity, she saw no one. There were just too many bristles and too many berries with no way of seeing or making it through, at least not for someone her size.

Am I being paranoid? Vista clenched her fists and looked behind her. She could still make out the pile of berries sitting on the ground.

Maybe I just miscounted? Embarrassment crept through her as she thought of all the fuss she had been making.

There's no one here. The thought that there was no one there was both a good thing and a bad thing. On the one hand, it confirmed she was safe, but on the other, it showed it had only taken two days on the ground to turn her into a crazy, paranoid mess of a fairy.

'Miss Vista? Miss Vista, where are yer? I caught us our breakfast.' Grecko's voice boomed through the forest, and Vista had never been more relieved to hear it.

With no way of stopping it, she let out the loudest laugh she had ever made. It was a laugh of shock and relief and made her sound completely insane. In truth, she did feel a little insane.

'Grecko, I'm over here!'

He pushed aside the bushes in front of her and his face creased in concern at her state.

'Miss Vista, yer alright? Yer don't look like yerself.' Kneeling down in front of her, he dropped two dead fish beside the pile of berries and looked her up and down.

'I'm fine now, don't worry. The forest managed to spook me a bit that's all, but it was just in my head. There's a small chance I might be losing my mind.'

'Aha!' Grecko's laugh bellowed out of him, awakening the forest and sending several stunned birds chirping from the snoozing branches. 'We're all losing our minds, Miss Vista, don't worry 'bout that. Every day we get a little bit older, an' a little bit crazier. That's why it's nice we got each other now ain't it?'

Vista continued laughing and shook her head slightly. It was tricky to tell if much of what he said made any sense but somehow just hearing him say it felt comforting.

'Yer ready ter go home now?'

'Yes, I'm ready.' She held Grecko's thumb snugly as he gathered up the berries and fish and stood. She was getting quite used to being carried around at this height. If she closed her eyes and arched her neck forward just right, she could feel the wind in her face and hear the birds all around her, it was nearly enough to trick herself into believing that she was actually flying.

Nestled against Grecko's fingers, Vista grinned, feeling ever so silly for getting so worked up before. Her eyes drifted back to the bush she'd been so dramatically searching through. Before she could blink, Vista was certain she caught sight of a pair of dark eyes staring straight back at her.

6

An Unexpected Gift

D *id I dream it?*
It had been days, but still the eyes haunted Vista. She found herself unable to think of much else.

During her walk home that day she'd decided not to say anything to Grecko about the eyes in the bush, nor did she bring up the missing berries. He'd seemed to be in such good spirits, grateful for her company, and she hadn't wanted to spoil that with stories of her paranoia.

For the most part, life on the forest floor had started to fall into a nice little routine for the two of them. Grecko was the hunter and gatherer, ensuring they had plenty of fresh fish and berries to eat, and Vista had become the homemaker. It wasn't much of a home to keep, but Vista did her best with what little she had.

She'd managed to convince Grecko that gathering berries was a bit too tricky a task for someone of her size, and together they agreed that she would be better off staying in the hut and keeping up with the cleaning. Every morning she would lay the sheet and blanket flat across the bed. This may sound like a quick job, but remember to take into account Vista's size in comparison to the bed. This task alone could take Vista the best part of a morning to get right!

She also cleaned the pots and pans, rather dramatically falling into the water a few times whilst trying to reach the very bottom, forcing her to hang on by her feet. There was nothing like the fear of drowning in a dirty pan to make Vista remember to hold on a little tighter next time.

Her jobs were rather small considering the adventures she had once imagined she'd be having. In truth, after seeing the eyes that day, whether real or imagined, it was enough to scare Vista out of the adventures she may have been planning to take.

She spent her nights wishing she could fly, dreaming endlessly of all the places she could go if only her wings worked. Her heart carried a dull ache whenever she imagined herself in flight. She thought of that morning collecting berries and how she could have just flown above the bush to see who was lurking inside it. Life could have been so much simpler.

Vista often wondered how the joy flower fairy had taken to life, when her wings had been taken and she'd been forced to live permanently in the Home Tree. Had she struggled to live without flight? Perhaps Vista was wrong to think life would be easier on the ground. Lying awake at night, tears stung her eyes as she sniffed quietly, not wanting to wake Grecko. Her mind always questioned why her wings had failed her when the others' had worked. She truly believed no one had wanted to fly more than she had, it just didn't make sense.

Occasionally, her mind drifted to Mila, Bess, and even Lorella, wondering what they were up to now, and if they even knew what had happened to her after their flights. Most likely they did - whispers between fairies were common. They probably thought she got what she deserved; she was the fairy who had so desperately wanted to leave, after all. She felt like such a fool, acting like she knew everything when it was clear now that she knew absolutely nothing.

One morning whilst Grecko was by the river collecting their breakfast, Vista stepped outside to gather up the clothes that had been hung out to dry. That is, she stepped outside to collect *her* clothes. The idea of lifting up Grecko's clothes created an image of slowly suffocating underneath one of his humongous tops, giving her a whole new kind of fear.

Vista had been surprised with her knack for making her own clothes, using anything she could find lying around. Her first creation had been a leaf wrap dress, made by taking a large leaf and wrapping it around herself, pinning it at the side using a twig from a fallen bird's nest.

The next one was made solely from flower petals. It was nowhere near the quality of her original water petal dress, but that one was now completely ruined and worn mainly when cleaning the pots. She did rather like her new flower dress, though. She had used white petals from a peace flower that she'd found close by. It was so rare to come across a peace flower, especially this far away from the hills, and she assumed it must be good luck. Treating it with all the respect it deserved, she carefully plucked off two of its petals and fastened them around her sides using grass stems (the same ones used for Grecko's roof). It turned out not nearly as bad as Vista had expected, and it was by far her favourite creation. Her only struggle was attempting to keep it white whilst living amongst such a large amount of dirt.

Holding the edge of her now clean petal dress, Vista paused. That feeling was back – the same niggling, gnawing feeling that made her want to run and hide. The inkling that something was watching her again.

Vista dropped the dress, dirtying it once more. She was determined to find out once and for all if she were truly going mad. Without a thought, she stepped directly on top of the dress as she marched towards the trees, pushing it deeper into the mud.

She couldn't say why she felt she was being watched again. She'd heard no noise, nor seen any movement but still couldn't shake the feeling.

Her jaw might as well have been wired shut, her teeth were clenched so tightly. Coming to a stop just in front of the trees behind the hut, Vista stood perfectly still. No movement. Her eyes darted over every tree.

She stared for a while, but after no sign of life, decided it was time to head back. Confused, she stepped away.

Maybe I am going crazy?

Vista forced herself to look away from the trees and turned back towards the hut, only to spot the filthy dress she had so elegantly crushed into the mud whilst in her strange trance.

'Urgh!' Her frustrated moan echoed through the forest, bouncing off the trees. The thought of trudging back to the river to clean the dress again disheartened Vista even further. She knelt down to pick up the dirty petals and that's when she heard it. Behind her, a crunch. The sort of sound that comes from stepping on a twig.

Frozen, her mind began to panic and she started to sweat, debating how much danger she may be in. Something was behind her, waiting.

Pulling herself up to her full height, she took a deep breath, feeling a knot twisting in the pit of her stomach. She forced her knees to stop shaking.

Why don't my wings work... This would be the perfect time for them to take me away!

Forgetting to release her breath, Vista spun around to face the trespasser. Her eyes blinked incessantly as she tried to make sense of what she was looking at. She saw nothing. There was no one there. Confusion muddled her brain, and the breath she had been holding on to came out in a loud, trembling rasp as large tears rolled freely down her flushed cheeks.

The crunch she'd heard had seemed so real that somehow being faced with no danger was more terrifying than any threat. She was becoming more and more convinced of her own madness.

Collapsing on the floor, she heaved dramatically. The forest was doing an excellent job of proving to her she wasn't strong enough to be on her own. Then, just as she wiped at her nose with her arm, she spotted it.

The thing was big, bigger than her and a deep emerald colour.

With the backs of her hands she roughly rubbed at her eyes, making sure she wasn't imagining things. When the object didn't disappear, she scurried to her feet and made her way cautiously towards it.

As she drew nearer, her fingers clutched her dress and she looked around suspiciously. Lying at her feet were handfuls of gorgeous emerald coloured fruit, the likes of which Vista had never seen before. They looked slightly similar in shape to bananas – except three times the size and a great deal more dazzling.

For Vista, the concept of eating something other than fish and berries was almost too good to be true. She looked around, but still no one was there. There was no way of knowing if they had been left as a gift or simply dropped by a passing creature startled at the sight of a panicking fairy.

Grecko will know what these are, she decided, forcing herself to step away from the tempting fruit. *They could be poisonous...*

The rest of that morning passed slowly as she waited for Grecko to return carrying his usual bundle of fish and berries. Vista focused on keeping herself busy, aware that every random sound caused her heart to skip a beat or two.

Whilst daydreaming about emerald fruit and strange visitors, Vista heard the slow plodding sounds of Grecko's footsteps heading back up from the river. Without even looking, it was clear that these were the plods of a very unhappy gnome.

'What's the matter?' Vista asked, walking towards a hopeless and exhausted Grecko.

He ran his fingers through his hair, and that's when Vista noticed his hands were empty.

'It's the weirdest thing, Miss Vista - there ain't no berries. It don't make no sense. I went ter where I always go an' normally there's loads o' berries, but now every bush is empty! I looked all over, but I couldn't find none. Not even them horrible shrivelled up ones. I jus' don't get it...' His face was solemn, no doubt afraid of delivering the bad news.

'Oh, well I don't know if this'll help, but I found these today while you were out fishing.' Leading Grecko towards the back of his hut, she pointed nervously towards the emerald bundle.

When he saw them his jaw dropped. He let the fish fall to the floor and rushed towards the fruits. 'Gubbling nibblets, where in Letherea did yer find doozles?' he cried, his exhaustion all but forgotten.

Vista laughed a little louder than she'd intended to, 'Grecko, I don't think I understood a word you just said?'

'Aha! Sorry Miss Vista, but where on earth did yer find these? I ain't seen 'em in the forest in forever. Used ter be me favourite once upon a time but they all got used up!' His delight was infectious, and before she knew it, Vista was kneeling beside Grecko, examining the precious fruit for herself.

'They just sort of... appeared today.' There seemed to be no better explanation for it without mentioning the part where she thought she was going insane.

'Well, wherever they came from, I sure is glad they came. They'll be the best thing yer ever tasted, jus' wait an' see!' Gathering up the four doozles in one hand, he rushed to get them inside.

Watching him run to the hut so happily, Vista hurried to keep up. *Must have been a generous stranger.* Seeing this kind of reaction from Grecko left her certain it couldn't have been anything else.

———

THAT EVENING, SITTING DOWN FOR DINNER, VISTA WAS PRESENTED WITH a plate of the most unappetising slimy green substance she had ever seen. Trying to be as subtle as possible, not wanting to offend Grecko after all his excitement, she suspiciously poked at the slime with her forefinger, half expecting it to jump up from the plate and smother her.

'Uh, Grecko, how exactly do I eat this?' Eyeing him quizzically, it was hard to believe his enthusiasm was caused by something that so strongly resembled snot.

'Well yer can eat it any way yer like, Miss Vista. Me, I like ter slurp it right off the plate. No need fer forks or nothing like that. All yer need ter do is put yer face right down next ter yer plate an' suck. Simple.' With this, he proceeded to demonstrate. His lips curved around the edge of his plate, and he made a loud, slurping noise as though he were trying to hoover up the entire table. As he sucked, the green substance slowly slid off the plate and straight into Grecko's eagerly awaiting mouth.

As he swallowed, his gleeful eyes met Vista's. Licking his lips he practically sang, 'mmm, takes me back years, it does.' He rubbed his belly and swung his head back, relishing the taste. 'Now yer turn. Try it!'

It was difficult to hide the disgust on her face as she stared down at her plate. Chewing the side of her lip, she carefully examined the green gloop as though it might explode at any moment. She was starting to realise that she could, in fact, be quite the dramatic little fairy.

She pursed her lips in the same way Grecko had done. Out of the corner of her eye she caught him watching, his face masked in smugness, so certain she was going to love it. With a large amount of dread, she shut her eyes (not wanting to see it coming towards her mouth) and slurped. As the fruit passed her lips, she braced herself, but to her complete surprise, the taste wasn't awful at all – it was actually rather incredible. It was sweet, but not so sweet that it left that sickly feeling in your stomach, and it was smooth, but not so smooth that it made you feel nauseous when it slid down your throat.

Looking up at Grecko, she couldn't help but smile, admitting defeat. 'Grecko, you're right, this is delicious!'

He clapped his hands together, 'yer see, I told yer it was good! Better than fish an' berries, right?'

'Ha!' She couldn't help but laugh, 'much better! How long has it been since you last ate these?'

Grecko paused for a moment, his gleeful face slipping slightly.

'They... they was me dad's favourite.' He swallowed hard and subtly turned his gaze from Vista. Her body tensed but she kept quiet, sensing he had more to say.

'Me dad was always me very best friend, yer know. We used ter 'av so much fun. He taught me how ter fish an' how ter build a fire. He was a good gnome, he was. Yer would 'av really liked him, I'm sure o' that.' He smiled toward his plate and blinked through glassy eyes, 'bin thinking 'bout him a lot lately. Reckon it's 'coz I got yer 'ere with me. I reckon he'd 'av bin so good at looking after yer. He would 'av known jus' the right things ter say an' do. He was so much cleverer than me.' Grecko's voice shook a little and, absentmindedly, he began poking at his food.

Vista so regretted asking her question. *Oh Grecko...*

'How long has it been since you've seen your dad?' she asked softly, not wanting to press him too much while he seemed so fragile. 'Maybe we could go and visit him some time?'

Grecko snorted and glanced down at Vista, 'Nah, we can't go see him, Miss Vista. Me dad ain't around no more, hasn't bin fer a long, long time.'

'What happened to him?' Vista stared at Grecko, her delight over the doozles completely forgotten.

'Let's jus' say he started messing with things he shouldn't 'av bin messing with. Gnomes is sposed ter be simple an' easy. He got his brain full o' these ideas an' reckoned he could change stuff. Didn't work out fer him in the end, though.' His voice broke off and he sighed heavily, 'It all changed after me mum went yer see.'

'Why did yer mum leave?'

Grecko snorted, 'Well she didn't leave...' he paused, searching for the best way to describe it, 'she got in an accident I s'pose yer could say.'

'An accident? What happened?' Vista's finger tips dug into the table's surface as she eyed Grecko nervously.

He glanced briefly over to her and continued, 'When I was young, no older than ten I reckon, me mum used ter make the best food around. She'd spend all day over a fire, making the best dinners yer could ever imagine. I wish yer could 'av tasted her cooking, it was better than anything else in all o' Letherea. We used ter 'av so many gnome friends as well, they would come from all over jus' ter eat supper with us, that's how good she was,' his face lit up, reliving happier days.

'She used ter make these soups fer everyone, they were full o' all sorts, I can't even tell yer what was in 'em, but I know it used ter come together like magic.' he took a sharp inhale. 'So there was this one day, she must 'av bin making soup or summit 'coz it was still bubbling on the fire. She used ter add these little nut things ter it, ter give it a crunch, but the problem was they were always up in these branches right near the tops o' the trees. Me dad used ter climb up an' get whole bunches of 'em fer her, ready fer her ter cook with. I still dunno why, but this one day she must 'av run out o' nuts 'coz she went ter go an' get some more. Now yer gotta know, Miss Vista, me mum wasn't a climber - dad was, but he was fishing down the river with me.' Grecko paused for a moment, trying to catch his breath.

'It was dark when we got back an' we first heard the screaming. We ran up there, Miss Vista... I don't think I've ever seen me dad run so fast in his life. He got there a bit before I did, I had smaller legs back then, see. Anyway, by the time I got there, there was this big group o' gnomes all circled in a group, an' me dad came running over ter me an' grabbed me. He was giving me this big, giant hug an' crying. I knew what he was tryna do, he was tryna stop me from seeing her, but it didn't work. I'd already seen her. She was jus' lying there, bent over with her arms an' legs all twisted up. Her face looked the same though. It jus' looked like she was sleeping. I wanted ter yell at her, ter scream 'Wake up!' Like maybe if I did she would 'av, but she didn't... I jus' always wished she'd waited fer me dad, if she waited then she wouldn't 'av fallen. Me dad was never the same after that day.'

Everything seemed to be moving in slow motion. Vista swallowed with great difficulty - her mouth having hung open the entire time causing it to dry up.

'I'm so sorry, Grecko,' she racked her brains for some words of comfort, 'I bet they were incredible. They'd have to be to have a son like you.' She laid her hand out in front of her. He was much too big for her to comfort properly, but luckily he understood her gesture and affectionately tapped her hand with his finger.

'That's very kind o' yer ter say.' He wiped at his eyes, dabbing them with the corner of his dirty old top. 'Wish one o' em taught me how ter make me own clothes, mind,' he chuckled, trying to lighten the mood, 'bin wearing me dads old hand-me-downs fer as long as I can remember.'

Suddenly, a lot of things began to make sense. Of course Grecko's clothes didn't fit him properly and looked so tattered – they weren't even his clothes. Vista thought again of how she wished she'd paid more attention when being taught how to sew. Although it seemed highly unlikely she'd ever find a flower with large enough petals to fit Grecko.

In a snap decision, Vista stood up on the table and walked across it to Grecko (something told her he wouldn't be concerned about table manners). When she reached him, she sat cross legged next to his plate and lovingly patted his arm. Looking into his face, she blinked away her own tears and sniffed. The sad truth was that there was nothing she could say; it was awful and she had no words that could help. She pressed her forehead against his arm and curled up next to him.

7

———

The Wing Thief

The day after the doozles had been a strange one. Neither Vista nor Grecko felt overly chatty. Vista couldn't help but worry over the prying eyes in the bush and she was certain that Grecko was feeling strange after talking about his parents.

'Miss Vista...' Grecko's voice startled her, but she was glad to hear it. 'I bin thinking we could do with some fun. There's somewhere I wanna ter take yer but yer bin so tired I ain't gotten a chance yet,' he paused, his face looking nervous. 'I get why yer bin tired though, don't fret. It's bin a lot o' change fer yer all this. I bin wanting ter show yer the flying fire. Do yer maybe wanna go an' see 'em?'

Vista's unease with Letherea grew daily, however she had to admit the idea of flying fire was intriguing. Her interest piqued, she asked, 'What do you mean by flying fire?'

'I dunno if it's their real name or nothing, jus' what I always called 'em. They look like tiny bits o' fire, so what else would I name 'em?' he shrugged his shoulders, slightly embarrassed by the name, but mainly pleased that Vista seemed somewhat keen.

Vista smiled, 'In that case, flying fire sounds like a perfect name for them! Do you want to go now?' Her willingness to go into the night surprised both of them. In truth, it was just nice to have something else to think about.

'Yeah, let's go now,' Grecko leapt up excitedly, 'lemme jus' wrap yer up a bit first. Gets cold outside when the dark comes.'

When the dark comes, Vista thought that seemed a very sad way to describe the night, like it was a foreign enemy invading the day.

Grecko gently yanked the bed sheet out from its neat and tidy corner and ripped the smallest section of it off to use as a shawl over Vista's dainty shoulders. Vista tried her best not to think about how long it had taken her to tuck that blasted corner in that morning. As she watched Grecko ruin what had been an almighty job for her, she reminded herself that he meant well.

Thanking him for the shawl, she tied it in a knot around her slender neck. Once again she held tightly to Grecko's fingers and closed her eyes as he walked, pretending her wings were doing the work.

'It ain't too far, yer can jus' relax an' enjoy the sights if yer like.'

In his free hand, he held a large stick and headed towards the fire. He dipped the end into it. Flames danced and kissed the stick until they clung on, and as Grecko lifted it the flames followed, glued to the end and making a perfect torch for a nighttime stroll through the magical forest.

Vista pulled the shawl tighter around herself, her breath quickening slightly. Looking up at Grecko, she relaxed a little – as long as he was with her, she felt safe.

'Oh! I've never been this way before,' she realised as they exited the hut and turned left.

'It's pretty at night, ain't it?' Grecko said with a smile.

There was no denying it – the forest's beauty was breathtaking. Looking towards the flame, Vista noticed the light was attracting all sorts of flying insects. They danced towards the flame, moving away at the last second to stop from getting burnt. Each insect was decorated in the most alluring colours, shining and reflecting against the light, creating a glow around themselves.

To Vista's astonishment, she saw that these glowing bugs had nestled themselves in every tree and scattered themselves across the entire forest floor, creating the illusion that the ground itself was glowing too.

How haven't I noticed these before? Vista couldn't believe she'd been so ignorant as to miss out on the most incredible sight. Everything else remained dark; tall trees cast shadows over the ground as the torchlight bounced off them. It would have been scary had it not been for the bugs - wisps of colours sparkling, giving the trees and the forest the illusion that they'd been dipped in glittering dust.

'Oh, Grecko, look at them all!'

Grecko smirked and let out a chuckle, 'If yer reckon that's special, jus' yer wait until yer see the flying fire.'

Magic seemed to flow from everywhere - every dark crevice shone with it. Resting her chin in her palms, she relaxed and let her eyes follow the trail of shining bugs.

After walking for a short while, Grecko's voice roused Vista from her daze, 'Miss Vista, we're 'ere!'

Stirring in his palm, she blinked repeatedly, trying to make herself focus. Besides the light reflected from the fire torch, there wasn't much to look at from where they stood. It was just a clearing. She'd never admit it to Grecko, but so far she would have much preferred to stay walking on the path with the glowing bugs.

Not knowing what Grecko expected her to say, and worried he was waiting for some sort of reaction, she awkwardly responded, 'Wow, Grecko, it's beautif—' before she could say another word, Grecko's booming laugh cut her off.

'Don't yer start lying ter me now, there ain't nothing ter see yet – it's empty 'ere!'

Embarrassed at being caught out in a lie, Vista giggled nervously. She waved her hands aimlessly around her, showing she had no idea what to say next.

'Oh, yer a daft one, Miss Vista,' Grecko shook his head smiling, 'dear me, so very daft!'

He made his way over to a large rock and set Vista down upon it.

'Yer make yerself nice an' comfy now, show's 'bout ter start!'

Bringing her knees to her chest, she twisted her chilly hands up into the shawl, attempting to trap in the heat. Her eyes followed Grecko as he stood in front of her, one hand still resting in the dirt and the other confidently raising his fire stick into the air.

For a while, nothing happened. It was hard not to acknowledge how silly Grecko looked, but he didn't seem to care. He just stood there, perfectly still, with his left hand raised and his eyes darting all around.

Everything was silent, but it wasn't long before Vista heard a noise. It was quiet at first, like a distant whirring that gradually grew louder and louder as though heading straight towards her. It sounded almost like a humming, like a song of some kind. As more and more hums joined in, the sound began to change and transform into majestic, soothing music.

Vista's smile reached her ears, and she turned in every direction looking for the bearers of this mesmerising tune.

A bright light of orange and yellow zoomed past her head, followed by another, and another, until it felt like hundreds of tiny balls of fire were whizzing past her and dancing around Grecko's flame. There was no doubt whatsoever as to why Grecko had named them the 'flying fire' - they truly did resemble tiny flames with wings. Vista watched in awe as Grecko became encased in a swirling sea of fire-like balls. His eyes met hers through the mass of blurred orange, and she could just make out his smile. His hand remained high, the fire stick being worshipped by the flames. They weaved in and out around his entire body, hypnotised by the fire that he presented for them.

Slowly, they filled the sky, creating the illusion that the night was raining fire, all the while singing their soothing tune.

Vista's hand rested against her heart. She held Grecko's gaze for as long as she could and mouthed the words, 'Thank you.'

———

AFTER THE FLYING FIRE, VISTA WAS FINALLY BEGINNING TO FEEL Letherea's magic again. This came as a great relief, to say the least. After all, a fairy who can't fly doesn't do well being afraid of the ground.

Early the next morning, before Grecko had even woken up, Vista found herself wide awake and desperate to get outside. Checking on Grecko, it was obvious he was still in the deep stages of sleep.

Surely he wouldn't mind if I took a quick trip out by myself?

It was odd that she felt the need to ask his permission. It wasn't like he had told her to do so, just more that she didn't want him to worry. *I've definitely given him plenty of reasons to fret!*

A loud snore from Grecko made Vista jump, and she giggled at the awful noise – it was a wonder she got any sleep at all. Excited by the prospect of a magical forest outing by herself, she made her way towards the end of the bed, careful not to disturb Grecko in the process. Holding tightly onto the sheet, she climbed her way down, taking pride in how good at this climbing thing she was getting.

With a gentle thud, she landed on the floor, trying to be as quiet as possible. Patting her dress down, she peeked in Grecko's direction, satisfied he was still fast asleep. *I'll be back before he wakes up.* Decision made, Vista crept soundlessly out of the hut, eager to start her early morning adventure.

The magical forest felt different when she was alone, not good different or bad different, just changed somehow. The mud felt harder and the leaves rustled a little louder. Standing for a moment, she debated what she would do with her unexpected free time. It was clear that Grecko had been having a bit of trouble catching fish lately. He seemed quite puzzled by it all, claiming he'd never had so many days without a single catch in his life. Vista regularly caught him staring out towards the river, biting his fingernails down to their stubs, deep in thought.

It was obvious this 'dry spell' was making him nervous, and she decided it might be a good idea to spend her free morning heading down to the river to see how many fish she could spot – that way she could pass the good news on to Grecko when she returned. Satisfied with her plan, she skipped towards the river, going as quickly as her small legs could carry her.

As it turned out, the river did take a lot longer to get to when walking as opposed to being carried. When she finally arrived, she was sweating and working hard to catch her breath. *What if Grecko's awake by now?*

Vista rubbed her palms together and stared back in the direction of the hut. *He'll be fine once I tell him about the fish.*

She bent forwards, hands on her knees as if she'd just run a sprint and gave a small nod to the fish as she did so.

'Good morning,' she said jokingly to the river, doing a small curtsy.

'Good morning!' came a reply.

Vista shrieked and jumped backwards. She knew the river housed magical creatures, but surely the river itself wasn't magical enough to speak?

'I said, good morning...'

There it was again, that strange voice. Staring closely at the river, she tip-toed towards it and cast her eyes across.

'H... Hello?' timidly, she edged forward some more, but still couldn't see the owner of the strange voice.

'Well hello yourself!'

This time she was certain it wasn't the river. *Stop being such a coward, they sound friendly enough...*

'I'm sorry, I'm afraid I can't see you?' Straining her eyes, she stared across the water.

'I'm just over here, behind these rocks.'

Vista looked to her left. Not too far from her lay a cluster of boulders, not unlike the large rock Grecko had placed her on during the flying fire show the other night.

Swallowing the large ball now lodged in her throat, Vista crept towards the boulders until she found herself directly in front of them. Standing there, she heard a strange cooing sound coming from the river. It grew louder, as though echoed by hundreds of different voices all coming together. Not wanting to be rude, Vista turned away from the cooing and back to the boulder, peeping her head around it.

'Ah, there you are. Nice to meet you!'

The creature before her was crouched on the floor in front of the river, his skinny arms and legs bent awkwardly. He glanced at Vista briefly before returning his attention to something in his hands. She studied him nervously. He was about double her size - but still small in comparison to the forest - and dressed entirely in black with a hood that covered the majority of his face. Even through his clothes, Vista could make out the imprint of his bony elbows and scrawny knees. From her quick glimpse, she could see that his nose and chin both pointed downwards as though racing to the ground. She squirmed slightly, trying to hide her strange discomfort. He looked very out of place, sitting amongst the leaves with the flowing water before him – like a smudge on a delicate painting.

Several small critters buzzed around him, and he lazily swatted them away.

'N... Nice to meet you too.' Vista couldn't seem to shake the bad vibes he gave her. *Stop it, he's being polite!* Forcing herself to smile, she stood her ground.

Stopping whatever it was he was doing, he gave her a fleeting sideways glance.

'Please, don't look so nervous, I won't hurt you, I promise,' he grinned – the corners of his mouth turning down as he did so – and displayed a mouth full of foul, yellowed teeth. He continued to look out towards the river, 'What's your name, my lovely?' The critters continued to buzz around him, but this time he didn't react, seemingly used to the irritation.

'I'm V-Vista... what's your name?' cautiously, she took a step forward, distant cooing still echoing behind her.

'My name's Inigo, but you can just call me Iggy if you like.' He slid himself across a little, giving Vista just enough room to sit down beside him.

She turned to look back, aware that Grecko would most likely be awake and might be worrying about her right now. *I'll just sit for a minute or two*, she reasoned. After all, this was the first creature other than Grecko she had met since living on the ground.

'So Vista, if you don't mind me asking, what's a fairy like you doing living all the way out here, hmm? I don't think I've ever seen a fairy this far away from the Home Tree before.' As he spoke, he continued to work on... Well, Vista wasn't quite sure what it was he was working on just yet.

'You know about the Home Tree?' she asked surprisedly, hoping to avoid the rest of the question.

'Oh yes, I've been around all parts of Letherea,' – he waved a hand dismissively – 'but what I'm wondering about is how *you* got to be here?'

With a frown, Vista felt compelled to answer. 'Well, I can't fly,' she swallowed, slightly embarrassed. 'I live here with my friend Grecko. He takes care of me.' Speaking about Grecko made her aware once again of how much he must be worrying right now.

'Your wings don't work? That's a great pity, a fairy without wings must feel quite lost indeed.' He continued his work with his hands, still looking down.

Vista had no idea how to respond to this, it seemed incredibly personal. The truth was she didn't know how she felt about her wings anymore. It wouldn't be so bad if she knew the reason for them failing, but she wasn't any closer to figuring that one out. It certainly wasn't a subject she wanted to delve into with a complete stranger.

'It's not so bad,' she lied. 'I've gotten quite good at making a home down here on the ground.' She made a point of shrugging, nonchalantly.

'Ah yes, I've seen your housekeeping, it's quite good. Tell me, did you enjoy the doozles?' he asked, gazing out at the water and grinning slightly.

A cold chill ran down Vista's spine. 'That was *you?*'

Finally, he turned to face her properly and she was able to have a good look at his face. His skin was wrinkled and leathery with tufts of wispy, grey hair poking out from the side of his hood. He looked tired and pale, as though he barely ever entered the light, squinting at her as the sun shone down upon them. Their eyes met and Vista froze.

His eyes... the dark eyes from the bushes.

'Yes, that was me. Did you enjoy them? They've always been a favourite of mine, and I thought you might have been getting sick of your fish and berries every day.' Once again, he continued to work on whatever was in his hands.

'How did you know about the fish and berries? Have you been *watching* me? Did you know I'd be here today?'

'How could I have possibly known that?' Iggy paused, picking up on the panic coming from Vista. 'I'm sensing I've startled you in some way? Please believe that I don't mean you any harm,' he held his palms up in front of him. 'I suppose I have been watching you. But I only wanted to help. It was obvious you were hungry, so I thought maybe you'd like something different to eat. I see Grecko's been having trouble catching fish lately as well.' Again, his attention returned to his busy hands.

'Do you have something to do with the lack of fish?' she asked.

Iggy looked up at her with a hand over his mouth, feigning surprise. 'Vista, that's *so* insulting! All I did was give you food. What possible reason would I have for holding back the fish?'

As much as she hated to admit it, Iggy did have a point.

'Look, I don't want to frighten you, but clearly that's what I'm doing. All I was trying to do was help you, I swear! If it makes you feel safer, I'll just leave.' Gathering up his things, he began to walk away, back into the forest.

'No, wait!' Despite her reservations, she felt a strange urge to keep talking with Iggy. He seemed to want to help her, despite his odd way of doing so. 'I'm sorry, I'm a little on edge these days since leaving the Home Tree. I, uh...' Vista searched desperately for something to ask him. 'I was wondering what you had in your hands?'

'Oh, this?' Iggy stood a little taller, his hood falling back slightly as he proudly strutted over to show her what he was carrying. 'This is something *very* special. I use it to catch fish when I'm feeling peckish.'

Instantly, he'd grabbed Vista's attention. Iggy laid it out flat on the ground, but to Vista it just looked to be an ordinary net. *If that was full it'd easily carry ten fish or more!* As exciting as that thought was, Vista reasoned that just because the net was big enough, didn't mean any fish would swim into it in the first place.

'How do you get the fish to go into the net?'

'With magic, of course.' Iggy said nonchalantly.

'Magic?' Vista wanted to make sure she hadn't misheard him. Her heart raced looking at the plain net on the ground.

'Yes, magic. Do you think I'd ever try fishing *without* magic? Ha!' Iggy laughed. 'Oh no, I'm afraid magic is the secret to everything, in my humble opinion. The days just aren't long enough to get anything done without it.'

'But how does it work?' Vista didn't want to get off topic. Kneeling down beside the net, she waved her fingers over it, ignoring the nervous feeling Iggy still gave her.

'I'll show you, my lovely. You see these ropes here?' Iggy pointed, gently stroking each rope like an old friend. 'Each one of them is laced with magic. The magic whispers hypnotic tunes to the fish, causing them to swim directly into it without knowing any better. Then, once I've got enough of them happily swimming around inside my net, I simply lift it out of the water and as easy as that I have my supper.' He jumped and clapped, doing a happy sort of dance and swaying side to side, clearly incredibly proud of his invention.

'But how did the magic get into the ropes in the first place?'

'Well, I put it in there.' Iggy stopped his dancing and stared at her in amusement. 'My dear, you do know I'm an Imp, right? Now if there's one thing that Imps are very good at it's magic... or at least it's something *this* Imp is very good at!' As he spoke, he moved nearer to her face and slouched slightly, until he was so close she could practically taste his breath.

'You're an Imp?' she asked, ashamed to admit she knew next to nothing about these creatures.

'Indeed I am, and once again might I add, it is a pleasure to meet you.' Iggy bowed dramatically and held out a hand that Vista shook straight away.

'Could you show me how the net works, please?' Vista stared at it laying between them, desperate to get back on topic. *Just a dirty old net*, she mused, knowing that it must be so much more than it looked.

Iggy nodded, his smile broad. 'I was hoping you'd ask!' Bending down, he scooped it up and without bothering to look or even aim, threw it directly into the river behind him. Vista gasped, certain the net would be carried away and never seen again, but Iggy looked unphased.

He chuckled at her startled face. 'Oh don't look so concerned, dear. It's magic, remember? It won't go far.' Looking out over the river, he shaded his eyes with his hand and squinted. 'Ahh, there it is. See it?' he exclaimed, leaning closer and pointing. Following his finger, Vista couldn't help but gasp once again: the water in front of them seemed to be shining. She couldn't hear any whispering calls to the fish, but she could feel the vibrations it was giving off, drawing the fish towards it.

'Shouldn't be long now.' Iggy put his fingers to his lips and smiled.

Before she could respond, the shining net began to move back towards them.

'It can't be done already, can it?' Vista asked in disbelief.

Iggy gave a nod. 'Told you it wouldn't take long.' Every inch of him oozed in smugness as he reached into the water and, needing both hands this time, dragged a net full to the brim with flapping, flailing fish back onto dry land. There were more fish inside than Vista had ever seen Grecko catch with those sharp spears of his.

'It's as easy as that.' Iggy grinned.

He chortled with glee as he opened the net, releasing panicked, floundering fish everywhere.

'Oh!' Vista hopped back, 'You're not really going to eat all of these, are you?' The lives of all these innocent fish hanging in the balance making her feel uneasy.

'Nah, I'm not even that hungry, to be honest. I'll just throw them back in the river, I guess. Only caught them to show you how it worked.'

Relieved to hear this, Vista gladly assisted Iggy in the long process of returning each fish back into the water. The majority of them were actually bigger than she was, but she helped as best she could.

'If Grecko had a net like this, I know his days would be so much easier...' She hadn't meant to sound like she was hinting, but that's how it sounded all the same.

'How about you take this one?' Iggy stopped hauling the fish and turned to face Vista. There was no suggestion on his face that he was joking.

Unsure of how to react to this offer, Vista scratched self-consciously at the back of her neck and tried not to meet Iggy's eyes. 'No, I really wasn't suggesting we take yours! I couldn't do that, it's too much. How would you eat without it?'

Iggy scoffed, 'Believe it or not, my dear, there are other things to eat in Letherea besides fish.'

Her cheeks flushed with embarrassment and she looked away, not wanting to face Iggy's amused expression.

'Although... thinking about it, you do have a point.' Iggy went on, 'Say I wanted to eat fish one day but didn't have my net, well then I'd be missing out on something, wouldn't I?' He threw the last, distressed looking fish back into the water and bent over, rubbing his hands in the dirt to rid them of their fishy smell. 'What if instead of me just giving you the net, we made a trade? That way you wouldn't feel like you owed me anything, and I wouldn't feel robbed of some-thing useful to me.'

Vista took a subconscious step back, growing slightly uneasy all of a sudden. 'But what could you possibly want from me? I don't have anything to give you.'

'Oh, that's not true...' Iggy stroked his chin, thinking for a while. 'How about your wings?' he asked breezily, tilting his head to one side. He made it seem like asking for someone's wings was the most natural thing in the world.

'My *wings*? But they don't even work, they're useless. What possible reason could you have for wanting them?' Vista asked, reaching her hands back and touching their silky surface. 'I don't understand?'

'Well that's the beauty of the trade – you don't need to under-stand. The only thing you need to know is how much my magical fishing net is going to help poor Grecko catch his fish. The rest doesn't need to concern you at all.' He stepped towards Vista, closing the gap between them.

She tried to make sense of it all in her mind. Of course there was no question she wanted to help Grecko; he'd done so much for her that surely this was the least she could do for him in return. The problem was the idea of giving up her wings. Wings - even broken wings - were what defined her as a fairy. Her mind drifted back to the whispers of the joy flower fairy - wingless and stuck in the Home Tree.

'Besides,' – Iggy interrupted her thoughts – 'it's not like your wings are working anyway, is it? Would you really turn down such a useful net for a pair of broken wings?'

Vista stroked them again and glanced at them over her shoulder, a thing she had once been so excited by the thought of doing.

'Well?' Iggy tapped his foot impatiently on the ground, breaking Vista's train of thought. Her throat felt dry and she fidgeted uncom-fortably with the end of her dress. 'I... I d-don't kno-'

'Vista this is an *excellent* deal. You'd be foolish to turn it down,' he interrupted, 'just think of Grecko.'

With every ounce of her body fighting against her, Vista ignored her instincts and went with what she felt should be the obvious choice – helping Grecko. 'I guess you're right, my wings aren't much use to me. I honestly can't think of any reason why you would want them, but...' she paused, blinking back tears, 'If that's really what you want for the net, then okay.'

Iggy clapped his hands together and hopped around on his heels victoriously. Quickly, realising this seemed a tad insensitive, he promptly composed himself.

'I think that's a very sensible decision, my dear. Would you mind turning around for me so I can take a good look at them?' he asked, his lip twitching into a smile. Holding out his forefinger, he spun it in the air, indicating what he wanted her to do. Obligingly

Vista turned away from him, hearing him gasp and sigh as she did so.

'Oh my dear, they are just lovely, aren't they! Best thing we can do is take these off of you. Don't need any nasty reminders of your failures as a fairy now, do you?'

His words stung, and she bit down hard on her tongue to distract herself from his cruel remark. *It's no worse than what I've thought myself,* she figured.

'You might want to hold still. I'm afraid this is going to sting a bit!'

She tensed all her muscles and dug her fingers into the palms of her hands as hard as she could – the wingless fairy tale had never mentioned how it had *felt* for the other fairy to have her wings pulled off. Her eyes squeezed so tightly shut that she could see spots dancing in the darkness.

'Ready? Here we go.'

With Iggy's words Vista felt what can only be described as a white, hot pain. The skin on her back ripped as her wings shook violently, resisting with all their might. The pain radiated through her spine, culminating between her shoulder blades. Vista began to feel hot, as though being dropped in an oven – her wings trembling unnaturally fast. A scream forced its way out of her as she dropped to her knees – body rocking and tears soaking the ground. Between cries, Vista felt the shaking stop – her back suddenly still and burning.

Iggy stopped. Realising it was over, Vista reached a shaky hand behind her, feeling the place where her wings used to be. With instant regret, her hand touched her bare skin. Vista hadn't expected to feel this way – without her wings she was hollow. Empty.

An anguished cry escaped her as she thought of what a terrible mistake she had just made. She hadn't considered the way it would feel to have a part of your body ripped away. *What do you even call a fairy without wings?*

'All done!' Iggy whistled in a cheery, singsong voice. He was either oblivious to Vista's pain, or simply didn't care. He clapped his hands again. 'Well, this has been fun, I've got some things I need to get on with now though, so I best be off. Oh, and don't forget your net, my dear!'

To Vista's left, a bundle of rope landed in front of her with a thud.

8

A Spiteful Imp

Nobody had ever truly understood Iggy, and he was acutely aware of this fact. There was a time when he thought someone had, but that was a long time ago now, and he didn't care to dwell on the past.

No, Iggy was undoubtedly a 'focus on the future' kind of Imp. The more bleak the future seemed for others, the brighter it seemed for him.

As he skipped away from the spot where he'd left a devastated Vista with that pathetic net, he clapped his hands together with glee.

'I can't believe how easy that was,' he shouted aloud. 'She was practically begging me to rip them off her, stupid fairy!'

As he skipped, he whistled a happy tune. Iggy wasn't used to being in such high spirits, and he had to admit he was rather enjoying it. Even the pesky bugs that flew around him couldn't dampen his mood.

'Well done, Iggy. What a splendid performance that was,' he snickered.

It was common practice for Iggy to speak to himself. He'd been doing it for many years now – it wasn't like he had anyone else to speak to after all. His own company was better than anyone else's anyway.

Confident he'd made a large enough distance between himself and that snivelling fairy, Iggy stopped to rest for a while against a large tree, wincing slightly as the spiky trunk scratched at his back. He didn't move despite the scratching; he was used to Letherea's cruelty towards him by now. Pretending to be comfortable, he allowed himself to take a proper look at his prize.

'Oh my, you'll do nicely!' He held the wings in front of him admiringly. 'Just look at you. How shiny you are, how strong, how new... Too bad that *idiot* fairy didn't know how to make you work. What a pity,' Iggy smirked, a cruel thought creeping through his mind. 'I suppose I shouldn't even call her a fairy now, should I? Without these beautiful wings, she's nothing. What would you call a wingless fairy?'

In Iggy's opinion, being a non-magical being was one of the most disgusting things that someone could be. The fact that Vista had so willingly given him the very thing that made her special was preposterous to him.

'I know,' he exclaimed, 'she's nothing but a stupid *girl!*' He spat again, the very notion of Vista repulsing him.

'And don't get me started on that Grecko,' Iggy continued his one-sided conversation with the wings as though they were his new best friends. 'I feel like I've heard his name before. I can't for all the doozles in the forest remember where from.' Staring out over the trees, he tried his best to place the name but ultimately shrugged, admitting defeat. 'Probably just somebody I've hurt somehow,' he cocked his head to the side and laughed, a little too loudly for somebody with no company. As he laughed, his head fell backwards and smacked against the tree. In a flash, his laughter turned to menace and he spun furiously, growling at the trunk. He bared his yellow teeth and scrunched up his nose before slowly turning back and focussing on the wings.

'Oh, my dear,' he snarled, wiping tears from his eyes. Stroking the wings affectionately, Iggy marvelled at how despite the ordeal they'd been through, the only evidence was a few specks of blood near the base. Other than that they remained the same as when they'd been attached to Vista - their delicate swirls still catching the light with a silvery sheen. 'You have no idea how long I've been waiting to get a hold of you. You're my reward for being so patient!' he giggled, 'Those idiots will never see this coming.'

Iggy leant heavily against the tree and forcefully began bashing his head against it, attempting to hurt it for causing him pain. He pushed his back against the spiky surface and relished in what he thought was a thoroughly successful day.

'Right, time to get moving, my dears, say goodbye to the tree. It made an *excellent* resting post, didn't it?' Patting the trunk, he gave a dramatic bow of gratitude. Still chuckling to himself, he spun around several times on the spot, enjoying the dizzy rush it gave him before continuing on his walk.

'Won't be long now,' he said, patting the wings lovingly.

You wouldn't be wrong to assume that Iggy was completely insane. Years of solitude could do that to an Imp - or to anyone else, for that matter.

Iggy arrived back at his cave after approximately a half day's walk, which involved several stops for snacks and more one-sided conversations with the wings.

'Here we are, my beauties - home sweet home!' He stood in front of his cave, arms stretched out wide, presenting it like a palace.

To call it a cave was a bit of an overstatement; it would more likely be described as a hollow space between two rocks. It was a large gap in which two boulders had collided together, creating an area between them which was the ideal place for a small Imp and his possessions to shelter from the magical forest. The ground around it was dry and empty; whereas Grecko's hut was surrounded by flowers, Iggy's cave was surrounded by decay. His part of the forest was dark and dank, with any remaining plants drooping sadly towards the ground, never getting the chance to flourish.

The closer you got towards his home, the duller the trees became. Gone were the sturdy branches engulfed in luscious green leaves. In their place stood dark, empty trunks, their branches more like twigs that hung loosely by their side. He spat on each trunk as he passed, a greeting he'd clung to for years.

What must be clear by now was Letherea's obvious disdain towards Iggy. The magical forest had a way of sensing cruelty; it picked up on the bad, and Iggy was about as bad as they came. He took his gift of magic and manipulated it into something evil and wretched. All the years filled with spite had turned him into a creature that Letherea couldn't fathom. As a result of Iggy's misuse of magic, the forest around him suffered. The malnourished ground he walked upon was a sign of the pain he caused.

Iggy crawled inside his home, roughly dragging his new wings behind him. When safely inside, he stooped down and rested his back against the inner wall - his home not being big enough for him to actually stand up in.

'I know it's not exactly the Home Tree, but I think it's quite cosy.' Staring at the wings, he seemed to be waiting for a response and grew more and more impatient with their silence. 'ANSWER ME!' he screamed abruptly before composing himself. 'I'm sorry about that,' he mumbled. When they did nothing, Iggy took this as a sign of their forgiveness and approval towards their new home.

'You're right - no words needed. I'm so glad you like it here. I realise you won't be around very long, but uh...' he leaned in and whispered his secret, 'I still have a few more ingredients I need to get, so you stay comfy until then, okay?' His smile was so broad and crooked it made it difficult to tell if he was happy or angry. More than likely, it was a combination of both.

Rubbing his hands together, he blew into them for warmth. 'Bit chilly in here, isn't it?'

Clicking his thumb and forefinger together, he focused on the area between himself and the wings. Out of nowhere appeared an impressive fireball, levitating just slightly above the ground; it sparked and flickered brightly, giving the cave a warm orange glow. The instant heat satisfied Iggy, visibly soothing him.

'Ahhh, that's much better.' Admiring the fireball, he flicked his wrist from side to side, causing it to swirl and twist on his command. 'Impressive, right?' he smirked and nudged the wings with his elbow. 'Just a little trick I know,' he said, waving his hand as if brushing off imaginary praise.

'So...' Sitting forward abruptly, he tapped his hands distractedly against his knees. 'All that work this morning has made me rather hungry. Who fancies fish tonight, hmm?' Twisting his body, he crawled into the very furthest corner of his cave. Reaching a thin, bony arm behind one of the boulders, he pulled out a bag filled to the brim with all sorts of different trinkets and ornaments. Rubbing his hands like a greedy child in a sweet shop, he chuckled eagerly and rooted his arm through the bag.

'Just wait until you see this!' he said to the wings, grinning. With a jolt, he found what he was searching for and pulled out four magical fishing nets from the bag, identical to the one he had traded with Vista that very morning.

'Ha!' Iggy nearly fell backwards laughing. 'Remember how she gave you to me because she didn't want to take my *only* fishing net? Well joke's on her, I guess, eh!' he laughed maniacally, tears streaming down his face, which he wiped away with the sleeve of his top. Abruptly, he stopped laughing and glared menacingly at the wings, relishing in every word he was about to say. 'The best part is, only my magic can make the net work.' A smile crept across his face as he crawled right up close to the wings, his nose touching the surface of them. 'Oh my, it's a good thing that you, my dears, belonged to such an idiotic *girl*. Had she been slightly less naïve, I may have had to resort to other measures to get you from her.'

Still wiping away tears of laughter with his now damp sleeve, Iggy began crawling out of his hole, dragging one of the fishing nets behind him. Once outside, he turned back, calling to the wings, 'You stay there, my lovelies, I'll be back before you know it.'

As he skipped away, the only sounds came from the crackling fire-ball and the distant whistling of an Imp who finally felt that things were going his way.

9

A Wingless Fairy

What have I done?

Staring at the net, everything felt wrong. All that time spent wishing for wings, and now they were gone. Everything about her felt unnatural. *What am I?*

Her cheek rested against the mud, sinking in deeper as she began to sob. The net became blurred as tears flooded her vision. She hadn't been prepared for how it would feel after her wings were gone. Her back felt raw and burnt, the skin sizzling where her wings had once been. She shivered as the cold reached her. Bringing her shaky arms into her chest, she hugged herself tightly, rocking with every sob.

It took some time for her to even realise Iggy was gone, taking her wings right along with him. Woozy and lightheaded, Vista swallowed down her nausea and forced herself to move. Her back throbbed with every small movement and she winced through gritted teeth. Slowly, very slowly, she dragged herself to her feet. Staring at the net she'd given up so much for, it dawned on her that she had no way of even getting it back to Grecko.

What an idiot.

'What have I done?' Vista choked on the words. Turning to look around her, she winced yet again – the movement sending fresh waves of pain through her spine. With her eyes screwed tightly shut, she felt suddenly weak – it hurt even to breathe. Her knees buckled and slowly, she sank back into the ground.

'Miss Vista? MISS VISTA?'

Vista's eyes shot open at the sound of her name, 'Grecko?' *Am I dreaming?* Everything seemed surreal. 'Grecko... If you're there, I'm over here...' she called, taking short, shallow breaths. '...behind these rocks.'

It didn't take long for Grecko to come bounding into view, scooping her up in his arms with all the love and devotion of a worried parent clinging to their child. Despite herself, Vista cried out as she was lifted, the touch of Grecko's palm against her wounded back taking her breath away.

'Oh! Miss Vista, I bin so worried, I woke up, an' yer was gone, an' I didn't know where yer went...' He stopped, his eyes staring over her shoulders at where her wings used to be.

Without a word, his head shook side to side, tears rolling down his rough cheeks.

'No... Miss Vista, who did this ter yer? I should 'av bin 'ere, I could 'av stopped 'em!'

Slowly, Vista brought a finger to her lips and shushed, hoping to calm him down – the more he sobbed, the more she jostled in his shaking hand. 'No, no, shhh, Grecko please... It's alright. I let him do it.'

'What?' he cried, staring at her dumbfounded, 'Yer let who do it? Why would yer ever let anyone do summit so awful ter yer?' His eyebrows were raised so high they were almost escaping from his head.

Vista's guilt over making Grecko worry was nearly enough to make her forget about the net, the magical fishing net she was certain would solve all of their problems and make Grecko understand.

'Well...' she shifted position in his palm, trying to hide her discomfort, 'I did it for you.' Her eyes moved in the direction of the net – too afraid to risk moving her head again.

Grecko stared at it, waiting for it to explain itself. When it did nothing, he looked back at Vista who tried to explain.

'The net is magic.' His expression didn't change. 'We can use it to catch more fish... you won't even need your spears.' Grecko was staring at Vista as though she'd completely lost her mind, but she was too weak to defend herself.

'I know it sounds crazy,' she swallowed hard, the simple task of talking exhausting her. 'But it works, I saw it. You can catch so many fish... Trust me, please?'

If Vista couldn't get Grecko on board with the net, then everything she'd done had been for nothing. *This has to be worth it.*

'I don't see any fish?' Grecko asked, his voice sounding slightly more agitated than perhaps he had intended it to.

'Oh,' she sighed, sweating now and blinking rapidly as beads of it dripped from her eyebrows. 'Well, that's because we threw them back in the river... Don't worry, we can catch more if you—'

'Who was 'ere, Miss Vista? Who showed yer this net?'

'His name was Iggy and he was an imp... I think.' The pain in her back was causing her to forget the details. 'Yes, I'm sure he was an imp. He said he'd trade me his net for my wings.' Vista fell silent for a moment, holding back tears. 'My wings didn't work, so it seemed like a good idea.' she whispered quietly, her voice breaking.

Grecko clenched his jaw and looked out towards the river, away from Vista.

He'd never looked this angry before, and Vista didn't know what to do. The muscles in his cheeks pulled and he ground what few teeth he had left.

'Grecko? Grecko, please... Say something?' her voice shook and she trembled slightly. 'I thought you'd be pleased?'

'Pleased?' He swung his head violently around to face her, making Vista jump and instantly cry out. 'How could I ever be pleased 'bout summit like this? Imps is bad news, Miss Vista, very bad news!'

Bad news... The words hung in the air between them.

'It's all me fault,' Grecko said, 'I should 'av warned yer 'bout creatures like him. I just didn't wanna scare yer, that's all.'

He stopped talking, taking a moment to consider what Vista must
have been through. Slowly, his anger subsided and his face softened
at the thought.

'Oh, Miss Vista, yer wings! Does it hurt much? There must be
summit I can do.'

Guilt-ridden, Vista couldn't bear to tell him the truth so instead
she said, 'It only stings a bit, I'll be fine.'

'Lemme look at it.' Without waiting for her permission, Grecko
turned Vista around and studied her wound. She'd never before been
so grateful for the fact that fairies' dresses are designed to sit just
below their wings, meaning she didn't have to move or adjust
anything. Clueless as to what state her back was in, she chewed her
lip nervously, listening to Grecko's pitying sighs.

Before she knew what was going on, he placed her on the ground
and started to walk away. She stumbled as she tried to turn and see
him. The burning intensified and panic set in. 'Grecko, no, please.
Please don't leave me!' she cried, her voice hoarse as she helplessly
watched him walk away, barely able to move.

Stopping abruptly, Grecko spun on his heels, a hurt look on his
face.

'Miss Vista, I'd never leave yer. Don't yer ever think like that! I'm
jus' getting summit ter help yer with the pain, that's all. Wait 'ere, I'll
be right back. I promise!'

So Vista waited, too weak to move. She kept her head still and
followed him with her eyes, feeling like a total fool. She could see
Grecko in the distance, appearing to be searching for something.
Occasionally, he would move towards a group of trees, bend down
and sniff. It looked very odd indeed, but Grecko seemed quite certain
as he marched around sniffing the forest; Vista assured herself that
he knew what he was doing. After a while, he finally stopped, looking
satisfied.

He stood in front of a large tree – a magnificent giant of a tree, likely as old as Letherea itself – and placed an affectionate hand against its trunk.

What is he doing?

As Vista watched, Grecko gently stroked the trunk with one hand, and began to cut into it with the other, peeling a strip of bark away as easily as peeling the skin off an orange.

When he was done, he stepped back from the tree and bowed. Running back to Vista, he presented the tree bark to her like a trophy.

"Ere we are. This'll help with yer back, I promise. Turn round fer me, please, Miss Vista. I need ter see the wound again.'

Vista winced at the thought of turning, 'I'm sorry, I don't think I can...'

Grecko gave her a knowing nod and, without saying a word, shuffled his way behind her so she needn't move herself. Vista winced, not wanting to imagine how hideous it must look. What came next, however, was the most welcoming sensation of her life. She gasped, taking her first deep inhale since before Iggy had ripped off her wings. A cool rush coated her spine, instantly easing the burn gnawing her back. Cautiously, she raised her right arm and gently touched where the pain had been. Something rough was resting against her back and she recognised it as bark, turning her head to try and see it. Her limbs slowly gained strength again and she found herself able to move, tingles running through her arms as though they were coming back to life.

'Some o' the trees in the forest 'av healing powers,' Grecko explained. 'Me dad taught me how ter spot the right trees. They 'av a special smell, a bit like peppermint.' He left the bark resting against her back and then tucked it into the bottom of her dress to hold it in place. 'We'll leave that there fer a while. The bark's very clever, it'll know what ter do.'

'Thank you,' Vista sniffed, 'Why did you bow to the tree?'

She turned to face Grecko just in time to see him squirm at the question.

'The trees can feel stuff, Miss Vista, jus' like we do. They feel pain, an' when yer cut 'em they hurt too. I was jus' thanking the tree fer letting me hurt it a bit so that yer back could hurt less.'

Vista bit down on her lip, not wanting to cry. She didn't know what she had done to deserve a friend like Grecko.

Afraid to ask, but feeling she had to, she looked up at him.

'Why would an imp want my wings?'

Grecko sighed in response, 'I'm afraid I dunno, but I do know one thing - imps can't be trusted, so whatever he wants 'em fer, I'm sure it ain't good.'

Vista felt like the biggest fool in Letherea.

'Well, can we at least give the net a try?' she choked on her words, trying to hold back her tears - desperate to bring some good out of this mess.

Grecko snorted, 'Alright, we can give it a go, I spose.' It was obvious he'd agreed more out of pity for Vista rather than an actual desire to see the net in action. Either way, she was grateful for the distraction.

Patiently, Vista taught Grecko how to use the net – too nervous to attempt lifting it herself after the pain she'd been in not long ago.

'That's it, now all you have to do is lift it up and throw it into the water.' Vista smiled, excited for what was about to happen.

Grecko eyed her suspiciously but dutifully lifted the net and threw it into the water. Together they watched as it landed with a splash, droplets of river water spraying in their direction. Vista closed her eyes and inhaled, enjoying the smell of the river. *This will make it worth it.*

'Uh, Miss Vista. Is that s'posed ter happen?'

Vista opened her eyes and watched horrified as the net began floating away in the current, utterly useless and drifting out of sight.

It didn't work! The realisation she'd been tricked hit Vista like a hammer to the chest. 'B-But... It worked before. Why isn't it working?' she cried. Her eyes moved from the river to Grecko, desperate for an answer, but all she found was that same pitying gaze.

'Imps is bad news, Miss Vista.' Was all he said.

10

Iggy's Rage

'Arghhh!' Iggy let out a frustrated cry. 'What's wrong with you all?' he screamed at the objects before him. Growing more and more frustrated, he began smacking himself in the head, sparks of red shooting out from his fingers and singeing the tips of his hair.

Rubbing his head roughly with the inside of his hood, he dropped down at the back of his cave, hunching himself over his collection of ingredients. There was the feather of a wishing bird (native to the Home Tree), a small vial of blood taken from an innocent believer, and moss collected from the oldest tree in Letherea (Iggy had spent the longest time tracking that one down).

Sat staring at these objects, he willed them to merge. Irritated by their disobedience, he clicked his fingers and angrily clawed his hands down the cave wall, leaving scorch-marks. Iggy looked up and stared at the wings leaning casually opposite him.

'I need these ingredients for my plan to work.' His face turned blank, and his mind began to wander.

'I wonder...' he pressed his forefinger to his lips, leaving dark residue from the scorch marks on his chin, and started madly crawling out of the cave. Out in the open forest, he cast his eyes around, clamping his lips together determinedly.

'A little blood to strengthen the mix should do it,' he murmured, glancing toward the vial of blood in his hand. 'My blood, that is!' he mumbled, correcting himself and pocketing the vial.

Scanning the ground around him, Iggy searched for the perfect tool. His knees scuffed as he dropped abruptly and started furrowing through the dirt like an animal. Fingers clasping around a stone, he studied it carefully and growled in anger, judging it too smooth to be of any use. Continuing to furrow, he picked up a second stone and - with great pleasure - stroked its jagged edge, deciding it would do the job perfectly.

'You're just what I need!' he spoke to the stone, holding it close to his face. 'Bet you never *dreamed* you'd have such an important job one day, did you, hm?'

Holding the stone tightly in his hand, Iggy turned back towards the cave and scurried back inside, convinced his imaginary enemies were watching his every move.

Crouched down inside he felt calm, taking comfort in the darkness. He held the stone between his forefinger and thumb and pressed it against his right palm. Humming a tune to himself, he got to work.

Like a knife gliding through butter, Iggy slid the jagged stone across his palm and watched, hypnotised, as the blood ran free, a flowing waterfall of scarlet red. He licked his lips.

'Ah, that should do the trick.'

He clenched his fist over the now open vial of innocent's blood and squeezed. The blood dripped from his hand, mixing nicely inside. Once he was satisfied he'd done enough, he turned back to the wings, smiling.

'Time to shine, my beauties!' In a clumsy fumble, trying not to spill any of his hard work, he wiggled and stretched until his hand wrapped around the wings. Pulling them towards him, he noticed that their once beautiful, pristine surface was now beginning to look rather dirty and, thanks to his jagged stone, quite bloody as well. *That's better*, he thought.

'Do you know anything about where you come from? Hmm? Do you know how deceitful and wicked the Home Tree actually is?' Iggy glared at the wings, daring them to answer. 'No, of course you don't! You have no idea where you come from, DO YOU?'

'They're all just living up there, flying around, not having the faintest idea of what they're all really like. Their whole act of being 'friends of the forest' is nothing more than a lie,' he spoke through gritted teeth, red hot anger burning up inside of him.

'Do you even know where these fairies come from? They're born from the *flowers!*' Iggy let out a high-pitched shriek of disbelief, running his bloody hand across his chest. 'Yeah, that's right. The FLOWERS around the Home Tree birth them, and then that fraud Lilleth comes along and claims that they are HER CHILDREN!'

It's all just one big lie.

'You're the only things that make them special anyway,' he mused, gesturing at the wings, 'you're the only real magic they have, and the flowers give you that anyway.'

Idiots.

'They all just stay in their little area, with their precious *Lilleth*. I'm doing them a favour really – if you think about it. ALL THEY CARE ABOUT IS THEMSELVES!' Iggy smacked his head furiously, taking ragged breaths before staring at the wings. 'I'll make sure those fairies don't ever get to lie again.'

Hysteria mounted inside him, and in his small space, wooziness took hold. Iggy placed his hand on the wall to keep his balance.

'You think I've gone mad, don't you?' Swallowing down his nausea, he added, 'Well, I haven't, they're the ones who are mad,' pointing a crooked finger out of his cave. 'They flutter around their part of the forest thinking they're *so* special and *so* wonderful, but they aren't. All I want is to do Letherea a favour and rid it of those attention-seeking vermin once and for ALL!'

Iggy's voice peaked, and he stopped, suddenly composing himself. He coughed violently and shook his head, trying to clear it.

In a croaky whisper, he spoke again, attempting to sound calmer.

'So this is where you come in. I've been waiting a *very* long time for you. You have, without a doubt, been my most unattainable object. Fairies don't usually leave their part of the forest; I've been waiting a long time for a fairy to 'break the rules' and venture out a bit.'

Iggy's dirty hands stroked the wings, and then, in a moment of pure hatred, he pushed a finger right through the surface of one, causing it to tear. Despite looking so delicate, wings are known to be strong – they need to be, in order to fly. Iggy's burning fingers, however, ripped through them like tissue paper. As its delicate structure ripped, Iggy let out a gratified sigh. He felt immense pleasure from damaging these beautiful wings. However, he knew even greater pleasure would be the kind he'd experience when his plan was complete.

Using all his willpower, he pried his fingers away from the wings before he ripped them to pieces in a fit of rage. He pressed himself against the opposite wall, growling at them and trying to gain back some control. When he felt strong enough, he carefully placed them in the centre of his other ingredients, each one laid out in a circle around his feet. Raising his right arm, he slowly tipped the vial of blood, making sure to cover each ingredient equally, giving everything a murderous red tint. His eyes gleamed at the beauty of it.

'Sorry for the slight delay, everyone. Let's get started, shall we?' he said, placing his palms together and rolling his shoulders, releasing all his tension.

Completely focused on the task at hand, Iggy began to chant. As he chanted, luminous sparks of orange and white shot out from his fingertips, shining light onto the blood that dripped from his wounded palm.

It would be a long night for Iggy; he would be chanting for the majority of it. But he had no doubt, from the core of his rotten soul, that all his hard work would be worth it in the end.

11

Leaving the Hut

Grecko was pacing; he'd been doing that a lot lately, ever since the incident with Iggy.

Vista watched him nervously. 'I wish you'd tell me what's wrong.'

Hearing her voice, Grecko stopped pacing as though noticing her for the first time. 'Okay, Miss Vista, now I don't wanna scare yer, but I reckon I 'av ter go away fer a little while.' he said, walking towards her slowly and speaking as calmly as he could, like he was speaking to a frightened child.

The nervous, gentle tone of his voice made Vista's skin prickle, she was beginning to grow tired of being treated as though she was weak. *I'm not a youngling,* she thought, frustrated.

'If you're going anywhere, I'm coming with you!' Vista said, with as much assertiveness as her tiny frame could muster. Grecko raised his eyebrows and leaned back slightly, but Vista continued, ignoring his surprised reaction. 'Why do you need to go anyway?'

'Miss Vista, us gnomes is carers o' the forest. We know when summits wrong.' He sighed and rubbed his palms together, 'The forest knows a lot more than yer reckon it does. It's bin whispering ter me lately, an' I bin listening. It might not sound like a lot, but the bugs ain't jittering as much, fish ain't fighting back when I catch 'em, an' the trees are starting ter droop a little. It's Letherea's way o' telling me summit's wrong.'

Vista didn't have the same connection to the forest that Grecko did, making it harder to tell if he was being paranoid or if something were truly wrong. Either way, Vista was determined that she wouldn't be left behind. There was something about being told Letherea was in trouble that made her pulse quicken, adrenaline demanding she take action rather than sit and wait. 'As I said, if you're going then I'm going too.'

Despite himself, Grecko laughed. 'I don't reckon that's a good idea, Miss Vista. It's too dangerous fer someone like yerself. Best fer yer ter stay 'ere, where it's safe.' he smiled slightly and patted the top of her head, ruffling her messy hair.

'I can look after myself just fine,' Vista insisted.

'Yer got no idea what it can be like on the forest floor. It can be real dangerous,' he insisted, awkwardly averting his gaze. 'I reckon it's all got summit ter do with that Iggy.'

Vista's stomach dropped upon hearing his name. Despite the shame she felt for giving up her wings, she also knew that she had been tricked.

Vista stared defiantly at Grecko. In the days following Iggy and her wings, Grecko had become a lot more distant. He still spoke to her, but there was something about his tone that told her he saw her differently somehow.

'Well if you're ready then I think we should go now,' was all she'd allow herself to say in response. Vista crossed her arms and straightened her back, trying to hide her wince. The ability to do this simple action was already a huge improvement, but it didn't mean the pain was gone. It felt like a sharp stab if she moved too quickly, although subsided much faster than before. The tree bark had been incredible - her skin began healing straight away - and it still had the ability to cool the wound whenever it began to feel too hot.

Grecko's face saddened slightly and he rose, giving her a brief nod. An awkward silence fell between them as he moved around the hut gathering blankets from their bed, bundling them together with some leftover fish and then making his way back to Vista to offer his hand. He scooped her up, barely looking her way as he did so and she sat cross-legged in his palm, her eyes stubbornly focused on her feet.

Within minutes they were out of their home and heading into the forest. Vista took one last glance back at the hut surrounded by flowers, wondering how long it would be until she saw it again.

———

STEPPING AWAY FROM THE FAMILIAR SETTING OF GRECKO'S HUT AND moving through the forest felt like entering a dream. Paths disappeared, and seemingly dead ends vanished as bushes parted, allowing you to walk straight through the middle. Vista had so far mainly experienced the familiar trek to the river and back, and that had been incredibly straightforward indeed.

Whilst Grecko didn't seem surprised at all by Letherea's helpful antics, Vista was in awe. The main thing that stood out was how colourful everything was. The greens of the trees seemed more vibrant, the reds of the petals appeared deeper, and the yellows of the suns rays looked brighter. Everything felt like a mirage; as though if Vista were to reach out a hand and touch a flower, it would evaporate.

Despite the awkwardness between them, even Grecko seemed to relax a little as they walked. He wasn't smiling, but she could feel his hand was a little less tense than it had been when they'd first set off.

Glancing up, Vista was startled by something gently flying towards Grecko and briefly touching his nose, appearing to plant a kiss upon it. It was a speck of a thing, as fine as hair but with a wiry top and all of it only about the size of a gnome's eyelash.

Grecko smiled despite himself, 'Nice ter see yer, too!' he chuckled as it continued flying around his face.

Vista saw an opportunity to break the tension between them and took her chance to speak. 'What's that?'

Looking down at her, his smile faded, and his face turned back to worry again, but he answered all the same. 'They're called wisps, Miss Vista. The flowers give 'em out ter the forest an' they fly away, planting colours everywhere.' He looked to her and could tell she wasn't understanding. 'Ain't yer noticed how bright colours are round 'ere? The brighter the colours, the more chance there's wisps nearby. They got these tiny faces, an' each bristle on their end's got a tiny hand. They touch with these bristles an' bring beauty ter everything.' Grecko eyed Vista cautiously. 'These is the creatures that took over from fairies, yer see...'

Vista stared at Grecko, not really comprehending what he was saying. 'Took over from fairies with what?'

'Miss Vista, ain't yer ever wondered why fairies get wings if yer never allowed ter leave yer part o' the forest?'

It was true that she'd always found this odd, never understanding the other fairies' indifference towards exploring Letherea's vastness. She'd never dared question it with Lilleth or the others, assuming that was just the way things had always been.

Grecko continued, 'Did yer ever hear the tale o' the intruders?'

'Of course I did, the fairies and I used to whisper about it all the time before we slept... But it's just a made-up story. Right?'

Grecko sighed. 'It was way before me own time, Miss Vista, so I can't say fer sure. I do know Letherea sure felt it was real though – put up enchantments an' such, made sure it couldn't be found ever again. Fairies seemed ter reckon it was real too. They used ter spread the beauty jus' like the wisps is doing now. After the intruders, fairies decided ter stay close ter home fer safety I s'pose, an' so over time Letherea made wisps – summit 'ad ter carry on spreading the beauty, didn't it?'

Vista sat dumbfounded, clueless at how to respond. *Intruders. Fairies. Beauty.* Her brain felt dazed. 'I don't understand...' she mumbled.

'I guess that's all I know, Miss Vista. One day when this is done, we can find more answers fer yer if yer like.'

Just the talk of future plans made Vista feel better, knowing that despite the tension between them, he wasn't planning on leaving. Her mind drifted back to the wisps. 'But if they spread colours throughout Letherea, how come I've never seen one before?'

'They don't tend ter like being seen. If anyone ever caught a wisp, they could misuse its gift, misuse its way o' making things look beautiful. So wisps only come out when they know it's safe; they come out fer me 'coz I'm a gnome.' Grecko smiled slightly, 'Wisps an' gnomes, we get each other. Kind o' kindred spirits in a way, I s'pose!' he chuckled.

Looking to his right, he gasped. Relieved at the distraction, Vista followed his gaze. There was a peach coloured flower curling itself around Grecko's forearm and opening up in front of him. The petals seemed familiar to her. Her mind thought back to a painting she'd seen once back at the Home Tree. Fairies prided themselves on their knowledge of flowers and, though Vista hadn't exactly been the finest student, this particular flower had stood out to her for both its beauty and its fascinating gift.

'This 'ere's a daw-'

'A dawn flower, I know.' Vista interrupted, thrilled at the thought of knowing something without Grecko needing to teach it to her.

Grecko paused and grinned at Vista, nodding his head encouragingly. 'Yer know 'bout these do yer?'

'We learnt about them back in the Home Tree - they're incredible. The nectar they make gives energy to those who drink it. Do you think we could collect some? I've always wanted to try it.' She gazed at Grecko, her palms pressed together pleadingly.

'I reckon we can get some, hang on... I reckon I brought an empty pot with me...' Grecko reached into the pocket he usually used for collecting berries, the familiar smell wafting into the air. It turned Vista's stomach slightly - sickened at the thought of how many berries she'd eaten since living on the ground. He pulled out a very small pot and held it out in front of the flower. Its petals curved around the edge, and slowly but surely the nectar appeared. It was bright orange and thick like custard, appearing to roll off the petals rather than pouring out of the flower. The smell it gave off was subtle and Vista couldn't place the scent, but found her cheeks flushed as she breathed it in. After a moment the flower was done, producing about a thimbleful of nectar.

'Thanks very much,' Grecko said to the flower, affectionately stroking its petals. In response, the flower uncurled itself from his arm and crept its way back into the ground.

He wrapped some cloth tightly over the top of the pot and very carefully placed it back in his pocket.

'Amazing.' Vista whispered.

'That's Letherea fer yer.' Grecko smiled. 'We'll save this fer when we really need it.' He patted the pocket holding the nectar, and they continued on.

12

Torment and Trickery

'Today is a good day!' Iggy emerged from his cave victoriously, acting as though he'd been greeted by a crowd of adoring fans.

Standing proudly, he struggled to keep still. His limbs begged to stretch and dance, thrilled with the vast openness of the outside world after days spent hovering over his ingredients. He licked his lips, practically tasting his revenge.

'Time to make them pay.' Iggy sang, skipping into the forest and patting the bag carrying the potion.

He'd never much liked Letherea; in his opinion, it had too many trees and too many jittery birds - always flapping, always chirping. He knew Letherea didn't care for him either, but that didn't bother him all that much.

Whistling a tune as he walked, a noise in the distance made him pause. It was a low, rustling noise. As he stopped, the noise disappeared. He looked around until satisfied it was gone before shaking his head and walking on, continuing with his tune. Much to his annoyance, the moment he moved, the rustling started up again. Frustrated, he stopped and found himself back in silence.

'It's bad luck to sneak up on an imp, you know!' he yelled, looking around for the source of the noise.

The rustling continued, undeterred by Iggy's threatening question. Impatient and disgruntled, Iggy spun around, heading straight towards the direction of the sound. Crunching his way through auburn leaves, he fumbled and tripped amongst the darkening trees, all the while gripping his precious bag to keep it safe.

'I've barely started walking and you're *interrupting* me? Who do you think-' Iggy stopped dead in his tracks.

He was staring into his own face. Granted it was a much younger, smaller version of his face, but still there he was - skinny, hungry, and very, very cross. They both stood rigid, staring into each other's eyes, one filled with hate and the other with uncertainty.

'How?' Iggy didn't like being lost for words but, annoyingly, found himself struggling. The younger Iggy in front of him didn't speak, merely scowling in anger. This mute version of himself seemed to have almost as much hate inside him as the real Iggy did.

Finding his voice, Iggy shook his head and regained his composure. 'I don't know what kind of trickery this is, but it isn't going to work! I know all about this forest and its love of games.' Iggy's voice sounded confident but inside his stomach knotted.

When the mute Iggy made no attempt to move or speak, Iggy took the chance to retreat, slowly shuffling his feet backwards.

To his dismay, every step back Iggy took, the mute Iggy took two steps towards him.

Holding up a hand, he attempted to halt himself. 'Hey, hey! As much as I'd love to stay and chat, I really have got places to be...'

His eyes scanned around, searching for a way out. He gripped his bag strap even tighter, nervous that this younger - and no doubt faster - version of himself might get hold of the bag before he had time to run away with it.

They continued this silent dance for a short while - one big step back, two small steps forward - until, with great frustration, Iggy backed his way right up against a tree.

Has this tree always been here?

The younger Iggy closed the gap, their faces so close together that their noses touched. Putrid breath lingered between them. Iggy pushed back with his free hand, trying to gain some control.

'Are you planning on telling me *why* you're here? If you're really me, then you know I have work to do.' Iggy wasn't expecting a reply, but this time he got one.

The younger him spat, a foul smelling odour pouring from his mouth. 'Look at you – you're *pathetic*. You think you've got some big, clever plan that'll rid the forest of all its fairies? Ha! Just give up and crawl back to your cave, you'll never make it work!'

Iggy swallowed. It was strange taking criticism from yourself like this. Despite himself, he began to wonder... *What if the plan does fail?*

'NO!' It wasn't clear who he was screaming at: himself or this horrid, younger version - but either way he knew he meant it. 'You can't get inside my head, I won't let you... This plan will work! It's what they deserve. THEY ALL DESERVE IT!'

The younger Iggy chuckled coldly.

Rage swirled through Iggy like a river in a storm, 'How *dare* you laugh at me – you don't frighten me.'

With great force, he pushed the chest of the younger Iggy, urging him backwards. Younger Iggy resisted, grabbing his arm and twisting it firmly. Iggy grimaced, furious with humiliation.

'LET ME GO!'

The younger Iggy chuckled some more, 'Why? So you can go ahead and carry out your *pathetic* attempt at revenge? It's. Not. Going. To. Work. Iggy.' he laughed, emphasising every word with menace, 'You *know* it won't work.'

Iggy forced himself to block out the taunts, refusing to accept what he was hearing. Thinking quickly, he dropped his bag to his feet and used his now free arm to swing around, hitting his younger self directly on the nose. Younger Iggy stumbled backwards and moved his hand to where the punch had landed, still chuckling. 'I suppose that's the worst I can expect from an old, washed up imp.'

Iggy licked his lips, shaking his head, 'Not even close...'

Lifting his arm out in front of him, he squeezed his fingers tightly together. Younger Iggy's eyes narrowed. Magic was a dirty trick to play in a fight. Younger Iggy began to grasp at the invisible rope that was slowly tightening around his neck.

'You may be younger, but I *distinctly* remember magic being some-thing that I got much better at with age.' He stepped closer, relishing the sight as younger Iggy's fingers clawed at his neck. The two locked eyes. Iggy's heart raced, the way it always did when he felt himself holding power over another. Continuing to squeeze, he waited patiently for the sign of life leaving the younger Iggy's body.

To his dismay, the face he was so looking forward to watching perish slowly began to fade away.

'Hey! Where did you go?' Iggy dropped his hand, frantically scan-ning around him, 'WHERE DID YOU GO?' he screamed, demanding an answer that refused to come.

My bag... Iggy jumped, turning every way he could, desperately searching. When he spotted it no more than a foot away from him, he sighed with relief.

'Well at least *you've* been behaving yourself.' Bending over, he picked up the bag and cautiously peeked inside it, elated to see the potion still intact and safely tucked away.

Peering over his shoulder, he shuffled to his feet – no longer whistling. *Should have known the forest wouldn't make this easy,* he thought.

———

IGGY WINCED WITH EVERY STEP HE TOOK. HE'D BEEN WALKING A WHILE now and the grass beneath his feet had begun to harden whilst either side of him still looked luscious and soft. Each step felt like knives slicing at his soles.

'It won't work, you know,' he called for what felt like the

hundredth time. The sky was growing dark despite it being no later than midday.

Never liked the day anyway, he thought, trying not to let it bother him.

Iggy grunted as he tripped over a raised tree root, sending him hurtling into the dirt. Never before had he seen so many exposed roots – it was like they'd all come out just for him.

He growled and spat out mud, breathing heavily. 'Haven't you got anything better to do?'

It dawned on Iggy how strangely quiet the forest had become. Not just silent, but *unnaturally* silent. No birds chirping, no creatures scurrying by. He seemed to be completely alone.

He smacked his head furiously in annoyance as he reminded himself that he wasn't *entirely* alone - he never was. Letherea itself was all around him. It might have been able to keep the animals at bay, but it was making its own presence quite clear.

Not too far down the path, he paused. It looked... wrong. Rather than being clear, the path had become scattered, seeming to disappear completely in the darkness.

'Can't an imp catch a break around here?' he screamed. Clicking his fingers together, he smirked. *A little darkness can't stop me.* Walking forwards, he lit the way with his flame tipped fingers.

A rustling noise ahead made him stop. 'That other Iggy decided to come back for more, eh?' he called, a distinct tremor in his voice.

With his glowing fingers held out in front of him, Iggy waited. There was nothing there. As he took a few more steps forwards, pressure built up on either side of him as leaves pushed into his sides, trapping him to the spot.

'HEY...' he cried. 'LET ME GO!' Wriggling his shoulders and kicking his legs, he fought fiercely to free himself, but the leaves were too strong. Iggy clicked his fingers and touched a leaf. To his delight, it burst into flames, releasing its grip. He touched another, and another, watching them all burn until finally he could see his way out.

'HA! You thought that'd work, eh? It'll take more than a few leaves to stop me.'

Tree roots snaked across the ground, grabbing at his ankles, but he shot flames at each and every one of them, causing them to recoil as he laughed maniacally.

A gentle breeze brushed past his face but Iggy barely noticed it - until it got stronger. It blew faster and louder until the noise of it filled his ears, and he was no longer able to light a spark with his fingers – each flame evaporated the moment the wind touched it.

Being pushed along by its strength, Iggy found himself stumbling to keep his balance.

'MY BAG,' he screamed into the wind, clutching it tighter. Pushing forward with short, sharp breaths, he wrapped his arms tightly around his waist. *I've always hated this forest.*

As he reached a tree big enough to crouch behind, he threw himself down, attempting to shelter from the gale. Iggy cupped his hands over his ears and hummed, desperate to drown out the forest's deafening roars. Lilleth used to warn him about Letherea - she would always insist it was an entity all of its own. Unfortunately for Iggy, this was proving to be true.

It can't stop me, it can't stop me, it can't stop me.

'IT'S WHAT SHE DESERVES,' he called into the darkness, his eyes screwed tightly shut. 'IT'S WHAT THEY ALL DESERVE!'

———

THE WIND HAD CONTINUED FOR SOME TIME AFTER THAT AND, WHEN IT finally died down, Iggy moved with extra caution. *Just keep heading for the river,* he thought. The river could always be heard from the Home Tree.

'Do you know, this'll be the first time I set foot in the Home Tree in over fifty years. Bet they thought I'd never be able to break that pesky protection spell Lilleth got that witch to cast. How little they must think of me...' Iggy ground his teeth and repeated, 'Fifty years – ha! Wonder if they've redecorated?' he laughed to the trees, a pathetic attempt to hide his nerves. A gust of wind crashed into his back, causing him to trip again.

With darting eyes, he stared into bushes, beginning to feel a little mad. His mind scattered and drifted away. *Just think of the Home Tree.*

Up ahead, he spotted some light peeking through the leaves; it made a change from the gloomy taunts of the towering trees, and Iggy clapped eagerly. With a burst of new found energy he ran towards it, jumping over roots and jabbing at bushes with his flaming fingertips.

'Yes!' he shrieked, as he pushed his way through the trees and into an opening where they parted. 'Try and spook me out in the open. Ha! I'd love to see your little parlour tricks when there's no scary corners to trick me with.' Iggy sneered. The magical forest didn't scare him – at least that's what he kept telling himself. He filled his lungs with the crisp air, at last feeling free.

'Break time,' he whispered under his breath. With a hand on his bag, he dropped to the ground and absentmindedly stroked the grass upon which he sat. 'Ouch!' he cried, pulling back and sucking at his finger. *The sharp grass,* he remembered angrily. Quickly, he reached for his feet to assess the damage it had caused them but, to his great surprise, he found nothing there. His feet were perfectly fine, as was his 'just sliced' finger. Another mind-trick played on him by the dim-witted forest.

'Oh, *very* clever,' he called back, spitting on the grass as he did so.

His thoughts turned to the Home Tree and how close he was now getting. Grimacing, he imagined all the fairies flying around it and shuddered. His hands cupped the sides of his head, as though the memories alone could cause him physical pain. Shakily, he peered into his bag. Just looking at his potion - the potion he'd waited so many years to complete - was enough to give him comfort. Soon he'd have revenge. Soon he'd be able to sleep again.

13

Troublesome Pests

They walked for a long time after this, passing more trees than Vista could count. Grecko had fallen into his thoughtful silence once again, and the back and forth between moods was beginning to wear on Vista.

Finally, Grecko stopped, rubbing his feet. 'Would it be alright ter take a quick break, Miss Vista?'

Thrilled at the idea of staying still for a while, Vista smiled. 'Yes, that sounds like a great idea.'

Somehow, the magical forest looked different again. The trees had changed from green to a rich mahogany colour, almost like the seasons had switched whilst they'd been walking. The ground was coated by a blanket of leaves, practically begging for some happy forest creature to come scuttling along and roll around in it, enjoying the feel of the leaves beneath them.

It was clear that Vista wasn't going to be that lucky forest creature. Grecko was making it quite evident that this wasn't a journey that involved having any fun. Her fingers twisted in her matted hair that no amount of river water or vigorous brushing was making any more presentable these days.

He placed her down on a tree branch in front of him and swung his arm to bring it back to life.

'Grecko.' Vista said, feeling now was as good a time as any to break the silence. 'Can you tell me where we're going?'

After a much longer pause than Vista felt was necessary, Grecko turned to look at her. He sighed, plonking himself down on the leaves and rubbing again at his filthy, tired feet. She tried not to think about how he was sitting on the leaves that she so desperately wanted to roll in.

'We're gunna see an old friend o' mine,' he explained, staring at the ground and absentmindedly tearing at the leaves with his chunky fingers. 'Well, I say friend, but more like... jus' someone I know, someone pretty special. Ain't seen 'em fer a real long time, but they're good at giving advice. Reckon they'll know what ter do.'

'Why do we need advice?'

Letting the leaves in his hands fall, he looked up and stared straight at Vista. His eyes studied her, making her feel like a child about to be scolded. She shifted uncomfortably on her branch.

'Miss Vista, 'av yer got any idea why a crafty imp would be wanting a pair o' fairy wings?'

Vista had no idea how to respond. The truth was she had no idea why he would want the wings, and she couldn't understand why Grecko was so worked up about it. *It's not like the wings worked anyway.*

'No, I suppose I don't. Do you?' The question came out slightly cheekier than Vista had intended, but frankly she was getting a little tired of the constant blaming when all she had been trying to do was something nice for Grecko.

'No... I dunno, Miss Vista, an' that's the problem,' Grecko admitted. 'I'll tell yer summit I do know though – imps is bad news, very bad news! Me dad thought they could be trusted once, an' he was so wrong.' he swallowed hard, and Vista realised he was once again holding back tears. 'An' now I 'av ter find out what this *imp*,' he sneered at the word, 'is up ter an' stop him somehow.'

A strange buzzing noise cut him off, growing louder and speeding in their direction. Distracting them from their own problems, they turned their heads towards the noise.

Vista craned her head over the branch, the stabbing feeling in her back making her inhale sharply.

'What's that noise?'

Grecko was already on his feet and marching towards the tree branch, a frustrated look on his face. 'We need ter leave now!'

Vista's knees trembled slightly, nerves creeping in. 'Why do we have to leave?' she asked, her voice rising slightly as she spoke. 'What's coming? Is it dangerous?'

'No, don't reckon so Miss Vista... more like nasty pests but we ain't hanging round ter see 'em.' Grecko grabbed hold of Vista, bringing her back into the safety of his hand and pulling her close to his chest.

'What kind of pests?' Vista persisted, 'Grecko, what are they? *Please* tell me?'

'Urgh.' Grecko began to explain as he moved, 'They're called skizzes; a weird name fer a weird creature. They're these flying pests, an' once they spot yer, they won't leave yer alone - they feed on chaos. That's why we gotta go or we'll be stuck with 'em.' Grecko's face fell as what looked like hundreds of tiny, noisy bugs hovered above their heads. They encircled them, each one screaming to be the centre of attention.

'Oooh, is that a fairy?'

'Can't be a fairy, it's got no wings!'

'It's got *filthy* hair, though!'

'Look at the dress, who made that?'

'It's *so* ugly!'

'Who's the big one? Looks like the bodyguard's a bit of a grump, eh?'

There was no doubt these were the loudest, most irritating creatures Vista had ever had the displeasure of meeting. They were also incredibly bizarre to look at – they were smaller than her, which in itself was astonishing as Vista had never met a talking creature smaller than a fairy before. They were deep blue in colour, and their hair, which was navy, floated above them the way it would if lying in a pool of water. They had hands with fingers pointed at the tips and faces that curved at the chin, giving them the look of a creature that enjoys doing evil things, despite Grecko's description of them as 'harmless pests'.

'We were jus' leaving if yer don't mind.' Grecko attempted to brush the skizzes aside with his free hand, but they continued to swarm around them.

'Nah, you're not leaving yet!'

'We don't even know your names?'

'You're quite rude for a gnome, aren't you?'

Grecko gritted his teeth and Vista could tell how irritated he was getting. Her blood ran hot as she grew more and more annoyed by these pesky things herself.

'Excuse me, but he's right, we really *do* have to be going.' Vista piped in.

'What's your name, then?'

It was near impossible to single out one voice amongst the hundreds of them, so Vista decided to address them as a whole.

'Well, my name's Vista, and this is Grecko.' she said, gesturing her hand towards Grecko who glared at her with a look of frustration.

The skizzes all giggled in unison.

'Those are stupid names!'

'Who would ever hate you enough to name you something like that?'

'I'd be devastated if I was called Grecko.'

Vista's jaw fell open in shock by the sheer rudeness of these horrid creatures. Grecko just continued staring forward, avoiding their gaze, his jaw clenched.

Grecko was right.

'You're all being very rude,' Vista remarked, 'You don't even know us.'

Her outburst caused them to erupt into another fit of giggles.

'Ooh, this one's got an attitude on her.'

'She must be feeling special because she's got her big, strong friend with her.'

Vista seethed, 'I most certainly do *not* think I'm special. I just happen to think that you're all being horribly rude *pests!*'

Standing in Grecko's palm, for the first time in her life being able to use her height to her advantage, she pursed her lips and stared at them all in anger.

'Oooh, pests are we? How about we show you what us pests can do?'

From the crowd of skizzes, one emerged to the forefront, a wicked grin spreading across her small, pointed face.

Grecko curled his fingers around Vista. She had almost forgotten he was there—he'd been so quiet until now.

'If any o' yer dare try an' hurt Miss Vista, yer'll all be sorry!' Grecko called to the crowd.

'Hurt her?' they replied innocently, 'Oh no, sweet Grecko, we don't want to hurt her. We only want to play with her!'

With this, all the skizzes drew closer, creating a strange buzzing noise. The noise had a hypnotic effect, causing Vista to feel confused and slightly dizzy. The Skizzes were now so close to her face that as she tried to focus on keeping her balance, all she could make out were flurries of deep blues whizzing past her head.

To her horror, Vista felt her hair being lifted away from her neck and yanked upwards. She wrapped her arms tightly around Grecko's finger and cried out for him to help, but it was no use – the buzzing noise had sent Grecko into a dream-like state, and her cries were going unheard.

Vista's feet were lifted from the safety of Grecko's palm, and she felt the unnerving feeling of nothingness beneath her as she was raised higher and higher into the air. Screaming desperately, she kicked her legs and swung her arms in a hopeless attempt to free herself. Two of the skizzes had wrapped their wretched hands around Vista's tangled hair and were now flying higher than Vista had ever been in her life.

'VISTA?' Her name bounced off the trees as Grecko screamed from the ground below - waking from his dream-like state as the buzzing noise faded. The skizzes followed Vista upwards, a few still lagging behind to bounce off Grecko's nose and pull on his eyelids.

'GRECKO? I'm up here!' Vista screamed. 'Please, *please* don't do this...' she cried at the skizzes.

Hot tears scolded her cheeks, and she breathed harshly as her mind desperately searched for an escape. From the corner of her eye, Vista spied a skizz hovering just within her reach – the others were all above her now, looking up to the skies and giggling as they dragged her higher. Vista took a deep breath and kicked out with all her strength. Her foot made contact with the skizz to her side and it cried out in alarm.

'Oi! Cheeky thing you are, aren't you?' the skizz laughed, clearly unhurt by the kick. The laugh floated through the air and reached every other skizz, each of them echoing the giggle, mocking Vista even further.

'LEAVE ME ALONE!' Vista yelled, ignoring their taunts. She reached out her hand, trying to grab the hair of the skizz she had kicked. To her surprise however, as her fingers gripped it, she found that she couldn't – it was like trying to hold on to flowing water.

The laughter went on and they continued to fly, the skizz now slightly out of reach - clearly bored with Vista's attempts to fight back. It was becoming quite clear that her fate lay solely in the hands of the two evil creatures currently pulling her up by her tangled hair.

'So, what happened to your wings?' one of the skizzes asked, flying so close to Vista's face that she could smell it's surprisingly sweet breath. Vista's head pounded inside her skull, her hair ripping from her skin. She opened her mouth but found no sound came out - the terror of being so high rendering her speechless.

'Oh, will you stop your whimpering and tell us? It's so *boring* watching you cry.'

Vista swallowed, staring at the skizz. It seemed in her favour to cooperate rather than defy at this point.

'I... I gave them away.' she stuttered, wincing with the pain of being held up solely by her hair.

'You *what*? Why would you ever do something so *stupid*?'

Vista didn't have the energy to defend herself, 'they were broken...' Fresh tears blurred her vision, and she blinked furiously.

The skizz in front of her feigned surprise and grabbed at its chest. 'Wait a minute, you mean to tell me that you've *never* flown before?' it grinned, 'Oh, you have to try it, it's simply the best.'

Vista's eyes widened, terrified. 'No! No, please don't! Just let me go?'

The skizz smiled, staring straight into Vista's wide, fearful eyes. 'But my dear, that's exactly what we're planning to do.' Looking towards the skizzes holding Vista's hair, it smiled. 'Do as Vista asks - let her go.'

Before Vista could say another word, she felt her hair be released, and she was falling. Wind hit her face at great speed, causing any remaining tears she had to evaporate the second they left her eyes. Cold air filled her mouth as she screamed, her cheeks puffing outwards. Grecko's panicked cries became clearer as she neared the ground. Together, their terrified shouts merged into the most horrific cry.

Before Vista could hit the ground, however, she was abruptly grabbed by her hair once again and yanked back upwards.

'Argh!' Pain scorched through her head, now fully at the skizzes' mercy.

'Do you like games, Vista? We *love* games! Especially throwing games.' With this, Vista was thrown – not dropped, but *thrown* – through the air into the arms of another eagerly awaiting skizz. The strength of these miniature creatures was astounding.

'STOP...' This was all Vista could manage as she was hurtled through the air in every direction. When they were done toying with her, she would be dropped – that much she was certain of.

Her stomach lurched and twisted, the contents of her most recent meal spilling out of her mouth and decorating the leaves below. Every part of her body ached with the pressure of being grabbed and thrown repeatedly, and Vista's head developed its own piercing ring.

The cackles from the skizzes echoed around the forest - the only thing louder was the howling from Grecko, stood helplessly below.

Vista began to lose track of which limbs were hers and which were the skizzes'. The nausea made it impossible for her to scream anymore, her body a limp rag doll, tossed from one skizz to another. She kept her eyes shut, the constant movement causing her vision to blur.

BANG!

What was that?

Her eyes shot open, terrified of what was coming next.

BANG!

There it was again...

The skizzes stopped throwing Vista. She dangled upside down from the hand of an angry looking skizz, unable to regain her focus.

BANG!

This time she saw it. A skizz directly in front of her was hit by something, something much larger than her. It was too fast to see what it was, but regardless, it sent the skizz zooming backwards and out of sight at great speed.

BANG!

Grecko?

The skizzes stopped their giggling and started to panic. Imagine the chaos hundreds of panicking skizzes could cause! They flew hurriedly, crashing into each other, all the while taking Vista along for the ride.

'Grecko? HELP ME...' Squinting, she looked down to where he stood. In his hands he seemed to be holding a catapult of some kind. Scooping low to the ground, he grabbed handfuls of what appeared to be large pebbles and, putting one in, he aimed ready to shoot at the skizzes again.

'Let her go!'

BANG!

Another skizz was sent flying, straight into the nearest tree.

There was no doubt that falling from this height would kill Vista, but unfortunately, it was still her best shot.

'Alright, we'll let her go, you big lump. Just stop shooting at us!'

Relief flooded Vista, which instantly changed to terror as the skizz released her ankle, and she found herself hurtling towards the ground with no way of stopping.

Vista's arms and legs flailed madly.

'MISS VISTA...'

Grecko's voice grew louder the closer she got. She closed her eyes, bracing herself for the impact, praying Grecko would reach her in time.

Pain shot up Vista's spine as she landed in a crumpled heap but, opening her eyes, was elated to find herself safe in Grecko's clammy palm.

He caught me, I'm alive! He caught me! Pathetic wails left her as she tried to still her spinning head.

'Miss Vista, are yer alright? Are yer hurt?'

Despite the spinning, she was relieved to realise she was indeed unhurt. 'Yes, I'm fine. Grecko, thank you so mu—'

'Miss Vista, how could yer be so stupid?'

His outburst startled her, and she struggled to defend herself as her vision continued to spin. 'You... You said they weren't dangerous?'

'I told yer we needed ter leave! I told yer them skizzes were trouble, didn't I?' his voice rose as his face contorted in frustration, 'Yer could 'av bin killed, yer lost yer wings, an' now yer nearly end up dead! Everything's gone wrong an' it's all yer fault – why are yer doing such stupid things?'

'But you said they *weren't* dangerous!' Vista repeated, louder this time, 'I never would have stayed if I'd known that would happen. I just wanted you to tell me what was going on and stop acting like I couldn't handle things.' she cried, staring at Grecko. Her whole body ached as her vision came in and out focus.

He sighed and sat down, Vista still curled up in his hand. 'I know... I know, but why can't yer jus' stop an' think before yer do stuff, eh?' he said as he dropped her abruptly into the leaves. It seemed strange that not that long ago she had wanted so badly to sit amongst them. The ground swayed as Grecko paced back and forth, his hands and legs leaving mirroring paths amongst the leaves as he did so. He muttered under his breath and shook his head like it was all a bad dream. When he spoke again he kept his face to the ground, not wanting to make eye contact. 'Really, Miss Vista... yer making things so much harder fer me...'

It's not my fault, Vista wanted so badly to defend herself but the nausea was making it hard to focus.

'I know yer don't mean it,' he muttered a little louder, not necessarily to Vista but more about her. 'It ain't yer fault, I get that. But why 'av yer gotta do these things?' he sighed again and stopped his pacing, turning back to face her.

She sat amongst the leaves, moving her hands through the dirt. It reminded her of the last time she lay curled up in mud, disappointed and distraught after falling from the Home Tree.

'It's not my fault...You're doing it again,' she forced out despite her nausea, 'stop treating me like a child!'

Grecko kept silent and studied her, his face a mixture of guilt and sadness.

Regret hit her in the stomach - she'd never meant to hurt his feelings. 'I'm sorry, Grecko,' she mumbled.

He sighed deeply, kneeling to the ground and admitting defeat, 'No, Miss Vista, I'm sorry. I know yer ain't a child, I just worry 'bout yer is all.' He looked at her hopelessly. Slowly her vision steadied and his face stopped swaying.

Breaking the stare, Grecko opened his palm, inviting Vista to climb on.

'We better get going, the forest floor ain't no place fer a wingless fairy.'

Though she would never admit it to Grecko, this hurt her more than she was prepared for.

What would you even call a wingless fairy?

14

An Imp amongst Fairies

Despite Iggy's best efforts to deny it to himself, the Home Tree had once been his home too. He'd been found on the ground there when he was only a baby, wrapped in a small shawl which barely covered his shoulders. Lilleth had told him this story so many times when he was young. So many, in fact, that he could almost trick his mind into thinking it was an actual memory of his - not that he wanted it as a memory, of course.

Iggy could never be certain, but he believed that he was the only creature other than the fairies to have ever set foot inside the Home Tree.

Growing up he'd always thought of Lilleth as his mother, and the fairies as his family. As Iggy got older, however, their differences began to show. For one thing, Iggy had magic.

When he was young he'd have great fun practising making different colours spark out of his fingertips, and moving objects along far away shelves. As he practised, he'd occasionally catch glances from envious fairies and knew how jealous it made them. If he were honest with himself, that just made him want to practise even more. The idea of having something that everyone else wanted was thrilling; it made him feel like the King of the Home Tree. No matter how hard the fairies tried, they would never be as good as he was.

That, of course, was before they started to fly. Flying was something Iggy could not do. Just knowing that they could fly whilst he was on the ground made him feel pathetic.

He remembered, with spite, one particular morning when Lilleth had come to speak with him.

'Iggy, may I speak with you?'

Back then, seeing Lilleth always made Iggy feel calmer. She was his mother, his safe place.

'Yeah, of course. Everything okay?'

Lilleth approached the bed that Iggy lay upon and pursed her lips, as though bracing herself. 'I've had some complaints regarding disagreements between you and the fairies. Is it true that you've been using magic against them?'

Iggy felt himself panic; he hated disappointing Lilleth. 'Well... kind of, yes. But it's not as bad as it sounds. They give just as good as they get, I promise!'

Lilleth held up her hand to silence Iggy. 'That is beside the point, Iggy. The important thing here is that you have magic and they don't! Magic can be very dangerous.' Lilleth stared sternly at Iggy, 'You will never use magic against any of my fairies ever again, do you understand me? Remember, I hear everything, Iggy. I hear about flames coming out of your fingers and jars that fall from nowhere, narrowly missing a fairy's head. Why are you doing these things?' Iggy wasn't used to her voice sounding this way. Usually, she was so calm and steady, but now there was an anxious ring to her tone.

Iggy looked to his feet, hurt that he was getting all the blame and angry she could make him feel this. 'It's not my fault. They look at me differently. I know they do. Sometimes they even laugh at me when I walk by. They know how much I'd love to fly, and so they wait until I'm right in earshot before they start talking about getting their wings. It's not fair!' Despite not wanting to, he had started to cry. Giant tears rolled down his cheeks, soaking his clothes. Lilleth moved closer towards him and wrapped her arms around his shoulders. Forgetting his anger, he sought her comfort – he needed it more than anything else. As Lilleth hugged him, he fell against her, holding her close and burying his face into her neck. He hadn't meant to upset her - that was the last thing he'd ever want to do.

'I won't do magic anymore, I promise.' he said between sobs.

Lilleth hushed him with soothing tones, and gently stroked the back of his hair. They stayed like this for a while until eventually Iggy fell asleep.

Iggy had tried so hard back then to keep his promise to Lilleth. The problem was that, over time, it got more and more difficult to resist his magic.

It started out with the small things. He'd been watching some birds flying together one day and absentmindedly flicked his fingers – sending them spiralling away from each other. He knew they wouldn't be hurt, of course, but it did give him a chuckle - the thought of them spending the rest of that day trying desperately to find each other again.

After that, it was almost too easy to fall back into using magic. He'd reasoned with himself that if he didn't get caught, then it wasn't really breaking his promise. He would make sure to only perform small acts of magic - things like moving objects closer to him rather than getting up to grab them, or making his hands glow in the dark.

Iggy believed to this day that everything would have turned out just fine if it hadn't been for Jesabelle. Of all the fairies that had taken a dislike to Iggy, Jesabelle had disliked him the most. He also, for that matter, had no doubt in his mind that the 'complaints' Lilleth had received had all been delivered, or at least perpetrated, by Jesabelle.

He could even pinpoint the exact morning that his life had begun to fall apart.

It was the morning of another flying day. Iggy was bored waiting for the action to start and was playing with his magic to pass the time. He'd lined up a set of bowls in the empty kitchen and was attempting to knock them off the table one by one, using only his magic and a keen aim. If anyone were to notice a smashed bowl on the floor, he could simply say he'd knocked it over whilst cleaning up or something equally dull. The table stood in the centre of the kitchen, so Iggy placed himself upon the window ledge in the far corner of the room. Patiently, he began practising his aim, picturing the faces of all the fairies that had taunted him plastered on the bowls as he did so.

It was only when he finally managed to knock a bowl down that he spotted Jesabelle. His scrawny hands were raised up in celebration, but he quickly dropped them at the sight of her smug face. She stood in the doorway, arms folded assertively across her chest. Iggy had always felt she didn't have the right look for a fairy, and this stance proved it. As far as he could tell – and he felt he had quite a good sense for these things seeing as he'd lived amongst them for so long – most fairies tended to look quite similar to each other. Of course, they all had different hair and dress colours, but each and every one was still elegant and dainty. Iggy assumed this was a mechanical design – the larger the object, the harder it would be to make it fly.

Their faces all looked very similar as well; they had soft features, almost childlike. But this wasn't the case when it came to Jesabelle. She'd been born from a joy flower which, in Iggy's opinion, was very ironic indeed. She had a nasty habit of frowning, leaving her face looking constantly bitter. Her jaw was harsh, angular, and framed with a short black bob - complete with a fringe that sat on top of her permanently creased forehead. She was dainty like the others, Iggy supposed, but the way she carried herself was far from elegant – she stomped whilst they glided. When Jesabelle was created, something must have gone seriously wrong and this thought amused Iggy indefinitely. As far as he was concerned, that joy flower should have been cast out of the fairy-making business a long time ago!

Now however, perching on the windowsill, Iggy was feeling far from amused. He swallowed hard. Jesabelle had caught him using magic. This was something she'd been trying to do for the longest time, and now she'd *finally done it. Iggy had no doubt she would run and tell Lilleth at the first chance she got, and that petrified him more than anything.*

'Jes—'

'Don't bother. I think you'd better save your energy for when Lilleth comes, don't you?' she smirked.

'Please, don't tell her, Jesabelle! She doesn't really need to know, does she?' It was obvious he was wasting his time trying to reason with her. Her face looked as though she had finally won the prize for the best flower nectar at afternoon tea.

'Oh, I think she does need to know, Iggy. In fact, I think we should wake the others up right now so they can all know too, shall we?' She spun on her heels and stomped out of the room.

'NO!' Iggy yelled, running after her. His head raced, trying to work out what to say.

'Everyone, wake up, Iggy's got something to tell you all...'

Over the next few minutes, fairies slowly emerged from their beds, yawning but intrigued as to what Iggy had to tell them. For a while it was silent. Every fairy was looking at him, and he tried to avoid all of their gazes. This could have gone on for quite some time had Jesabelle not grown impatient and taken matters into her own hands.

'Oh for goodness sake,' she huffed, 'I caught Iggy using magic again!'

As soon as she'd said it, the room filled with gasps and excited squeals. Every fairy was whispering over what they thought would become of Iggy.

'Is this true, Iggy?'

Silence. Iggy forced down the urge to vomit and turned around. Nobody had seen Lilleth enter the room. Even Jesabelle looked surprised, cautiously blending into the crowd of fairies, her smug confidence paling under Lilleth's unfaltering presence.

Lilleth looked only at Iggy. They may as well have been the only two creatures in the entire magical forest at that moment. Her face was shrouded in disappointment; that was what hurt Iggy the most.

'You have let me down, Iggy. I want you to go to your bed and wait for me there. When the day is done, I will deal with you.'

His eyes shot up. 'But the flying... I always watch the flying!'

'Not this time.'

It was obvious this wasn't up for debate, and Iggy sloped to his bed, admitting defeat. Walking past Jesabelle, he caught the smallest glimpse of a smirk creep across her lips. That smirk was the first thing Iggy could remember filling him with rage. Later on, rage came easily to him, but that was the thing that had started it all. All Iggy had wanted to do was wipe that smirk off her face.

———

SITTING THERE, CONFINED TO HIS BED, IGGY'S RAGE AND HUMILIATION AT *being sent away only grew.*

How dare she! *All he saw when he closed his eyes was Jesabelle's smirk.* Why did she have to smirk like that?

Hatred ran through him, making it impossible for him to sit still. Back and forth he paced, trying to plan the perfect retribution for her smirk.

From his bed, he could hear the incessant giggling of the fairies in the other room.

They must already have their wings by now. *Iggy had watched the flying days enough times to know the routine by heart. To his dismay, he heard the faint sound of Jesabelle's name being called.*

How did I forget she was flying today?

This was a disaster. If Jesabelle flew away, then his chance for payback would be gone. The thought of her getting the last laugh twisted Iggy's stomach and made him sweat.

With no time to stop and think it through, Iggy crept from his room. He crouched down, slowly crawling along the ground so as not to be spotted. Annoyingly, he realised it wouldn't have mattered if he'd come out doing cartwheels - everyone's eyes were fixed on Jesabelle as she stepped out of the Home Tree.

The fairy younglings gazed at her in awe as she walked along the branch with her brand new wings. They gawped at her, as though she were the most amazing creature they had ever seen.

Iggy's skin crawled, and he clucked his tongue in disgust. So what if she has wings now? Can't they see what she's really like?

Warily, he peeked his head slightly further outwards, hoping to get a better view whilst trying not to be spotted.

The fairy elders were gathered around the branch, each offering their own words of encouragement. Jesabelle was facing Lilleth and smiling. From the corner of her eye she caught sight of Iggy. Subtly, so as not to be noticed by the others, she raised one eyebrow and smirked at him. She did it again!

Jesabelle knew how much Iggy would love to fly, and he had no doubt that was why she had smirked. Heat swirled through Iggy's fingertips, the magic inside him screaming to be let loose and teach her a lesson. In a way, Iggy felt almost powerless against his magic; when he got angry, it was the magic that was in charge. The magic wanted so badly to make everyone pay.

His forefinger straightened without Iggy even thinking about it.

He glared furiously at Jesabelle, watching as she removed one foot from the branch ready to fly away and leave his life forever. Without any hesitation, Iggy flicked his finger deliberately in her direction and before anyone could even blink, Jesabelle's wings were ripped away from her body.

The sound of hundreds of fairies gasping in unison followed as Jesabelle fell backward onto the branch.

She screamed as she fell, in pain and confused. Wildly, her head spun towards Iggy. 'You!' she yelled, pointing, 'y-you did this, all because you're j-jealous...' Her breathing quickened. 'You. Don't. Belong. Here.' she cried, blood now pouring down her back and staining her dress. Elder fairies from every direction rushed to soothe the now hysterical Jesabelle.

It was then that Iggy began to laugh. Not just a quiet, reserved giggle either. Oh no - this was an uncontrollable, booming laugh. The type of laugh reserved for things that were truly funny. This, however, was not one of those things, and the more Iggy tried to stifle his laughter, the more it came.

Fairy younglings near him began to step back, none wanting to be his next victim. Their mouths hung open in fear, and they grasped for each other's hands, knowing full well they were no match for this vicious creature's magic.

'IGGY!' This was possibly the one and only time anyone had ever heard

Lilleth shout. Even the fairy elders seemed slightly stunned by the sound, briefly looking away from the distraught Jesabelle.

Lilleth's scream was the thing that put an end to Iggy's laughter. Pathetically, he wiped away tears and waved his hands in front of him, showing everyone that the magic had gone and there was no need to worry.

He risked a peek towards Jesabelle. She was still lying in a ball, weeping helplessly over her injured back and ruined wings. The sight gave Iggy immense pleasure, but he tried his best to disguise it. Facing Lilleth, he did his best to look remorseful.

'Iggy, what do you have to say for yourself?' Lilleth stared at him, wide-eyed and unblinking. Her lips were pursed together so tightly that her mouth dissolved into a thin line.

Iggy mulled over his answer, debating what he thought Lilleth would most want to hear, 'I'm sorry. It was... an accident...'

Iggy would never say it to her face, but he felt that a part of the blame should lie with Lilleth. After all, if she hadn't tried to shut down such an important part of him - his magic - then maybe he would have had better control over his urges by now and be able to resist. Not that he was regretting his actions in any way.

'I know you, Iggy. You don't do accidents. Now tell me why you would ever do something as appalling as ripping Jesabelle's wings off? How could you even be capable of something so brutal? What is she going to do now?'

A smile crept across Iggy's face which he quickly hid with his hand. Judging by her question, it seemed as though Jesabelle wouldn't be able to get a second set of wings as Iggy had originally thought she might. Knowing this made his revenge even sweeter. That'll teach her to smirk at me.

'Iggy, how dare you smile over such a thing! You have ruined Jesabelle's life as a fairy - and for what? What kind of a monster are you?'

Iggy froze, his smile well and truly gone. Surely she couldn't really think of him as a monster? After all, she was his mother.

It was becoming quite clear just how far he'd pushed things this time and Iggy dug deep to show some remorse. Apologise, that's it! *If he pretended to feel guilty for Jesabelle, then Lilleth would have to forgive him.*

He went to step out onto the branch and towards Jesabelle - still snivelling like a baby - but Lilleth stepped in front of him, blocking his path.

'I'm trying to say sorry to Jesabelle...'

'It's too late for that, Iggy.'

Too late? He didn't understand. How could it be too late? 'But-'

'I've tried my very best with you, Iggy, truly I have. But my fairies must come first. I'm afraid the time has come for you to leave.'

Iggy stared at Lilleth, not understanding. He watched her sceptically, waiting for her to change her mind. After all, she loved him, there was no way she could ever throw him out.

'Iggy, I want you to leave now and never come back. You've become a danger to my children.'

My children... The words cut into him like a knife.

'But... What about me? I'm your child too...'

He refused to cry. An audience of fairies had gathered around them, and he would not give them the satisfaction of his tears.

Lilleth looked deep into Iggy's eyes. He noticed she too seemed to be holding back tears and was taking a few shaky breaths before speaking again. 'My fairies must come first, Iggy... I'm sorry,' she said, looking away.

'Sorry?' Iggy shrieked, 'YOU'RE SORRY?' Suddenly he didn't care one bit about how he was coming across to the others. 'How can you do this to me? If I leave, you'll regret it! You can keep your precious fairies, but just know that you'll regret this...'

Lilleth remained silent, not reacting to Iggy's shrieks and threats. Furiously, he spun around, heading straight for the window in the kitchen.

I'll show her! He'd spent countless days sitting at the open kitchen window, looking at the outstretched branch opposite and debating if he could make it over with a jump. This seemed like the perfect time to find out.

Reaching the window, he paused, ensuring he made the scene as dramatic as possible. Glancing back at Lilleth, he swung his legs out and teetered on the window ledge. Iggy wasn't sure what he expected to happen next - maybe Lilleth would call him back, or cry out and askv to leave with him. He paused a little longer than necessary just in case, but all that greeted him was Lilleth's stern, yet pitying, stare.

When no one moved or made a sound, Iggy turned his attention back towards the branch opposite. His heart pounded in his chest and he told himself that was just a normal reaction to the jump, but in reality he knew what it really was. He was afraid.

Not wanting anyone to sense his fear by stalling for too long, Iggy plunged forwards out of the window and across to the neighbouring branch. Fingers outstretched, he just about managed to grab hold of it. He peeked down at what would have been a very unpleasant drop and puffed out his cheeks in relief.

Hanging there, he breathed deeply and focused all his strength on holding on. Now what?

Swinging his nimble feet in front of him, he was able to press them against the bark of the tree, turning his body into a sort of half-moon shape. He hung there, rather embarrassed, clearly stuck between the branch and the trunk.

To his dismay, an audience had now gathered around the window to watch this rather impressive fail of his. Twisting his body he peered at the ground again, debating whether or not he could survive a fall from this height. His sweaty hands struggled to maintain his grip, and he curled his toes firmly into the tree.

Cool air brushed past his face. He could hear birds chirping in the tree above him. Shut up! He resisted the urge to scream at them out loud, knowing full well he still had an audience of fairies watching, and no doubt judging him, from the window. If he were to fall and die, he didn't want his last words to be wasted shouting at some chirping birds.

His hands slipped a little, 'Lilleth? LILLETH!' The moment he called her name he regretted it. He'd have liked to think he'd rather die than show any kind of weakness, but it was quite clear that was merely a lie he told himself in order to feel tougher. Arching his back, he saw Lilleth appear at the window ledge. The fairies had scattered, allowing her a path through without her needing to ask.

Her eyes widened for a moment at the sight of Iggy, arched and dangling between branch and trunk. Without a word she flew through the window towards him, her wings shining in the mid-morning sun. She wrapped her arms around Iggy's waist, her strength remarkable for someone of her size, and pulled Iggy tightly towards her. Held close in her embrace, they gently floated towards the ground. Despite himself, Iggy rested his head against her chest, closing his eyes and breathing her in, wanting to commit her to memory.

To Iggy's disappointment, they reached the ground quickly. Lilleth slowly released her grip on Iggy, and he stumbled backwards clumsily. Standing in front of her like a naughty school boy, he took in his new surroundings. Everything was so big on the ground, making him very aware of how small he actually was. Slowly, he reached his pointed fingers out and stroked the stem of a nearby flower. It felt soft against his dry touch, and he recoiled instantly. Flowers appeared to be everywhere around the Home Tree, he noticed. Behind Lilleth, however, there were bushes. Great, big, giant bushes that an imp like him could easily disappear into. If Lilleth is serious, that's the way I'll go. Even the thought of it made his throat tighten.

He dared a look at her face, pleased that she hadn't flown away the instant they'd reached the ground.

'Thanks for helping me...' Iggy mumbled, scuffing his feet on the soil.

Lilleth merely nodded. They stood there for a while, neither really wanting to leave.

'Do you really want me to go?' Iggy asked, breaking the silence. He continued to kick his foot nervously into the mud, surprised by the feeling of it. It was soggier than he'd imagined it being from up in the Home Tree.

'It's not a question of what I want, it's a question of what is best.' Lilleth sighed, 'You don't belong with us anymore, Iggy. Imps and fairies are just too different. I think it's for the best if you try to find your own kind now.' she paused and swallowed. Iggy was glad to see she was struggling with this; he hoped it might be a sign of her changing her mind. 'Iggy... I should have taken you to your own kind the moment I found you... It was wrong of me to have kept you.' she looked into Iggy's eyes sadly, 'I'm so sorry.'

There was that word again. Sorry. For some reason that was the word that seemed to anger him the most. Sorry... like she'd spilt the last of the honey or something, rather than throwing him out of his own home.

'So that's it then? You're really just going to leave me down here?' he asked, his heart aching with betrayal. When Lilleth didn't reply, he continued, 'You have no idea how sorry you'll be!' With all the force he could *muster, he stormed past Lilleth towards the giant bushes. As he passed, he let his shoulder bash into her side, setting her off balance briefly but able to steady herself before tripping. Pity, Iggy thought.*

He forced himself to keep walking without looking back. When he reached the bushes, however, he stopped. He knew without even checking that if he were to turn around, Lilleth would still be standing there. He didn't turn around, though. That was the first time Iggy recalled ever feeling true hatred towards his mother.

15

Grecko's Pain

'Miss Vista, I reckon it's time ter drink the nectar now.' Grecko stopped, feeling they had walked a significant distance away from the skizzes.

Vista felt shaky but nodded her head in agreement – anything to make her feel slightly less nauseous.

He rooted through his pocket and produced the small pot. Gently pulling the cloth back from the top, he offered it to Vista first. 'Don't forget, yer jus' need a sip.'

Vista opened her mouth, allowing Grecko to lift the pot's edge right to her lips and tilt it slightly. She slurped slowly and waited. It tasted incredibly sweet, like syrup or honey. She savoured it on her tongue for a moment, relishing the distraction from her ordeal with the skizz.

Grecko took the pot away and had a sip himself. The pot now empty, he popped it back in his pocket and watched Vista expectantly.

As they waited, she began to feel a tingle in her arms. It felt as though they were finally coming to life after being dead for quite some time. The tingle spread throughout her entire body, and gradually she felt the strength returning to her limbs. Looking from her arms to Grecko, she smiled shyly, grateful for this help.

'I feel stronger already, thank you. Is it helping you too?'

'Aye, it'll work in a bit, I'm sure. We'll keep moving while it kicks in.'

Grecko and Vista continued their wade through endless paths. Thousands of trees separated them from Iggy's madness and hatred, but the leaves still seemed to tremble with its echo.

As they walked, the occasional fruit would fall at their feet - an offering from a friendly tree. They would give their thanks by stroking its bark, and then fill their stomachs gratefully.

'Miss Vista,' Grecko said as he noisily munched, 'there's summit I never got 'bout fairies.'

Her interest was immediately piqued, the idea of teaching something to Grecko rather than the other way around amusing.

'Where do fairies come from? I mean, I know yer don't exactly 'av mothers like other creatures do, do yer?'

The mere mention of mothers sent Vista's mind straight back to Lilleth. Despite not being that long since she last saw her, so much had happened; it felt like it had been years. She considered how seldom she thought of Lilleth and the other fairies now, and her cheeks flushed with shame. It was hard imagining she'd once been a part of their family. She wondered if Lilleth ever thought of her, and for Lilleth's sake hoped that she didn't - the thought of causing her more upset was too much for Vista to bear.

'Well, yes, we do have a mother.' Vista replied, 'She's called Lilleth. She's mother to all the fairies actually. She's the first fairy we meet when we're brought up to the Home Tree, and she's the one who sends us on our way when we're ready to take flight.' Grecko had the decency to look away, knowing it must stir up painful memories for Vista of her first flying experience.

'I see.' was all Grecko could think to say.

Despite it being a sore subject, speaking about something she knew as much about as the Home Tree made Vista feel strangely safe whilst surrounded by so much uncertainty. She shrugged away her guilt and animatedly began to delve into the history of the Home Tree and the fairies.

'Well, we obviously aren't born in the conventional way that most other creatures are born. Fairies are actually created by the forest,' she explained, staring confidently at him and chuffed at being able to teach a thing or two for once.

'I did hear that before, ' Grecko answered sheepishly.

Undeterred by his surprising knowledge, Vista continued, 'We can be created in lots of different ways - for example there are certain flowers called onamas, but we just call them luck flowers. They're great big plants with petals the size of your hands!' she chuckled, 'The petals are red and green, and smooth like velvet. Every now and then they give off a little tune, almost like a lullaby, and that's the signal to Lilleth and the other fairies that there's a new youngling waiting to be collected from its petals.' She smiled at the memory, 'my friend Mila was created by a luck flower. You would have liked her, she was so positive about the fairy life and their beliefs. She would have been a lot less trouble for you than I am,' Vista shrugged, trying to ignore the slight glimmer of guilt.

'That could be true, Miss Vista, she sounds sensible,' he mused, glancing at her and raising an eyebrow playfully. 'Bet she ain't half as much fun as yer are though!' He snorted and Vista couldn't help but laugh with him. She had to hand it to Grecko, he did have a knack for making her feel better.

'So, what flower were yer born from then. Not a luck flower I take it?'

Vista grinned, lying back in Grecko's hand to continue her story. 'No, I'm not a luck flower fairy,' she paused. Describing herself as a fairy at all felt odd without her wings. 'I was actually a water flower fairy, known as an aleeran.' Vista giggled as a thought struck her, 'I wonder who came up with these bizarre names?'

'I s'pose someone with too much time on their hands?' Grecko laughed in response.

Vista nodded in agreement. 'Yeah, you're probably right. Anyway, what was I saying? Oh that's it, so I'm a water flower fairy, that's why my dress is made up of blue petals.' Vista looked down at her stained, filthy dress. 'Well, it used to be made up of blue petals, before all of the dirt that is.'

Grecko chuckled, 'An' Lilleth was the first fairy yer saw then?'

'Yes, she was my mother who came and collected me from the flower. She brought me up to the Home Tree, and I stayed there until my flying day.' Her eyes glazed over and she blinked irritably. It seemed hypocritical to cry over a place she'd been so desperate to leave not that long ago.

'Yer must miss yer mother very much.' Grecko said, sensing her sadness.

'It's not like that Grecko, all I ever wanted was to leave. I don't think I ever took the time to appreciate what I had until I'd lost it.' She was now more grateful than ever not to be alone in the magical forest.

'It's alright, Miss Vista, I know how yer feel.' Grecko kept looking forward as the path steepened slightly. 'I miss me own mum as well.'

Vista froze, unable to speak. *How could I have forgotten about Grecko's mother?*

'I'm so sorry... I didn't think...'

Grecko had stopped walking and looked down at her. He smiled sadly through his watery eyes. Again, Vista wished she were big enough to hug him properly. She gripped his thumb tightly and leant into his chest - all the while trying to dodge the occasional large tear that rolled off his chin and splashed his hand, each one large enough to soak her completely.

Grecko shrugged and sniffed, puffing out his chest heavily. 'Sorry Miss Vista, I wasn't expecting that. I'm alright now - was a long time ago. Besides, I ain't lonely no more, I've got yer 'ere now, right?'

He curled his hand tighter around Vista and she gripped his thumb, squeezing back as hard as she could.

'Always,' she promised, and she really meant it.

———

It didn't take long for Grecko to start walking again. Pulling himself together, he quickly felt strong enough to move. As he trudged forwards through the forest, he did his best to avoid looking at Vista too often, the sadness in her eyes too much for him to take. When she finally curled up and fell asleep, he breathed out in relief, unable to take much more pity.

As often happened in quiet moments, his mind tried to wander back to his younger days, and the horrible moment which had marked the end of his happiness.

Remembering his mother felt like reliving a dream. Over time, he found small things would fade from his memory – the smell of her hair, or the off-key tunes she would absentmindedly hum while she cooked.

Wanting to avoid the memories, Grecko decided to sit for a while. Vista was asleep anyway, so it seemed like the perfect time to rest. Slowly, he edged his way down the trunk of a nearby tree until he was on the ground, his back against its smooth bark and his legs outstretched before him, all the while careful not to move his arm too quickly and disturb the sleeping Vista. When confident she wouldn't stir, he allowed himself to close his eyes.

That's when he heard it. The trees. They were whispering again. Now, trees don't whisper the way one would expect them to – the whisper tends to come out more like a tune that only gnomes can hear. The type of tune it makes and the way it sounds can say a lot about its feelings in that moment. Gnomes also have a unique ability to communicate with the forest through images as well - the trees are able to put visions into their minds.

Grecko didn't see visions often anymore. In fact, the first and last one he'd seen for a long time was the morning before he'd found Vista. Grecko had been watering his flowers as usual when an image of the Home Tree, clear as anything, came into his mind. He knew straight away that the forest wanted him to go there. Grecko tended to avoid that part of Letherea - too many bad memories - but it was obvious that the trees needed him there, and as soon as he saw Vista, he knew why. She was important, and for whatever reason he knew he had to protect her. Sitting there with Vista sleeping in his palm, he'd never been more grateful for a vision in his entire life.

The image had surprised Grecko at first, he'd almost forgotten it was even an ability of his. He used to see them all the time when he was around other gnomes, but after everything that had happened to him, he'd shut himself away from the others, and somehow this had made the images harder for him to spot.

Sitting there now, the tune was the first thing he noticed. With his eyes closed, a melancholy sound pooled through his ears. It wouldn't wake Vista, he knew that for certain – there was no way she'd even hear it. But it forced Grecko to open his eyes and listen. Ever since he had found Vista down by the river, her wings ripped from her back, he'd had a horrible feeling. He knew imps were bad news, but he couldn't be certain just how bad this particular imp was. Without any proof, he had chosen to simply bide his time and wait until the forest told him more.

The tune flooded over Grecko, and his eyes prickled with the sting of fresh tears as he felt the full force of Letherea's fear. He allowed it to wash over him, knowing it needed this as much as he did. What happened next, however, he hadn't expected. An image came to him. It formed in his mind as clear as if it were right there in front of him.

Iggy.

He'd heard Vista say the name, but couldn't be sure of the connection until now. It was the same Iggy. The same Iggy who ruined his life all those years ago. The same Iggy capable of such evil. Letherea was confirming Grecko's worst fears, and all he could do was sit there and cry. He cried as silently as he could, trying his best not to wake Vista - but with no such luck.

Slowly, she stirred in his palm, and her face dropped as she looked up at him.

'Grecko, what's happened?'

He took a deep breath. 'It's nothing, Miss Vista,' he lied. 'Don't worry 'bout me. Jus' a bit tired, yer know?'

Grecko wanted so badly to protect Vista, but it was only a matter of time. It was obvious how serious this was, but he wasn't ready to put that kind of worry on her shoulders just yet. He allowed her to hug his thumb and whisper sweet words of comfort as the forest continued to play that melancholy tune which only he could hear.

16

An Old Friend

'Miss Vista, wake up! We're 'ere.'

Grecko's voice stirred her from her sleep, and she rubbed her eyes sluggishly.

'Where are we?' From what Vista could see it was the same old forest she'd fallen asleep in.

Grecko smiled, but despite his best efforts, there was an obvious sadness to it.

'Look over there...' He faced her towards a big mound of dirt in the ground with a large hole leading into it. It looked similar to a badger hole, except a great deal larger than any badger a human would know. Vista stared at it, unsure how to react. Grecko still hadn't told her why they were here, nor who they were coming to see. She didn't understand the need for all this secrecy but frankly, after finding him so upset, Vista hadn't wanted to press him any further.

The journey had become a quiet one. Vista had tried her best to comfort Grecko, but he hadn't wanted to speak, and she had ended up falling asleep again. Now she was worried that by sleeping, she had let Grecko down.

Pushing these thoughts from her mind, she focused again on the dirt mound in front of her. 'Grecko, who exactly have we come to see?'

He seemed to hesitate and Vista waited, confused as to why he was so reluctant to tell her. He'd brought her with him after all, so it couldn't be that big of a secret.

'Oh for goodness sake, Grecko, stop making her so nervous,' Vista spun her head around at the sound of a voice emerging from the hole, 'I live here, Vista, and it's a great pleasure to meet you at last.'

From the hole appeared a lady. She rose from the earth with a certain air of dignity that seemed completely out of place amongst all the dirt. As the lady approached them, she smiled kindly, holding her palms outwards as a sign of greeting.

Vista glanced up at Grecko, puzzled. 'How does she know my name?'

A brief, fleeting smile crossed Grecko's lips as he replied, 'This 'ere's an old friend o' mine. She's a witch, Miss Vista' he said, as though that explained everything.

Many people imagine witches to be haggard, elderly women with warts on the end of their noses and a broom at their side. This, however, couldn't be further from the truth. In fact, witches are considered to be very beautiful - one of the most beautiful creatures in all of Letherea.

Their bodies are surprisingly long (not a hunchback in sight) and they're so tall that they tend to loom over every creature they meet. This left most feeling quite intimidated in their presence (through no fault of the witch, of course). Witches are also known to be extremely kind, only ever wanting to help others and spread love. In that way they're quite similar to gnomes.

The witch approaching Vista and Grecko seemed to fit the description of beauty perfectly. As she walked, the forest stirred around her, leaves raising around her bare feet whilst flowers and trees arched closer to her side. The magical forest seemed in awe of her. Her skin was smooth, and her eyes sparkled like blue crystals.

Long, auburn hair hung loosely at her waist, brushing lightly against her moss-coloured gown.

Witches are also known to favour solitude, despite being perfectly pleasant enough to warrant some company. It was merely that they preferred to live alone. It's funny how solitude can affect creatures so differently.

The witch stopped in front of them, and Vista marvelled at how soft her skin looked – how flawless. Feeling she should speak, Vista subtly cleared her throat, 'I'm sorry, I'm a bit dumbstruck. I've never met a witch before, I wasn't expecting you to know my name...'

The witch waved her hand as if the statement was amusing to her, 'Oh, don't be silly, I know so much more than that.' she laughed, tickled by Vista's bewilderment and turned her attention towards Grecko. 'I'm so glad you came to me, I knew that you would. We don't have much time, I'm afraid, you'd both better come inside.' She took Grecko's free hand and without another word, led them both into the hole.

Vista wasn't sure what to expect being led into a pile of dirt, so she braced herself for what might come. Stepping into the hole it grew dark, but a soft golden flame coming from the witch's palm lit their way. Vista noticed they were being led down a winding staircase. *How deep are we going?*

After a few turns around the stairs, they came to a stop, the steps opening up into a large room. For an underground home, it was nothing like Vista had been expecting.

'Wow...' she whispered softly - she didn't know what else to say. Everything was spotless, and there was actual furniture! In the far right corner a fire crackled, giving the room a warm glow. In front of the fire were armchairs, padded and comfortable looking with not a speck of dust in sight. To the left she could see a tunnel, presumably leading to other rooms that Vista hoped she might get a chance to explore later. What grabbed Vista's attention the most, however, was the table. Directly in front of them lay a table filled with food – more food than Vista could ever possibly eat. There were scones and cakes and all kinds of different fruit. Her mouth salivated at the mere sight of it all.

'You must both be hungry after such a long journey. I have plenty of food to fill you up, so please sit down and build up your strength. *Both* of you.' Vista saw the witch look directly at Grecko, who was already looking past the food and pacing, clearly in a hurry to keep moving.

'Sorry, Layla,' Grecko said sheepishly.

Layla – that must be her name!

'It's jus' that we don't 'av time fer any o' this! I need ter know what he's planning.' Grecko continued to pace, the movement making Vista feel slightly nauseous.

Layla moved closer to Grecko and placed a hand upon his shoulder, squeezing it affectionately. 'I'm going to help you as much as I'm able, but first you must rest and build your strength up. Now eat.'

With a meek nod of defeat, Grecko perched himself on a stool next to the table and placed Vista down beside the food.

Layla continued to speak as she came to join them, 'It's a great burden, being able to see what's to come and yet being unable to act,' she glanced towards Vista, 'it's a weight us witches must bear as servants of the forest. Letherea tells us its woes and we must trust that what we see will come to pass the way it is supposed to, without our interference. That's why I'm so glad you're here.' Layla smiled at both of them in turn and Vista awkwardly diverted her gaze. Her eyes landed on the biggest scone she had ever seen in her life; it was almost the size of Grecko's fist, making it about double the size of Vista's entire body. *Those honeysuckle scones have nothing on this!*

Layla placed a bowl down in front of Vista, so big she could have bathed in it. 'Eat as much as you like, Vista.'

With as much composure as she could muster, Vista stretched out a hand and ripped away a part of the giant scone. When it reached her mouth, the taste was so sweet and such a welcome change from fish and berries that all her table manners were forgotten, seeming pointless. *If Lilleth could see me now!* She snorted at the thought of the state she must look. Neither of her present company seemed to notice, however, as they busied themselves with other things. Grecko buttered a slice of bread, his mind clearly elsewhere, and Layla had briefly moved toward the corner, brewing a pot of tea that made Vista tingle with excitement. She couldn't remember the last time she'd drank tea.

'So, what do we need ter know, then?' Grecko asked through mouthfuls of bread as Layla joined them with a bubbling pot.

Perching on a stool opposite Grecko, she went about pouring the tea and eyed him nervously. 'It isn't good news, I'm afraid. I'm sure you've figured out by now that this is, of course, the same Iggy?'

Iggy. His name hung in the air between them – a little too long.

Grecko got to his feet, nodding uncomfortably and staring at the floor. He held back more tears and avoided Vista's gaze. 'Yeah, the forest jus' told me.' he sniffed, still looking down. 'I'm so sorry, Miss Vista, I didn't want yer ter find out jus' yet fer same reason I didn't tell yer 'bout Layla. I wasn't ready fer yer ter know everything...'

Layla approached Grecko for a moment and laid her hand upon his arm, giving it a reassuring squeeze.

Vista was so confused. *How could Grecko have not mentioned to me that he'd met Iggy before? What more don't I know?*

'Grecko, I know this is hard for you to hear, but I feel that you must know. Everything that's happening now is linked to your past. Your dad was a part of the puzzle, just like Vista's wings are now.'

The mention of her wings sent a chill down Vista's spine, her wound throbbing at the memory. Layla appeared to know everything that was going on – possibly more than Vista. She averted her gaze in shame.

Layla turned to Vista briefly, 'I'm so sorry you had to go through that with Iggy, by the way. Imps can be deceptive creatures, and Iggy is a prime example of that.'

Vista awkwardly looked down at the scone in her hands, not particularly wanting to relive the memory, 'I should have realised I couldn't trust Iggy...' she began - words she'd heard from Grecko many times before.

'Vista, it's important that you understand none of this is your fault. Iggy made sure he understood everything about you long before you met. He knew how guilty you felt and how much you wanted to help Grecko, and he preyed on those weaknesses. It's what he does best, unfortunately.' Layla looked towards Grecko who had stopped pacing and was now leaning against the wall taking deep breaths. 'I know you've had a hard time Grecko, but I feel you need to understand this. Iggy *tricked* Vista. He wanted her wings and he would have resorted to anything to get them. We should be grateful Vista gave them so willingly, it could have been much worse for her had she not.' Layla's eyes bore into Grecko and his head fell in shame. Slowly, his watery gaze met Vista's and she braced herself for what was coming next. Vista knew it hadn't been her fault, and having Layla stand up for her made something inside her settle at last.

'I'm so sorry, Miss Vista.' Grecko spoke, his lip trembling through his words.

Her heart broke as she watched him, 'It's alright Grecko...'

Why is he so upset? We've had some disagreements, but... Vista suddenly felt very sick, a thought striking her like a lightning bolt. 'Wait a minute... Grecko, you said your dad was messing in things he shouldn't have been... Did Iggy have something to do with your dad's death?' The question came out of her mouth before she could stop it, and she inhaled sharply, filling with regret.

Grecko remained mute, but, with his face to the floor, he nodded. The room fell silent for a while.

When Layla spoke again, it was aimed at no one in particular – more meant as a warning for the entire room. 'Iggy is seeking revenge against the fairies, especially Lilleth. He feels that she betrayed him, and he is incredibly angry,' she looked towards the stairs and shuddered slightly, closing her eyes, 'so very angry.'

'He wants revenge on the *fairies*? But why? None of the fairies have even met an imp before, we haven't done anything to him!' Vista's rage burnt her insides. *How dare he!*

Grecko, reacting to Vista's rage, began to pace the room again, shaking his head emphatically. The room quickly turned more and more chaotic.

Gently, Layla raised her palms, calling for silence and calm. 'Vista, look at me. There is so much that you don't know and I need you to listen.' she paused, 'There is more at stake than you could possibly realise. Letherea needs you.'

'What?' Vista choked, forgetting her resolution to stay calm, 'Why would Letherea need me? I'm not even a real fairy anymore, I haven't got any wings. I can't help anyone.'

'Of course you're a real fairy!' Layla pressed on, 'Being a fairy isn't determined by whether or not you possess wings – it's determined by you. It's in your blood, Vista. You are a fairy because that is the family you were born to be a part of. Whether or not you have wings is beside the point. Would a tree still be a tree if it had no leaves?' Layla's voice was stern and focused.

Vista's cheeks flushed as she thought of her scarred back. Fairies didn't look like she did. 'I know you're trying to help, but I'm not a fairy. I can't even fly...' Her wide eyes looked at Layla imploringly. A single tear rolled down Vista's cheek and she blinked fast before brushing it away, determined not to cry. From the corner of her eye, Vista saw Grecko move towards her, but Layla turned to him and shook her head. He pulled back obediently.

'Why do you believe you can't do anything?' Layla asked. 'You've been living on the forest floor now for quite some time. You've even faced Iggy – had one of the worst things that could possibly happen to a fairy happen to you and not only did you survive, you *grew*.' As she spoke, Layla rose to her feet and looked down at Vista. 'If I were to push you from this table right now, what would happen?'

Vista froze, *surely she won't push me...*

'Would you fight back? Would you try and stop me?'

'Yes?' Vista responded, more as a question than an answer, still unsure of where this was going.

Layla leaned forward and prodded Vista in the shoulder with her finger causing her to stumble, 'You are so much smaller than me, Vista. What's preventing me from pushing you?'

Vista glanced over to Grecko, uncertain of how to respond but Grecko looked helplessly on - this was down to Vista alone.

Again, Layla prodded her shoulder. It didn't exactly hurt, it was more uncomfortable than anything else. Her feet slipped on the polished table's surface and, with a third poke, she found herself falling backwards and landing right into a spoonful of jam, presumably laid out for the scones. The jam clung to Vista's hands and she felt her fingers stick together. Vista grimaced and rose to her feet, scone crumbs itching her skin as they clung to the jam. Vista looked up just in time to see Layla's finger coming forward to shove her a fourth time. This time, however, she was ready and quickly ducked to avoid it. Layla's face looked pleased and Vista hoped that meant it was over but no such luck.

Layla's hand moved across the table in a sweeping motion, sending food flying in all directions and causing Vista to run. As the hand moved closer towards her she jumped, just managing to clear it. With no time to congratulate herself, however, the hand swiped behind her and she soon found herself on her back again.

'Vista, you need to fight back. Grecko won't always be able to help you.'

Fine! Vista could feel herself getting angry, she'd been so looking forward to eating the scone which was now crumbled on the floor. She looked towards Layla and saw a finger move to prod her a fifth time. The table was now filled with leftover crumbs, remnants of the lovely food that had been laid out before. The sight made Vista nervous, picturing herself soon as useless as the crushed food on the floor. As Layla's finger came close, Vista ducked and it moved straight over her head, landing in a lump of jam on the table. Vista looked behind her and smiled at her win. Quickly, she bent down and picked up two fistfuls of crumbs. As Layla bent forward to swipe at her again, Vista pulled her arms behind her and launched the jam-covered crumbs as far as she could. The crumbs smacked Layla in the face, and Vista was pleased to see some had even managed to stick to her nose. Layla paused and blinked a few times, crumbs falling from her eyelashes. Without thinking too much about her next move, Vista jumped and swung onto Layla's finger at the next incoming jab, quickly scurrying her way up her arm. With the skills of a spider, Vista surprised herself by climbing over the folds in Layla's clothes as Layla hurried to try and stop her. Vista's size now seemed an advantage as she turned and gripped tightly to the clothing, quickly finding herself up on Layla's shoulder, unsure how exactly she'd managed such a thing.

Vista prepared herself for what was to come next, but to her great relief Layla just smiled and held out a hand to help her down. 'Do you see how strong you can be when you stop relying on others?'

Vista landed back on the table, feeling quite shaken. Her fingers were white at the tips and stiff from the effort of climbing up Layla's arm, she forced them to open and close a few times in an attempt to loosen them.

'Grecko, it's okay. Vista isn't hurt.'

Vista spun her head around to look at Grecko, who was looking shell shocked in the corner, clearly struggling to process what had just happened.

Neither of them spoke.

'I think we should set the table again, don't you?' Layla said and with a wave of her arm the crumbs magically disappeared and the table was once again set, as though nothing had happened.

Layla handed a scone to Vista and gestured for Grecko to join them again. 'I understand it's a lot of pressure, but can you see how strong you are now? I need you to believe you can do this and keep that fighting spirit alive.'

Vista forced her body to relax as she thought over what she'd just done. Grecko sat quietly beside her, looking down in surprise. She suddenly felt rather cold but tried her best not to show it. 'What do I need to do?'

'Rest. Eat. You'll know before long what it is you must do.' Layla smiled encouragingly, gently tapping Vista's shoulder with her finger and making Vista flinch, bracing for another prod. 'Vista, the reason I'm so calm is because I know you can do this – I've seen it.'

In all the excitement, Vista had forgotten about Layla's burden. 'You've *seen* it? How?'

Layla grinned, 'I'm a witch, remember? I see all sorts of things. Everything becomes easier when you have magic.'

'That's strange, that's the same thing Iggy said to me when I first met him.' As soon as she'd said it she knew she shouldn't have. Cupping her hand over her mouth, she bit her tongue. 'Oh Layla, I'm so sorry, that was so rude!'

Layla had paused, clearly slightly taken aback by the comment, but promptly she composed herself again. 'No matter, I suppose Iggy and I can agree on one thing... What's important is that the way we use our magic differs greatly!' No one in the room could argue with that.

'How long before we 'av ter leave?' Grecko asked.

'I'd say leaving before sunset would be wise.'

Vista stood up and began pacing the table, absentmindedly kicking scone crumbs with her feet as she lost herself in thought.

'Iggy won't take long. In fact, if I'm not mistaken, he is already very close. The forest will be difficult for him, it certainly doesn't like what he's doing, but we both know that the forest can't stop him. He'll get there.' Layla turned back to Vista, startling her from her anxious pacing, 'You won't know this, Vista, but Iggy once lived in the Home Tree. It was an exceedingly long time ago, of course.'

Vista paused. In fact, it felt like the entire forest paused. *But only fairies lived in the Home Tree. Surely we'd have known?* Then a memory popped into Vista's head - the whispers of fairies late at night when they were telling stories - *Lilleth once had a child who had taken a dark path...*

Vista stared at Layla. Was it possible that Lilleth had once been a mother to an imp?

'But... that was just a rumour!' Vista said, as though Layla could read her mind.

'All rumours start from somewhere; they begin as stories and over time we choose whether or not we believe them. This has been kept a secret from all the fairies for the longest time. Not just fairies, in fact – this is Grecko's first time finding out as well.'

Vista turned to Grecko and was relieved to see he was looking just as confused as she was.

'Lilleth was once a mother to a non-fairy child.' Layla went on, 'She rescued Iggy when he was abandoned as a baby and raised him as her own in the Home Tree but, unfortunately, it was not to be. Iggy feels betrayed by Lilleth and the other fairies. I know it's hard, but try and see it from Iggy's side. Imagine feeling betrayed by the only family you'd ever known. It must have been terribly hard for him.'

Grecko gave a loud snort, turning his head away in disgust. 'No one should ever feel sorry fer that imp. He's evil an' Letherea's better off without him.'

'I'm sorry Grecko, I meant no disrespect. I was simply trying to make Vista see that sometimes, in order to defeat our enemies, we must first understand their reasons for doing what they do.'

Grecko snorted again, this time even louder, and looked directly at Layla. 'I don't 'av ter understand him. All I 'av ter know is this imp is the reason me dad ain't around no more. Me dad trusted him an' got tricked! We can't let him do it again, we can't let him hurt no one else. He's gotta be stopped!' Tears trickled down Grecko's face, and he turned his back to Layla, not wanting her nor Vista to see him cry again.

Cautiously, as one would approach a wild animal, Layla rose to her feet and stepped towards Grecko. She wrapped her arms gently around his shoulders and, to Vista's surprise, Grecko spun around and allowed Layla to hug him. Soothingly, she stroked the back of his head as the sobs he'd been holding in broke their way through the surface. 'It's going to be okay,' she heard Layla whisper.

'Grecko, listen to me.' Layla pulled away to face him, 'There are things I must tell Vista, and I'm afraid they're going to be too difficult for you to hear. Around that corner is a bed; it's warm and safe, and I want you to go and rest. It really will do you the world of good. Go and get some sleep,' she took a glance behind her, 'for Vista's sake.'

Hearing Vista's name seemed to bring Grecko back to himself. He shot a glimpse across the table at her, embarrassed by what he'd allowed her to witness. Dutifully, Grecko exited the room through the tunnel at the end. Vista watched him go until he was out of sight, desperately wanting to follow him and make sure he was alright, but knowing that Layla wouldn't allow it. She seemed to have other plans for Vista.

Trying not to show how distracted she was, Vista turned her attention back towards Layla, who was now seated and smiling kindly at her as though Grecko's breakdown had never happened.

'Are you ready to hear what I have to tell you?' she asked, fingers interlocked on the table in front of her.

Vista swallowed, her lips sticking to her teeth with nerves. 'I'm ready.'

Taking a deep breath, Layla closed her eyes. 'Now, Vista, in order for you to fully understand, it's easier for me to show you something first. I'm going to show you a memory; it's not my memory, nor your memory, but Grecko's. I'm going to allow you to witness a very painful time in his life so that you can understand what you're up against a little better.' She opened her eyes, looking slightly hesitant. This didn't seem like something she was entirely comfortable with doing.

Vista was equally hesitant, finding this to be a horrible invasion of Grecko's privacy. 'Do you think Grecko would be okay with us doing this?'

'No, I don't imagine he would be,' Layla admitted, 'but the reality is that it needs to be done. I need you to close your eyes now.'

Despite her unease, Vista obeyed. There was something about Layla that made you feel she was working in your best interest.

'That's good, Vista. Now breathe deeply - and stay calm.'

17

A Visit to the Past

Layla raised her arms above her head and beautiful sparks of colour engulfed her glowing hands. She looked towards their magnificent gleam and closed her eyes once again.

As they sat, both perfectly still, neither making a sound, a bright worm-like white light crept out of Layla's fingertip. It tumbled through the air and landed on the table in front of her. Layla peeked down, bringing her mouth close towards the light. She whispered a few words and blinked in Vista's direction. The worm-light twisted and turned itself several times, until it managed to face her, stopping just short of Vista's feet. Carefully, the light wrapped itself around her legs and crawled its way up to her torso. From there it twisted and creeped until it reached her neck, where it gladly found Vista's ear and began to wriggle its way inside, giving it an alarming orange glow.

Vista gasped. It felt as though an insect were tickling her brain, and she scratched at her earlobe. It persisted to tickle so she shook her head vigorously, opening her eyes in the hope Layla could reassure her this was all normal.

To her shock, when she opened her eyes she was no longer sitting with Layla but back at home – on Grecko's bed. She blinked, trying to make sense of how she'd ended up back here, when a figure ran into the hut. No, not a figure... a gnome. Grecko! *Relieved by the sight of her friend, she tried to rush towards him, but found she couldn't move. Trying her best not to panic, she slowly focused on Grecko. As he came closer, she was surprised to find it wasn't Grecko at all. This gnome had a face she had never seen before and yet recognised all at the same time. It was Grecko, but it wasn't.*

'Guess what, son, I've got amazing news!' He came bounding towards the bed in which Vista lay.

Son? A coldness ran through her as she realised what it was she was seeing. Standing in front of her was Grecko's dad – their similarities were shocking.

If that's his dad... does that make me Grecko?

Catching sight of the legs sprawled across the bed, she stifled a cry when she saw not her own dainty fairy ones, but a pair of large bulky gnome legs complete with a set of bulbous gnome feet. As they clearly didn't belong to her, she watched in a daze as they began to move, and she found herself leaning towards Grecko's dad. It was a strange feeling – being trapped inside another's head. It felt as though you were that person and yet had no control over anything they said or did. Vista could only lie dormant in Grecko's mind as an unwilling observer.

'What if I told yer I'd found a way ter get yer mum back?' Grecko's dad continued.

Vista felt sickness rise up inside her and quickly realised that this was in fact Grecko's reaction. What kind of cruel trick was this?

Grecko threw himself back down on the bed without a word, forcing Vista to lay with him in his mind.

'No, Grecko, I swear I ain't tricking yer, it's real! As real as me name's Hermon Trotts.' Vista felt a heavy hand rest upon Grecko's shoulder, pleading with him to turn around.

Cautiously, Grecko rolled to face his father. Vista knew this would end badly – she already couldn't bear to watch.

'Why would yer believe we could bring mum back? She's dead, Dad...' Vista could feel the pain in Grecko's words and knew this likely wasn't the

first time he'd had to remind his dad of that fact. She felt the lump form in Grecko's throat, his mouth drying up to create a sponge-like sensation on his tongue.

"Coz it's true, son. I met someone who can help us. He says he 'as magic!' Hermon smiled eagerly, 'He says his magic can help us bring yer mum back. His name's Iggy. He's an imp, jus' a little thing, bit odd looking, but seems friendly enough, an' he wants ter help us...'

'An imp?' Grecko's voice echoed through Vista's skull, 'But we dunno nothing 'bout imps. Why would he even wanna help us? It don't make no sense...' Despite everything, Vista couldn't help but feel proud of Grecko for being so cautious towards Iggy – it was more than she'd managed after all.

'That's the best bit, he's helping us 'coz he needs our help as well. Ain't that great?'

'But what help would he need from us?' Grecko continued with his questions suspiciously.

'Well he says he's bin tryna find the fairy Home Tree fer a while now... Reckon he had some friends there or summit. Dunno how he lost it though, ain't like it's moved, an' the fairies never leave it no more...' Hermon looked confused for a moment, but quickly brushed past it. 'Anyway, I said I could show him the way, an' it jus' so happens that the stuff we need ter bring yer mum back is right next ter the Home Tree! What are the chances, son? Everyone wins, am I right?'

His dad's look of joy broke Vista's heart – or maybe it was Grecko's heart. It was getting tricky to tell the difference.

'Dad... Don't yer reckon it all seems a bit... dodgy? I mean... I ain't ever heard o' no one who can bring back the dead before?'

Hermon sighed, clearly disappointed by his son's rejection. 'Son... We jus' don't make no sense without yer mum. Yer know it's true. If there's even a chance this could work, then we gotta do it.'

Grecko exhaled. It was obvious that his dad's mind couldn't be changed.

'Yer know I'll help yer, dad.' His voice bounced through his head and Vista ignored the queasy feeling it gave her. 'We'll do it together,' he said, but Vista could feel the unease and fear creeping inside him.

'Son, yer ain't gunna regret this, we're gunna get yer mum back!' Hermon jumped up, clapping his hands together and spinning with as

much grace as a gnome with oversized limbs could manage. 'Let's go, Iggy said there ain't no time ter waste - he's waiting fer us down by the river.'

With that, Vista found Grecko standing up and following his dad out of the hut. He took one last look behind him, reminding Vista of when she and Grecko had left not so long ago, both wondering when they would next see their home again.

As Hermon and Grecko approached the river, a voice called out. 'Ah, good, you made it.' That voice... Vista would recognise it anywhere. It was a voice that could make the trees cower. A voice filled with so much menace that even when trying to sound polite, it still sent a chill down her spine. How she hadn't noticed this the first time, she'd never understand. Her own stomach knotted as she watched a delighted Iggy jump up eagerly as Hermon approached. Vista saw Grecko's eyes looking Iggy up and down - not that there was much 'up' involved. Just the sight of Iggy made Grecko uneasy, and Vista couldn't blame him.

'Wait a minute...' Iggy held up a palm, 'Who's that?' He pointed a crooked finger at Grecko with a look of disdain on his face. It seemed obvious this was a glimpse of Iggy's true self, but Hermon seemed determined not to see it. He was so blinded by hope.

'Oh, this 'ere's me son, Grecko. Don't worry 'bout him, he's a good boy. He's so excited yer gunna bring his mum back fer us!' Hermon smiled, oblivious to the atmosphere around him, and Vista couldn't stand it. It was all so unfair.

Iggy stared at Grecko for a moment and then, with a shrug of defeat, spun on his heels and began walking away from the river straight into the forest. Vista noticed that even back then, he still had plenty of critters buzzing around his head.

Without another word, Hermon obediently followed, leaving Grecko to pick up the pace from behind in silence.

As Vista watched nervously, she felt a strange pull in the pit of her stomach. Everything blurred for a moment before coming back into focus. It seemed the memory was jumping forward.

She blinked, trying to figure out where she was now. She was still in the magical forest, that much was certain, she could feel the forest floor beneath Grecko's bare feet and it felt amazing. She'd gotten quite used to being carried everywhere, so the feeling of being able to walk and feel the earth beneath her toes, or rather Grecko's toes, was very freeing.

'Keep going son, ain't much further.' Grecko's dad called, a short distance ahead.

'Hermon, is that son of yours still holding us up?' Repulsed by the sight of him, but still having to watch through Grecko's eyes, she could just about see Iggy barrelling forward, Hermon and Grecko doing everything they could to keep up.

'He's still with us, don't worry. Ain't yer, son?' Hermon looked back in Grecko's direction.

'Yeah dad, I'm 'ere.' Each time Grecko spoke his voice echoed through his skull. Vista swallowed down a fresh batch of nausea.

'See, Iggy, he says he's coming...' Hermon was still looking back at his son, his face creased with concern, 'Maybe we could 'av a quick break, aye? It's a long walk, ain't it! Grecko ain't used ter so much walking, poor lad.'

As Hermon suggested a break, Iggy came to an abrupt halt, his back still facing them. Whirling himself around, he scrunched up his face in annoyance. 'Listen, Hermon,' Iggy emphasised his name mockingly, 'I don't know about you, but I'm serious about our deal. Now, do you want your precious wife back, or don't you?' His cruel words came out slowly, as though Hermon was so beneath him he was barely worth speaking to.

"Course we do! It's jus' that me boys tired - be nice fer him ter 'av a quick rest is all. Jus' fer a bit?' Hermon seemed to almost be begging.

Iggy took another step closer to Hermon, cocking his head like he was about to tell him a secret. 'No.' he snapped. There was no mistaking the fact that Iggy felt he was running the show.

Anger boiled inside Vista, it consumed all of her until she was filled with a furious rage. Why am I so angry? Suddenly, it dawned on her that it wasn't her anger she was feeling, but Grecko's. The way Iggy treated his dad was just too much, and Vista could tell he was about to explode.

'YES!' Grecko yelled.

Both Hermon and Iggy stared at Grecko. Despite discussing him, they seemed to have almost forgotten he was there.

'Excuse me? Just who exactly do you think you are, gnome?' Iggy stomped over to Grecko, prodding him with his finger. Vista could feel

Grecko's fury. Whatever Iggy was capable of, Grecko either didn't know or didn't care, because she felt no fear from him whatsoever.

'Me dad said we need ter rest an' I agree with him. Now yer need our help ter find the Home Tree, right? So either we rest now fer a bit or we go home an' yer don't get our help at all!' Grecko's eyes fixed on Iggy, and Vista could see how infuriating he was finding the disruption.

He ground his teeth loudly as he stood there considering Grecko.

Hermon hovered in the background, wrestling between his loyalty to his son and his desperation at seeing his wife again. 'Please Iggy... Don't listen ter Grecko. Course we'll help yer find the Home Tree. Grecko don't know what he's saying. He's tired that's all, makes yer say daft stuff, don't it?' he mumbled, giving a nervous laugh.

Vista felt Hermon's betrayal as a blow to her own gut. Grecko's tears stung her, and she felt the pull on his heart as his dad gave in so easily.

Hermon stared at Iggy, who hadn't yet turned his gaze away from Grecko.

'Did you hear that? Your daddy will help me with or without you, so if you really need to rest then that's fine with me! Actually, I encourage you to rest... It'll keep you out of my hair. Me and your dad will keep moving... You can do what you like!' Hate poured from his smug face, and he strolled away from Grecko, chuckling with every step. Grecko stared at his dad who submissively followed Iggy, avoiding his son's gaze.

Despite every part of Grecko wanting to leave, he began to walk again, like the loyal son he was. Just one foot in front of the other and Vista could feel Grecko's pain with every step he took.

Another pull hit Vista like a rocket, and she found her vision blur, coming into focus again in another part of the forest. She didn't know how long they'd walked for, but she would have safely guessed the entire night based on how exhausted they both appeared.

'This, I'm afraid, is where I have to stop. I can't walk any further.'

Vista was confused, but still wasn't sure whether it was her confusion or Grecko's. The area they had stopped looked no different to any other part of the forest. Why would he need to stop here?

'What happens now then?' Hermon asked, his face pale with exhaustion.

'Well, you see, I physically can't pass through this part of the forest. There's been a spell cast against me, a blockage spell that prevents me from passing through and getting anywhere near the Home Tree. You can walk through easily, but for me... There might as well be a sky-high brick wall in front of us.'

'Fascinating...' Hermon gazed upwards, as though if he looked hard enough, he might be able to make the brick wall appear in front of them.

'If you say so... Anyway, this is the part I need you for. You see, if you were to walk over there and then invite me to join you then BAM. Just like that, I can walk right on through!' He clapped his hands together, eager to get on.

'That's all I need ter do?' Even for Hermon, who was so desperate he'd believe almost anything, this seemed a bit too simple.

'Yep, that's it, so easy, right? Even you couldn't mess it up!' Iggy chuckled.

Hermon scratched the back of his neck and for the first time since the incident earlier that night, looked over at his son. 'If it's that easy, then how come no one's ever helped yer before?'

Iggy sighed, rubbing his eyes impatiently with his calloused fingers. 'Did I say that was any of your business? Hmm? You're just here to help me get through, that's all!'

'How come someone put a spell on yer?' This time it was Grecko who spoke. It seemed like a valid question, and quite frankly, Vista was surprised Hermon hadn't thought to ask it himself.

This time when Iggy answered, he did so through gritted teeth, clearly irritated by the sudden onset of questions. 'It doesn't matter why they did it, what matters is that you want your mum back, right? Now if you help me get over there, I'll bring her back for you. If you waste my time asking any more questions, then get ready for a lonely life without her...'

Vista hated Iggy. She despised him. He was a vile, evil little creature who didn't deserve to be breathing the same air as Grecko.

'No! No, we'll let yer through. No more questions... we were jus' wondering, that's all. We're sorry.' Hermon was irritating Vista more and more every time he spoke, so willing to let Iggy belittle Grecko like this.

She wondered if Grecko's mum would have dealt with this differently, *or on second thought, maybe Grecko was the one wondering this? It was getting more and more difficult to separate their thoughts.*

'That's more like it. Now, Hermon, all you have to do is walk forward, turn around and invite me to join you. If you can do that, I would be exceedingly grateful.'

Hermon coughed nervously and began to walk forward, counting his steps under his breath to make sure he'd passed this 'wall' Iggy had mentioned.

'That's great Hermon, stop there. Perfect, now invite me to join you!'

Hermon turned around, shuffling awkwardly from foot to foot, embarrassed by the thought of public speaking. 'I uh... Invite yer ter join me, Iggy.'

Vista didn't know what she was expecting to happen at this point, but she had been expecting something... A bright light perhaps, or some kind of earthquake beneath their feet. Either way, she was surprised and a little disappointed as she saw that nothing happened at all. No fire, no smoke, no falling clouds. Nothing. The magical forest remained just as still as it had done moments before, not seeming to realise the disaster that was Iggy finding his way back to the Home Tree.

Despite everything looking the same, things definitely seemed to have changed from Iggy's perspective. He hopped back and forth excitedly, waving his hands in the air and singing. 'That's it! That's it! I'm in! Haha!'

He closed his eyes, and Vista watched in horror as he took one step, and then another, and then another, until he had reached a part of Letherea that the blockage spell had never intended him to go to again.

He grinned impishly and looked up at Hermon, 'Well done, you did it.'

Hermon grinned broadly back, pride and relief falling over him like a warm shower.

Despite Grecko's doubts, Vista could feel that even he was getting a little excited at the possibility of getting his mum back.

Now came the part that Vista had been dreading. She knew Grecko wasn't getting his mum back, and for whatever reason, Layla felt this was something that Vista needed to see. So far, one thing was abundantly clear – there was no way this Imp was getting anywhere near her Home Tree.

'Oh, you have no idea how long I've been waiting to see this place again.' Iggy sighed, spinning joyfully in circles, arms outstretched.

In all honesty, it was hard to tell what Iggy was so excited to be seeing. As far as Vista - and Grecko for that matter - could tell, it looked no different here than it did in any other part of the forest that Iggy hadn't been banished from. 'Oh, my friends, this is a great day!' Iggy continued to spin.

'Um, Iggy?' Hermon interrupted his celebration, 'Now that I've done me part o' the deal... Do yer reckon maybe yer could go ahead an' bring Evie back now?' He stood sheepishly a few feet away, twisting the corner of his crumpled top in his hands and looking nervous. He scanned around him anxiously, as though Evie might pop up from behind a tree at any moment, all smiles and praise for her boys for managing to bring her back to them.

Iggy grinned, 'All in good time, Hermon, but please, I haven't even caught sight of those snivelling little bugs yet.' He rubbed his fingers together like he was squashing a fly and crept noiselessly in the direction of the Home Tree.

Vista knew nothing would happen to the fairies yet – this was a memory and if something had happened, then she was certain she would have learnt about it. Even so, watching Iggy creep this close towards her home made her insides twist nervously, bile rising in her throat.

It's not really happening, it's just a memory, *she repeated over and over to herself, as the Home Tree came into view. As it appeared before her, her breathing stopped momentarily. She had never seen the Home Tree's beauty from the ground before. There was no doubt it was the grandest tree in all of Letherea, standing tall and strong, surrounded by hundreds of flowers that decorated it so lovingly. Vista felt great pride looking up at her home, followed quickly by shame for how much she had disregarded it when she had lived there.*

Once again Iggy let out an excited squeal and promptly covered his mouth, not wanting to be spotted. The three of them crouched together, hidden behind some berry bushes and watched.

'Pathetic, aren't they?' Iggy spat, glaring at the fairies as they flew around the Home Tree. He studied them with a furious intensity, scrutinising every move they made. Vista couldn't understand what gave him so much hatred towards them. She may be biased, but she was certain that fairies were viewed as friendly and useful members of Letherea.

'I dunno... I always thought they looked kinda nice?' Hermon said, and

Iggy scowled at him with the same level of intensity he seemed to hold exclusively for the fairy community. It was obvious Hermon had said the wrong thing.

'I agree with dad, can't see nothing wrong with 'em meself.' Hearing Grecko say this was exactly what Vista needed to hear. Realistically, she knew he wasn't talking about her, but it did make her feel like he'd been her friend long before they'd even met – possibly before she'd even been born.

The silence that followed went on much too long, and it was clear Iggy didn't know how best to react. Without bothering to answer, Iggy crawled backwards until he was safely out of sight of the fairies, then stood to his full height which, granted, wasn't much.

Hidden from the fairies' view, Vista could see (as Grecko looked back) Iggy waiting patiently - or as patiently as an Imp could - for Hermon and Grecko to join him. He rubbed his palms together, a warm red glow forming between them, random sparks shooting out from gaps within his hands.

'Sorry ter keep asking, but is it our turn yet?' Hermon asked again as they joined Iggy, impatience written all over his face.

Iggy didn't reply straight away, he merely stood still, observing Hermon. Glancing between the two of them, Vista could feel every inch of Grecko's unease.

When he finally spoke, his voice came out soft and soothing, reminding her of the Iggy she had met down by the river that day. It felt like a warning alarm for Vista, more so than if he were to scream and shout. His voice now was calculating – Iggy knew how to speak so as not to start a panic.

'Oh Hermon, you have no idea how grateful I am for what you've done for me today. Of course I'll help you. Come over here and sit with me for a moment.'

Hermon followed Iggy gladly, but Grecko paused, uncertain. Vista was proud once again of Grecko for seeing through Iggy. Iggy was a master of trickery, he'd tricked her that day by the river and by the looks of it could trick mostly anyone just by finding out what it was they wanted most. The fact that Grecko remained so cautious was admirable.

Hermon sat down next to Iggy, resting his back against a tree trunk and smiling to himself. With Hermon sitting comfortably, Iggy continued to speak, 'So, here's the thing, Hermon... This is the part where our deal gets a little bit complicated. It's complicated, because I lied to you. The truth is I can't bring back the dead - no one can. It's an incredibly well known fact! Dead means dead, there's no coming back from it. I'm actually a bit shocked you didn't realise this sooner...' Iggy smirked as Hermon looked around bewildered, trying to make sense of what Iggy was telling him. He shook his head and mumbled under his breath, not understanding what this meant for Evie. Grecko, meanwhile, didn't need any time to understand. He'd been waiting for this since the beginning and was already marching towards Iggy, fists clenched.

'No, no, no! We're not having any angry gnome vengeance today, thank you very much.' Iggy waved his hands and Grecko and Hermon were promptly frozen in their place. Vista felt Grecko's strength as he fought against Iggy's magic, but it was no use – he was completely stuck. He couldn't even speak.

'That's better. Anyway Hermon, as I was saying,' Iggy turned to face Grecko's dad who sat unblinking and motionless. Iggy knew, however, that both were still able to hear him perfectly well. 'I don't want you to worry. This wasn't a wasted trip for you. You're here because I need you and not just to help me find the Home Tree. You see, it's not just that I wanted to find the Home Tree, it's that I want to destroy it.' He paused for dramatic effect, 'But in order to destroy it I need to make a spell, and the tricky thing about dark magic spells is that they have quite unusual ingredients. For example, I'm currently in need of the blood from an 'innocent believer' – in simple terms that means someone who would be considered a do-gooder of sorts, such as yourself, with the ability to trust in anyone. You'd be surprised how many suspicious creatures there are in this forest, Hermon! Just take a look at your son here...' he said, gesturing towards Grecko before crouching down in front of Hermon, 'So you can imagine how frustrated I was when I found out about that juicy little ingredient, hmm? Where, oh where, was I going to find an ingredient like that?' Iggy tapped his chin sarcastically before climbing up Hermon's legs and moving closer, their faces inches away from each other, 'and then I met you. It was like Letherea was sending me a gift. There you were, so desperate, so innocent! You believed so wholeheartedly in me that I barely had to do a thing. Just a few false *promises here and there and bing bang boom I had you hooked. Who am I to refuse such a useful gift?'*

Vista couldn't bear to watch, but it was no good, she had no choice but to see through Grecko's eyes. She wanted to scream at them to run, run away as fast as they could, but she was stuck herself. Doomed to watch as the horror unfolded before them.

Iggy stepped back from Hermon and turned his attention to Grecko. He walked in taunting circles around him, smiling lazily, relishing in the fact that no matter how much Grecko wanted to, he couldn't do a thing to stop him.

'Now Grecko,' he glared up at him, 'you were the only real threat to my plan. You were the only one who could see that what I was offering was impossible. For a fleeting moment I was worried you'd manage to turn dear old dad against me and make him doubt my abilities. But, as luck would have it, his desperation turned out to be much stronger than anything you could throw at him.' Iggy cocked his head sideways, considering Grecko, 'It's a shame really...'

Vista seethed with rage. There's no way this imp feels any genuine sympathy.

Shaking his head, Iggy stepped between the two gnomes. 'So this is where things get a bit personal.' Iggy addressed Hermon again, 'I'm afraid I'm going to be needing your blood now, Hermon.'

Grecko's terror and panic hit Vista. She was choking in his fear.

'Don't worry, something you should know is that this won't hurt you at all. Small mercy, I suppose...' Iggy smiled, 'It'll be more like falling asleep. You never know, if you're the type that believes in an afterlife - and something tells me that you are - maybe Evie's waiting for you on the other side?' Iggy jerked, pulling his head back amusingly. 'Ha! I suppose if that's the case, you could say I did come through on my promise then, eh?' He bowed to imaginary applause and then stood tall, his fingers pointing straight at Hermon's body.

'Once again, I am sorry about this, Hermon...' he swished his hands chaotically and to Vista's horror, the leaves stirred in response to his command. They deliberately rose and began to swarm around Hermon, encasing him inside. He floated away from the tree and the leaves spun

around him, rapidly creating a cocoon that was difficult to see through. Hermon, still frozen inside, was unable to move, nor make any kind of protest. He kept completely still, in a deep slumber. Vista could feel Grecko's agony slowly crushing her chest. Hermon's stillness did nothing to dull the pain.

The leaves whirled faster and faster until Hermon's silhouette in the centre began to fade. His shape dissolved into the leaves themselves, disappearing into the wind. Within a few moments, Hermon was gone and the leaves fell, settling themselves back into their original resting place. The only clue left behind was a small vial lying just where Hermon had been. It was filled with a deep red liquid that Vista realised horrifically was the blood of Grecko's 'innocent believer' dad, all neatly packed and ready for Iggy to take on his merry way.

Crouching to the ground, Iggy patted the leaves appreciatively. 'Thanks for the help, friends.' He curled his wicked fingers around the vial and stood, grinning horribly at his prize.

Turning, Iggy peeked at Grecko from the corner of his eye, almost forgetting he was there. Grecko was frozen, fists still clenched and unable to make a sound, but inside Vista could hear his screams. Iggy spotted a single tear running down his cheek, and calmly climbed up his leg and wiped it away with his finger.

Vista felt Grecko's revulsion to Iggy's touch, it was like a flame burning the side of his face. Through Grecko's eyes, Vista could see where his dad had sat. The grief was unbearable.

All at once time seemed to stop as if someone had hit pause on the world. Every inch of Grecko ached, and Vista felt it right alongside him. He so badly wanted to scream, to lash out, to run to where his dad had been and dig through the leaves in hopes of finding him hidden underneath.

'Your dad's with the forest now. If you're a believer too, then maybe you'll see him again someday. Something tells me you're not a believer though, are you?' It seemed like Iggy couldn't just leave - he had to dig a little more, and prove he'd won.

'Now Grecko... you understand that I'll only unfreeze you once I'm a safe enough distance away that I know I won't be chased and killed by that angry gnome rage that's no doubt building up inside of you, right? I know you can't answer me, but I'm sure you'll understand this; don't try and look for me. You'll never be able to find me, and even if you somehow managed to, well,' Iggy scoffed, 'you've seen what I can do!'

Vista watched through Grecko as Iggy backed away, not once taking his eyes off him, as if he were afraid Grecko might have figured out a way to unfreeze himself. When he was far enough away and no longer worried for his own safety, he spun around and disappeared into the forest, leaving behind a frozen gnome and a bundle of leaves.

18

Vista's Acceptance

Vista gasped. Without even realising it, it was over. She looked up, relieved to see Layla's face concerned and watching her intently.

'Welcome back.'

'Welcome back' – it seemed a strange thing to hear after such a nightmare. *Not a nightmare - Grecko's memories,* Vista corrected herself.

'I can't believe Grecko went through all that, it's awful.' This time she knew she wouldn't cry; every worry she'd ever had paled in comparison to what he'd been through. 'What happened after Iggy left? How did Grecko get home?'

Layla peered over Vista's shoulder, conscious of Grecko resting just a few feet away. 'Well, after Iggy left, Grecko unfroze. He wandered the forest for a while, not in any particular direction. I believe he was in a state of shock. It's possible his mind was fogged and he had gone searching for his parents in his confusion.' Layla stopped, listening for Grecko. Satisfied he was still asleep, she continued, 'He ended up stumbling upon my home. I don't think he even knew what he was doing when he wandered inside. The thing I remember most is how tired he looked – he was so incredibly pale. Fortunately for him, I don't need to be told other's stories, I can already see them. They're written all over them like the pages from a book, and Grecko's book was so very, very sad. He was just standing there in my home, looking lost and in desperate need of some rest. I warmed him up and took care of him. He'd wanted to leave as soon as he'd slept, but I wouldn't allow it until I was certain he was strong enough.' Layla swallowed, 'He stayed with me for two whole weeks. After he left, I was anxious for him, but Grecko was determined to get back to the river – it was his home, after all. He never went back to his parents' hut, but he built his own close by. I often thought of him as time went on. When I heard Letherea whispering about an evil imp, I knew straight away who and what was coming. Iggy's story is a strange one, but that's for another time... Another meeting, perhaps.'

Vista nodded. A surge of adrenaline was coursing through her and she bit her lip, trying to keep calm. 'I still don't see how I can stop him, though. I don't have magic.'

Layla smiled, 'Magic isn't everything, Vista. When the time comes, you'll know what to do.'

Tired of Layla's cryptic responses, Vista glanced behind her, hoping Grecko would wake soon. She needed to see him and hug him – or hug his thumb, at least – and make sure he was alright.

She continued to remind herself that what she had witnessed had happened a long time ago, but to her it felt fresh, like it had just occurred that very day, leaving her utterly confused as to how she should react. Still trying to keep her mind steady, she twiddled her fingers - longing to ask more questions but knowing it was pointless.

'I do need to give you one warning, Vista.' Layla's face looked grave, 'There will come a time where you will need to make a choice. Choose wisely, because you will not get a second chance.'

Vista tensed. *What kind of a warning was that?* Fighting against the building pressure inside her chest, she cleared her throat. 'Wh—What kind of a choice?'

'I'm afraid I can't tell you that. If I did, it would no doubt influence your decision, and it *must* be your decision. My input would only hinder you.'

Vista grimaced, no longer trying to hide her frustration with Layla's puzzling warnings. She twirled her hair and instantly felt nauseous, realising that her hair no longer 'twirled', but merely clumped together as she turned it in circles. Layla appeared to notice Vista's revulsion – not that it was difficult to miss.

'Perhaps you'd like to clean yourself before Grecko wakes up?'

The thought of washing made Vista feel giddy; she so badly wanted to be clean. 'I'd love that!' she smiled graciously.

Layla held out her hand and Vista climbed aboard, worrying slightly about any lingering odours she may leave behind when she jumped off.

Layla strode to the far side of her home and through a passage leading from the end tunnel Grecko had walked down. They took a right and entered a small room complete with a wash basin that Vista could comfortably bathe in. To her delight, Layla clicked her fingers, and the basin instantly filled with sweet-smelling rose water, accompanied with a clean cloth and some honey wash to soak her tangled locks.

Vista gawped, causing Layla to laugh. 'Magic.' she explained with a smile.

Carefully, she placed Vista down beside the basin and helped her with her tattered dress. 'Let me wash this for you whilst you bathe. You'll feel like a brand new fairy in no time.'

A lump formed in Vista's throat. Hearing herself described as a fairy despite her lack of wings gave her great comfort.

Clumsily – not wanting to reveal too much of her scarred back to Layla – she handed over her dress and carefully placed her left foot into the water. All her tension dissolved as she melted into its warmth. Closing her eyes, she thought of the Home Tree and Grecko and Iggy. Bringing her knees to her chest, she allowed herself a moment to cry. It felt good, and made her feel stronger. As she soaked her hair in honey wash, Vista tried to imagine what might be coming next. There was one thing she felt certain of: if Iggy wanted a fight, then she was ready to give him one.

A short while later, Vista was roused by a gentle tapping on the wall outside the room. The softness of the tap told her it was Layla rather than Grecko.

'Vista, I'm sorry to disturb you, but Grecko's awake.'

Splashing her face with the water, Vista noted how much it had cooled and wondered how long she'd been soaking for. She rinsed the honey wash out of her hair with record speed as she called to Layla to come in, wrapping the cloth carefully over her wounded back.

Layla entered with Vista's dress draped over her fingers. If Vista hadn't known any better, she'd have thought it was brand new. 'Oh wow Layla, how did you get it so clean?'

Layla chuckled, not really answering the question but diverting her gaze so that Vista could put on her sparkling dress, feeling like a new fairy.

With her hair clean and smelling of rose water, she cheerfully climbed into Layla's hand, then promptly reminded herself of the situation they were in and to hold back her smiles before facing Grecko.

As they entered the main room, Vista spied Grecko near the table and was immediately comforted. He looked rested. Vista hadn't realised how tired he'd been until seeing him after some sleep. Her eyes misted up, and she swiftly blinked to clear her vision.

'Grecko, I'm so glad you're awake!' Trying hard to disguise her pity, she coughed, 'Did you sleep well?'

Grecko grinned, seeming just as pleased to see her. 'I did, Miss Vista, thanks. Might I say yer looking lovely. So clean an' neat.' His voice was tinged in sadness, it was obvious Grecko had noticed her appreciation for the comforts in Layla's home.

'Thank you,' – Vista blushed – 'I do feel a lot better.' She looked back to Layla. 'Are we leaving now?'

Layla nodded, 'I'm afraid so. I've shown you what you needed to see to understand what Iggy is capable of. The rest is up to you now.'

The rest is up to you now. The words rang through Vista's head like a tune you can't stop humming, and Vista was surprised to find she wasn't as frightened as she'd assumed she'd be. She looked back at Grecko who was busy filling his pockets with extra scones and cakes for the journey and smiled, glad to see she wasn't the only one sick of fish and berries.

'Grecko, could you please go out the front and ensure there's enough clean water collected for the journey?' Layla asked, distracting him from his food scavenge. Without complaint, Grecko turned and left.

Suddenly, Vista noticed she was being walked away in the opposite direction. 'Layla? Where are we going?'

'Hush now, I must tell you this quickly whilst Grecko's distracted,' she uttered quietly – so quietly in fact that Vista had to strain to hear her. Pressing her mouth as close to Vista's tiny ear as she could, Layla whispered.

What Vista heard made her heart stop; everything slowed, and her skin paled. Having no idea how to respond, Vista nodded her head and looked over to where Grecko had been. What was she going to do?

19

Letherea's Goodness

Stepping out into the forest again seemed bizarre. Despite spending so much time within it, Vista had quickly grown used to the comfort of Layla's home.

Layla led the way and the three of them walked through the trees, Grecko following closely behind with Vista perched upon his hand.

She rested her head against Grecko's thumb, breathing in the smell of his chest as he held her close, taking comfort in his presence. She tried her best not to think of Iggy, too nervous of what might be coming.

All Vista could see were trees and leaves. Every noise, whether it were a passing bird or wind rustling the branches, made Vista flinch, and every time she flinched, she felt Grecko's fingers curl around her a little tighter. Layla, however, moved through the forest as though she was a part of it. Vista couldn't help but notice how trees and flowers seemed to bow in her presence. Absently, Layla stroked and patted the heads of various plants in her path.

'You know, Vista, you belong here in the forest. All the plants agree.'

Vista chuckled, unsure how to respond.

'It's true.' Layla continued, 'The flowers whisper of your presence. I understand it's not common practise for fairies to move away from the Home Tree anymore, but I feel you belong out here.'

Grecko winked at Vista, clearly pleased with this idea.

'It's a shame the fairies no longer venture into Letherea – they once were so useful to the forest. I can tell it misses them a great deal.' Layla continued to stroke the flower petals as she walked, 'In order for there to be a change, someone must first step forward and be willing to stretch the boundaries.' She stopped and turned around, her eyes sparkling, 'You might just be that someone, Vista.'

Vista blushed slightly but movement in the distance distracted her before she had time to respond. 'Grecko, what was that?'

He looked in the direction of the noise and grinned. 'It's alright, Miss Vista, it's jus' a kirgle, see?'

Vista followed his gaze towards the bushes. They rustled, the leaves alive with movement as something very large made its way through them. She swallowed, gripping her fingers around Grecko and urging herself to be brave – the thought of Layla seeing her scared embarrassed her greatly. *Whatever's coming can't be that bad if no one else is afraid.*

'How big is it?' she asked, her eyes staring straight into the rustling leaves as she tried to sound calm.

'Umm, pretty big, I s'pose. Bigger than me, anyway.'

Vista gawked at Grecko. *Bigger than him!* Considering Vista's small size, anything bigger than Grecko was humongous. She tried to focus on taking steady breaths, suddenly feeling quite faint.

Before she could fret any more, a creature bigger than anything Vista had ever seen emerged from the bushes ahead. It slid across the ground, leaving a trail of slime behind it. To an outsider in a regular forest, this creature would look similar to a snail, but a great deal larger than any snail a human would ever encounter.

The kirgle's eyes protruded from its body on rigid sticks, hovering above a large head easily the size of four bowling balls. From Vista's angle, there didn't appear to be a mouth, although she assumed it was merely hidden somewhere beneath the bulbous head. Its skin was speckled grey, and resting upon its back was a large shell that looked almost as beautiful as Vista's wings had the first time she'd seen them. The shell's surface was white with fine swirling lines of rich sky blue. The lines looked like they'd been hand drawn especially for it.

Grecko noticed Vista admiring the shell. 'All kirgle's shells is different. Every year they age another marking appears. That's why this one's shell's got so many blue lines, must be very old indeed.' Grecko spoke in soft, gentle tones, displaying the utmost respect to the creature in their presence.

The kirgle being so old surprised Vista. When she thought of something old, she pictured withering and decay. Looking at this creature before her, she had no doubt her impression of age was very much mistaken. This kirgle proved that with age came character and stories. Everything about it was fascinating.

The kirgle paused, noticing them in its path. After a brief hesitation, it continued forward, straight in the direction of Vista and Grecko. Vista was delighted; the thought of talking with such an old, interesting creature made her feel a small bit of magic return to Letherea. She turned to Layla, who stood slightly away from the kirgle but bowed her head towards it graciously as it approached.

'Hello,' Vista smiled awkwardly when the kirgle finally reached them, 'It's so lovely to meet you.'

Stopping in front of them, the kirgle didn't reply, but its eyes began lowering from their stalks until they peered very closely at Vista. She looked to Grecko, unsure of what was happening.

Grecko giggled slightly, 'Uh, Miss Vista, this is how they greet yer. They don't speak like we do.' Vista heard Layla softly chuckling behind them.

The hopes of any conversation washed away as she smiled at the creature, trying to hide her disappointment.

The kirgle closed its eyes, revealing long, thick lashes. It used them to gently brush Vista's cheek, tickling her and making her snort self-consciously. 'What's he doing now?'

Grecko petted the large creature's head as he spoke, 'Kirgle's is very special. They have the power of empathy. See, a kirgle can sense sadness an' pain – they sorta seek it out – ter try an' help fix it in some way I s'pose.'

Vista's eyes welled as she stared into the kirgle's, his whole reason for existing to show compassion to others. 'So, he can tell how we're feeling? Just by looking at us?'

Layla offered an explanation as Grecko continued to pet the gentle giant. 'Very close Vista. They have the ability to see feelings on you. The way we see faces, they see colours.' Vista looked confused, but Layla continued, 'They can't see features, but we all have a certain colour around us all the time. When someone's anxious or upset, they send out a colour that the kirgles' can see; the same goes for if someone's happy or excited. The kirgles' problem is that it can't speak – it makes it difficult for them to comfort properly.' Layla smiled at the creature as it rested briefly between them.

'I guess it's nice jus' knowing someone cares enough ter come sit with yer, even if they can't say nothing, yer know?' Grecko added, the lines on his face deepening.

The kirgle turned one eye towards Grecko, blinking its long lashes against Grecko's cheek the same way he had with Vista's. Vista wondered what colours they were shining and whether they shone the same or a mixture of colours, mixed together in a rainbow of nerves.

Grecko smiled and patted it some more, 'Alright, big fella, yer done a good job. We feel a lot better now we seen yer.'

The kirgle's eyes moved back to their original position. Vista watched as it did one final slow blink before edging away from them, heading back the way it came.

'It was lovely to meet you!' she called, hoping it might understand.

They stood together in silence watching until it disappeared from sight. It dawned on Vista how much beauty there was living in Letherea, and how wrong it seemed to have it all be at risk because of one spiteful imp.

20

A Mind Gone Mad

Iggy smacked at his head viciously, trying to escape the past. His memories bore into him, hurting his mind and making him cry out in pain.

'Stop it, stop it, *STOP IT!*' he screamed.

Muffled voices in the distance brought him back to the present; Letherea was playing tricks again.

Oh, how it loves its trickery. It was whispering about his upcoming failures, Iggy knew it was. The forest was so convinced he was going to fail that it wouldn't even listen to his reasons why he was going to succeed.

'Stop it! I can hear you, you know.' Iggy whirled around raging, desperate to pinpoint the exact tree that was starting all the rumours, 'Why are there so many of you?' Iggy cried, 'Too many trees...'

His fingers glowed a familiar red as his anger bubbled.

'What's your plan, Iggy?'

He knew that voice. Spinning frantically, he froze as a figure emerged from the trees.

'Jesabelle.' He cursed her name. He knew there was a chance she was just his imagination, another cruel trick brought on by the forest. The forest he now hated *almost* as much as he hated Lilleth. Nevertheless, even the possibility of Jesabelle standing in front of him fuelled a brand new wave of anger, refocusing him and steering him onwards.

'You're going to fail. You know that right, Iggy? Remember what happened the last time you tried to get back at a fairy? You got kicked out of your home by your own mother.' Jesabelle smirked, the very same smirk that had started all this.

'I'd hoped you were dead,' Iggy muttered, walking nearer to her, so he could wrap his hands around her throat if he needed to.

'Ha! I didn't die - they let me continue living in the Home Tree, which is more than they did for you. Wings or no wings, Iggy - you still lost!'

'What are you even doing here?' he snarled.

Jesabelle laughed, 'You really have gone mad, haven't you? I'm not really here, you fool. This is all in your head! But it's nice to know you haven't forgotten about me, I must have been *very* special to you.' Bile rose in Iggy's throat at the sound of her laughter, but with great difficulty, he swallowed it down.

Sparks pricked his fingers, but Jesabelle wasn't finished yet. 'You think you're so terrifying and tough, but the truth, Iggy, is that you're just a pathetic little imp screaming at himself in the middle of the forest.' She cackled then, her shrieks echoing and bouncing off the trees whilst Iggy cupped his hands over his ears to escape the sound.

'How *dare* you!' he screamed, throwing his hand forward to tear at her throat, wanting more than anything to feel the touch of his hot fingers burning through her skin. But as he lunged, his hand swung at nothing. He blinked, confused. She was gone.

'What? Where are you? NO! Bring her back, we weren't finished!' he demanded, hollering at the trees.

A low chuckle rustled through the leaves, filling the air and pooling into Iggy's ears.

He dropped to his knees and huddled into the dirt, not quite defeated but entirely exhausted. Absentmindedly, he began drawing line after line in the mud, lifting his finger every now and then to examine the dirt that gathered beneath his nail. Slowly, in a daze, he dragged the wet muck from his finger down the side of his sweaty cheek. In a fit of sheer insanity, Iggy then placed both hands into the mud and began to smear it all over his face.

'Be the forest... Be the forest... Be the forest,' he muttered repeatedly as he covered himself in more and more dirt.

It didn't take long for Iggy's face to become completely covered in a mask of thick, dried mud and leaves. Only then did he proceed to lie on the ground and roll side to side, coating his clothes and the rest of his body. The mud squelched beneath him as he rolled. He could feel the weight of himself bearing down on it, creating dips in the dirt as he pushed in deeper. It squashed between his fingers, drying quickly as it settled on his burning hands.

When he felt he was sufficiently covered, Iggy stopped moving.

'Are you happy now?' he called to the trees.

Lying there on his back, enjoying the quiet, he giggled to himself. He giggled like a child, incessant and uncontrollable. He giggled until it turned into a laugh and then that laugh turned into a cackle. He cackled until his throat hurt and his voice turned hoarse. Day turned to night, and night turned to day, and still Iggy cackled.

Letherea and everything that lived within it filled him with hate, turning his stomach into a fiery whirlpool of rage. He was ready to go now, he just had to make sure that the fairies went first.

Using every ounce of strength he had left, he rolled onto his side and flopped onto his stomach, gazing around the area.

There was movement in front of him, but it was small and likely harmless, so Iggy paid little attention to it. He was certain it wouldn't be Jesabelle. She wouldn't dare come back and face him again. Tightening his fingers around his bag, as he often did when he felt nervous, he pulled himself to his knees and from there pushed himself up to standing.

Maybe I should eat something? He thought, struggling to remember when he had last had a meal. Reaching into his bag, he searched for his magical fishing net but, to his dismay, realised that going towards the river would only take him further away from the Home Tree, so he quickly decided against that idea.

Scanning his surroundings, he smirked. He remembered learning a long time ago from someone (not wanting to admit it was probably Lilleth) that tree bark could be a good source of sustenance in an emergency situation.

Iggy smiled, also remembering that trees feel pain when you cut them. He recalled also being taught that you should always thank them for their sacrifice.

'Ha! Good luck with that one,' he snarled in response.

With a few painful steps he managed to reach the trunk of a large tree, standing tall and strong.

'Hope you don't mind if I cut a few slices?' Iggy chuckled, pulling out a knife from his bag and slicing into the tree.

Iggy could have used magic to do this but he did enjoy the idea of causing the tree as much pain as possible.

He cut four unappetising chunks out of it and held them tightly in his hands.

Without even acknowledging the tree's sacrifice, Iggy turned his back to it and placed the first chunk of bark into his mouth. The taste instantly made him gag - it was like vinegar mixed with sticks - but Iggy kept on chewing. The texture on his tongue was dry, the bark soaking up all of his saliva, and he gagged as he forced himself to swallow. Whilst picking bits out of his teeth, he looked back at the tree, irritated that it was getting the last laugh as he struggled to eat it.

Placing the second chunk into his mouth, Iggy gagged again as it broke apart, splintering his gums. Not wanting to give the tree any more satisfaction, he began to walk away, bark in hand. His body ached with fatigue and his tongue stung with gashes from that wretched tree bark, but at least his stomach didn't feel so hollow.

Iggy dragged himself forward, cupping his hands over his ears to block out the roaring winds as they rushed past his face, despite not a single leaf moving in the breeze elsewhere.

Grunting angrily, he hopped for a moment as his left foot stepped down and he felt a crunch beneath his skin. Looking at the ground, he was shocked to find that he'd just stepped on and broken a twig from a honeysuckle bush, unmistakable due to its caramel-like colour.

Now, normally a broken twig would have been easy to ignore, had Iggy not known that the honeysuckle bush only grew in one particular part of the forest. It only grew near the Home Tree. Iggy scooped up the broken twig and kissed it elatedly, spurred on by a newfound energy that only comes when the finish line is in sight.

Iggy ran.

He ran for what felt like hours, until up ahead in the bushes, the Home Tree came into view.

When a place has existed only as a memory for the longest time, that memory can sometimes alter the reality of the place. In memories, colours can appear brighter, smells can seem sweeter and sounds can be musical. This, Iggy found, was not the case for him.

The Home Tree was just as beautiful and majestic as he had remembered it to be. Its trunk stood strong, looking like it held the entire magical forest together. Its leaves were the brightest of greens and filled with dozens of sweet singing birds - the sound of them making him snarl in disgust. Breathing in, the scent of fresh flowers and honeysuckle tickled his nostrils and he blew out angrily. Everything about this place made Iggy nauseous. He was certain he'd have felt better had it not looked so delightful. He'd been hoping to find a dank, lonely looking tree decorated in Lilleth's shame and regret at letting him go.

Glaring upwards, he could see fairies swooping in and out of the Home Tree's entrance. *Maybe they were having lessons?* The thought of this made him snigger, picturing how many of them might be gathered inside, completely oblivious to what was coming.

With sweaty palms - his weary legs and dirt-covered face long forgotten - Iggy stepped out from the bushes. Looking up at the Home Tree, he did one final check to ensure his bag was safe and, placing one determined hand against the trunk, began to climb.

21

Return to the Home Tree

It was quiet for a moment or two after the kirgle had left. Layla and Grecko stood still - Vista still in his palm. All of them were briefly lost in their own thoughts.

'Layla?' Vista was first to break the silence, 'Is Iggy—'

'Shh!' Layla had stopped moving. Looking to her right, she stared closely at a nearby tree trunk, 'Grecko, a nosey, there!' Layla pointed straight at the tree and, without any explanation needed, Grecko slammed his hand against the trunk, causing a creature to appear out of nowhere and tumble straight towards the ground.

'What is that?' Vista cried out.

'It's a nosey, Miss Vista.' Grecko kept his eye on it as it scuttled out of sight, as fast as it could possibly go. 'Awful things, they are. Can't be trusted at all. Don't worry though, I didn't hurt it, jus' gave it a scare that's all.'

Vista remained still, baffled by what had just happened.

'A nosey is an untrustworthy creature, Vista.' Layla explained, 'Did you notice how it appeared as soon as Grecko smacked the tree? They have the ability to hide from sight, and they use this ability to their advantage. They like to hide and hear secrets throughout the forest. Did you see how small it was? That helps it sneak into the smallest of spaces. They're fast too; if they hear a secret, they can spread it throughout the whole of Letherea before you even know they heard you.'

'Like I said, awful things. Yer lucky yer didn't get a proper look at it. I reckon they go invisible fer another reason as well – ter hide the fact they're so ugly. They're scaly an' wriggly, an' they got these long tails that swish back an' forth, urgh!' Grecko shuddered, 'Ugly on the inside, an' it shows on the outside, I reckon.'

Vista chewed her lip, unsure of how to respond. 'Oh...'

'They might seem alarming but they can't physically harm anyone. They're certainly a nuisance, however. I'm afraid we mustn't discuss anything else regarding 'a certain imp' out here. It's simply not safe. We can't risk secrets getting whispered into the wrong ears. At the moment the element of surprise is still on our side.'

Vista swallowed, admitting defeat and accepting that she knew all she was going to know for the time being.

'How did you see the nosey?'

Layla shrugged, 'Being a witch can have many benefits. A nosey hides itself using magic, and magic can always sense other magic. It's one of the perks.'

Grecko scoffed under his breath; no words were needed to understand his views on magic.

A noise ahead of them broke the moment, drawing all of their attention to it. It sounded like laughter – giggly and cheerful.

'What's that?' Vista asked.

'Oh, it's the children o' the forest,' Grecko smiled, 'Ain't the chattiest o' folk, but they sure is happy.' Grecko steered them towards the laughter, Layla following behind.

'We shouldn't stop, Grecko.' she reminded him.

'It's alright, Layla, I jus' wanna show Miss Vista fer a minute.'

Stepping into a small clearing, Vista was faced with two small children running through the grass. The only thing that made them different to regular children was the fact that they were almost completely see-through. As they ran, they came in and out of focus, butterflies and other flying critters flying right alongside them. They laughed and played, running and rolling in the grass, seeming not to notice the others' presence at all.

'Hello!' Vista called, enjoying the sight of so much happiness.

'They can't answer yer. They can't even see yer. But it's still nice ter watch 'em play, right?'

'The children of the forest are the very essence of nature,' Layla explained, 'They can't be communicated or played with, but their presence represents the joy of the forest, and they're always cheerful. Their existence is proof of Letherea's goodness.'

As Vista watched them play and laugh with each other, a tree to her left began to swirl and take on a body-like shape, with long branch-like arms and leaves falling like hair. It moved towards the children and waved its arms high above them, back and forth. As the branches waved, flurries of leaves fell like waterfalls over the children, causing them to shriek with delight. The leaves shimmered in the sun, glistening as they spun and twirled their way towards the ground. The children danced and skipped, running through the raining leaves as the sound of their laughter filled the air. As they giggled, the tree figure continued to sway, showering the children in its love.

Without Vista needing to ask, Layla explained further, 'Those are the tree folk, they're like the mothers of the forest and take care of the children. They're the only ones who can communicate with them.'

The three stood quietly and watched them for a moment or so. The tree mother continued to sway her branches and float her leaves, much to the delight of the forest children below.

'We must keep going now, just over this hill,' Layla said, bringing them out of their trance.

To Vista's disappointment, she was led away from the giggling forest children and the tree folk, forced back into reality.

———

AFTER A SHORT CLIMB, THEY WERE OVER THE HILL AND LAYLA STOPPED. Resting before them was a large rock, seemingly ordinary-looking - but as Vista was quickly realising, nothing in Letherea was ordinary.

'This is your way back to the Home Tree,' Layla gestured towards it.

Vista stared, bewildered. *How?* She focused on the rock, trying to figure out what made it so special. It was a weathered grey colour with scattered darker patches, and as Vista watched, she could see a forest insect or two scuttling across its surface. *Doesn't seem too different from any other rock...*

'Rocks are much more powerful than you realise, Vista.' Layla interrupted her thoughts, appearing to sense her confusion, 'They have been around a long time and absorbed the power of many that pass them. This one here is incredibly old and a great source of power for me. It grounds my magic and helps me to focus it.'

Vista knew better than to ask Layla to elaborate.

'Now, when you're both ready, I want you to close your eyes.'

'Wait, wait! What if I can't do it? What if I can't save them?' Vista's confidence suddenly felt shaken, her moment was approaching much faster than she'd thought it would.

'Don't worry, Miss Vista, yer got me, remember? I ain't gonna let nothing happen ter yer.' Grecko smiled reassuringly.

'You promise you'll stay with me?'

'Promise!' Gently, he brought his forehead close to her and closed his eyes.

Vista was amazed at Grecko's ability to remain so calm. He put her to shame, that was for sure. Following his lead, she closed her eyes and braced herself.

Bringing her slender arms forward in one fluid motion, Layla spoke her final words to them, 'I wish you both the very best of luck.'

Vista's stomach knotted; she'd never been sent anywhere by magic before. Her lip stung as she bit into it nervously, and she quickly debated how she would know when to open her eyes again. Not long after wondering this, however, she felt an almighty crash against her chest, as though something very large had smacked her in the ribcage and sent her flying away from Grecko.

Winded and dazed, her eyes shot open. Vast arrays of colour whizzed past her head at great speed. She looked to where Grecko had been, but with a panic realised he was gone. She tried calling his name, but the speed at which she was travelling made it difficult to speak, her breath catching in her throat every time she opened her mouth. All sense of control left her as she found herself flying at a rate that was increasing by the second. It was like hurtling through a rainbow - flurries of colour flooded her vision and her eyes stung from the sheer brightness of it all. Her head whirled unsteadily as she tried to determine which way was up and which was down.

Nauseous and woozy, Vista's limbs began to grow heavy under the weight of her own body. She felt herself being pulled down to earth and screwed her eyes tightly shut, trying to brace herself for another crushing blow to her chest.

With an immense thud, her body crashed and rolled its way to the ground.

Lying perfectly still, it took a moment or two for her to realise that it was over. Cautiously, she unfolded her arms, drawing quick breaths and glancing around her, relieved to see that the flurries of colour had vanished.

The sound of familiar birds filled her ears, and in that moment she knew she was home. Memories came flooding back of days spent sitting at the window ledge above, dreaming of how wonderful everything would be once she was free. The next thing to hit her was the smell - it filled her nostrils and tickled her insides, teasing her with memories of freshly baked scones and warm honey. She was definitely back.

Vista found herself crying and panting to catch her breath.

'Miss Vista?' Grecko's voice boomed from behind her, 'Are yer okay? Landing's a bit rough, ain't it?'

The sight of Grecko hobbling towards her made her smile - clearly she wasn't the only one who had had a sore landing.

'Did you hurt yourself?' she asked, feeling bad for smiling in case it was serious.

Grecko stopped walking and looked down at his knee, as if noticing his hobble for the first time. 'Huh? Oh yeah, I s'pose I did a bit. Not ter worry. More like a scratch, I reckon. How 'bout yerself?'

'No, I'm fine,' Vista lied. Pulling herself up to her full height and still not reaching further than Grecko's ankles, Vista looked up towards the Home Tree. 'Do you think he's up there yet?' she asked, not wanting to say his name – it seemed disrespectful to Grecko to use it somehow.

'Hard ter say. If he was, surely we'd hear some kinda noise or summit, don't yer reckon?'

As though hearing his request, several stifled screams came rushing down from above. Vista and Grecko's eyes shot upwards.

'Answers that I s'pose. What now?' Grecko asked, looking cautiously to Vista.

Vista's forehead felt clammy and she rubbed her hands distractedly against her dress. *What now, what now?* she thought and began whispering nervously under her breath. They needed a plan and so far, they had nothing.

'Vista?'

Both of them jumped at the sound of her name. Looking behind her, Vista staggered slightly at the sight of yellow hair and a red and green dress.

'Mila?'

Mila rushed towards her, tears pouring down her face, arms outstretched. They embraced each other, Vista hushing Mila's sobs.

'Where have you *been*? Everyone's been *so* worried about you! Do you have any idea what's happening up there?'

Vista had forgotten how fast Mila could speak when she was panicking.

'That's why I'm here. This is Grecko.' Vista gestured behind her and Grecko smiled, waving awkwardly at Mila and looking quite out of place indeed.

Mila drew back slightly upon seeing Grecko, somehow missing

him before. Without a word in his direction, she turned back to Vista. 'What are we going to do? There's an *imp* in the Home Tree! There's been calls to all the fairies from all over the forest to get to the Home Tree immediately. The imp must have done it. He keeps yelling at everyone, and he's *screaming* at Lilleth! Vista, he has magic...' Mila had begun pacing, but suddenly stopped, noticing something, 'Where are your *wings?*'

Grecko tutted loudly and Mila, once again, stared at him for a moment before turning back to Vista.

'There'll be time to explain all that later. Mila, listen, can you fly me up there?'

Grecko shot a look at Vista; they both knew this meant she would be going up alone. Neither needed to acknowledge the unfinished business there was between Grecko and Iggy, but there was no way that Grecko was fitting inside the Home Tree. So, avoiding Grecko's gaze, Vista stared firmly at Mila. This was the only option, and she couldn't let Grecko sway her.

'Well... Yes of course I can, but what are you going to do?'

'Just get me up there and you'll see.' Vista did her best to look confident, praying Mila wouldn't ask her any more questions - truthfully, she had no idea what her next move was.

'Okay, then let's go,' she said and wrapped her arms tightly around Vista's waist. Vista felt her feet lifting away from the ground and couldn't help but think how much nicer it felt than being lifted by those awful skizzes.

'Miss Vista, STOP!' Grecko's call startled Mila and Vista felt her jolt in mid-air. This was when she realised that Mila may have thought Grecko was a mute until now.

'Can you take me to his eye level, please?'

Obligingly, Mila flew Vista to Grecko's face and politely averted her gaze in an attempt to give them some privacy.

Vista gently cupped Grecko's cheek and swallowed hard. Placing a soft kiss on the tip of his nose, she whispered softly to her friend, 'I'll be back, I promise!'

Grecko squeezed his eyes shut, trying not to cry and appreciating her closeness. He couldn't bring himself to speak, only managing a small nod. They stayed there in silence for a moment.

Coughing as subtly as she could, Mila reminded Vista of their need for urgency. With a slight wave, she continued their flight upwards, pulling Vista away from Grecko.

The nearer they got to the Home Tree, the clearer the muffled voices became, until Vista had no trouble telling them apart. The sound of Lilleth's voice sent a shiver down her spine, her nerves at seeing her growing with each flap of Mila's wings. The only voice that evoked a bigger reaction for Vista was Iggy's - so cold and callous, you could feel his hatred with every word he spoke. Vista still couldn't understand how she had ever trusted a creature with a voice like that.

They perched on the branch, and Vista felt her mouth dry up as her heart pounded in her chest. Mila tightened her grip on Vista at the sight of Iggy in their home, her fear causing her hand to twitch. Iggy was pacing the room, waving his hands wildly as he yelled, his body and clothes filthy as though he'd just crawled out of a muddy trench. All around him, fairies recoiled and screamed, their faces shrouded in panicked confusion as they huddled together, trying to make sense of what was happening. Their home - their safe place - was being invaded. Vista heard Mila sob quietly behind her, letting go of her arm and shuffling her feet backwards. Vista's body tensed as she forced her legs to move forwards slightly, still hidden from view.

Peeking into the entrance, Vista could see the inside of the Home Tree. It was bright - contrasting the dark tone within the room. The sunlight shone through the window, casting a warm glow in the centre. Iggy, pacing up and down, passed through it as he walked and Vista thought how wrong it looked, him being in the light. He was taunting the fairies, screaming at them as they wept. He walked slowly around them in circles, crouching down to smell the fear they were giving off. No one had spotted Vista yet, standing just out of sight on the branch.

The smell of sweat and salty tears hung in the air as the fairies crammed closer together, clutching at each others' hands. Vista looked around at the faces of her family and then at Iggy. He was smirking at the chaos he was creating, and the sight made Vista ill. Her palms grew clammy and she focused on keeping her breathing shallow, afraid of being heard. Her home felt violated, every step that Iggy took left behind a muddy footprint that directly went against the fairies love of beauty, turning their home into a dirty, ugly scene. The noise inside grew louder as the fairies cried harder, each one shaking as Iggy became more and more chaotic. He skipped around the room, growling and screaming at them all, occasionally smacking his own head in fury - appearing to be arguing with himself while he spoke.

The sight made Vista's heart jolt. The last time she had stood on the Home Tree branch she had been so unsure of herself, so weak. But not this time. Now she found herself ready.

Turning to Mila, she gave a small smile despite the noise behind her. It reminded her of their flight day when Mila had smiled at Vista from the branch. Vista pressed a finger to her lips, indicating for Mila to keep quiet and then, with a deep breath, made her way into the Home Tree. As she stepped into the entrance, a hushed silence fell over the room as, one by one, each fairy caught sight of her. It was Iggy's silence, however, that held the most weight. While every face in the room rested on Vista, she saw no one but Iggy.

22

Vengeful Magic

'Vista?' It was Lilleth's voice that broke the silence, her face a mixture of confusion and relief. Vista paused as she caught sight of her, previously hidden in the corner. *Lilleth?* She looked just as frightened and fragile as the other fairies, and Vista looked at her in shock. For a moment it seemed that the imp's presence had been forgotten.

Iggy's surprise quickly turned to anger as he watched, 'I don't have time for interruptions. What are *you* doing here?'

Mila whimpered from the branch, but Vista coughed in the hopes of covering the sound, not wanting Iggy to spot her friend.

Unexpectedly, staring into the eyes of the imp who had tricked her and done so many evil things didn't fill her with the fear she had thought it would, but rather fuelled her strength.

In an act of either bravery or stupidity (she hadn't decided which yet), Vista took a step towards Iggy. 'I-I'm here to stop you.'

Hushed whispers frantically passed throughout the room between scared and bewildered fairies. Lilleth in particular looked extremely confused, her hands trembling slightly as she looked on.

Iggy, on the other hand, laughed. It was a dramatic, mocking sort of laugh. A laugh that Vista tried to block out.

'You're going to stop *me*?' Iggy scoffed, 'How exactly are you planning on doing that, hmm?'

Seeing as Vista hadn't quite figured this out yet, she decided to stall for a while first. 'You tricked me and stole my wings!' she said accusingly.

Iggy smirked as each fairy subconsciously turned their wings away from him - none wanting to be his next victim. Pressing a finger to his chapped lips and walking in tiny circles, he chuckled to himself, 'Don't pretend like you weren't happy about that - you were *desperate* for me to take them from you.' Giving Vista no time to respond he continued, 'You're just angry because you made a bad deal. What kind of a fairy would trade her wings for a fishing net?' he sneered. Every fairy in the room gasped, setting off the incessant whispering and murmuring all over again. Vista's heart dropped, she tried to hide it from Iggy but this hurt. *They hate me.*

Her throat swelled as she fought back the tears, she could feel every eye in the room upon her. The judgement of every fairy seeping through her skin and suffocating her.

Iggy waved his hands around him incessantly, encouraging everyone's tutting and angry looks towards Vista to continue. His face wore a serene look as he embraced the growing chaos.

'That's right, everyone, you heard me correctly. Vista *traded* in her wings. She said she didn't need them anymore. She didn't need the very thing that made her a fairy!' Everyone continued their panicked whispers and Iggy turned back to Vista, 'Even your family can't stand you now,' he sneered, 'Maybe we have something in common after all.'

Her eyes darted quickly around the room, the faces watching her a mixture of puzzlement and betrayal. Not one of them was able to make sense of a fairy who would go against her family and willingly give up her wings. *They'll never understand.*

'Iggy, stop it.' Lilleth's voice trembled as it rose above the chatter, easily shutting it down as though pressing pause on the scene, 'Vista, we could never hate you; you're one of us.'

Vista looked to Lilleth, not knowing what to say.

Taking a deep breath, she forced herself to step closer to Iggy. He smiled at her as she approached, his eyes filled with menace. Either side of her she could hear the scuffling noise of fairies, shuffling backwards to clear her path.

'So, what's your big plan then?' Iggy stepped towards Vista, quickly closing the remainder of the gap between them. He was so close now that she could smell his putrid breath against her face. She tilted her head back slightly from the stench, hoping he wouldn't notice and mistake it for weakness. The room felt darker than it had when Vista had looked in from the branch, despite it still being midday. Leering over her, Iggy certainly managed to cast a shadow, and Vista thought it seemed fitting that Iggy would bring in the darkness. Glancing at the fairies around her, Vista noticed every head was tilted in her direction. Most of them had sunk to the floor now and their arms were wrapped tightly around their legs. It was clear Iggy wasn't the only one keen to hear her plan. Vista pictured Mila shuffling nervously on the branch outside, and wondered if she were fighting the urge to fly away.

'Whilst you try and think of a plan, how about you take a look at mine?' Iggy grinned wickedly and took a step back, creating an open space between them.

'Iggy, please...' Lilleth stepped forward - one of the last standing fairies - and attempted to touch Iggy's arm, invoking instant rage within him.

'DO NOT TOUCH ME!' he screamed, making the entire room jump and edge backwards, 'You're the reason I'm having to do all of this.' He stood, panting and pointing at Lilleth, every word to her tasting like poison in his mouth. 'This is all your fault. YOU SHOULD HAVE PICKED ME!'

'Oh, Iggy,' Lilleth looked at the ground and began to sob. The light from the window glinted off her white hair, showing loose strands falling from her normally immaculate bun. Never before had Vista noticed a hair out of place on Lilleth. Her face was damp with tears and she dabbed at her eyes with the back of her hand.

Every fairy in the room turned pale, unsure how to react to the sight of their mother weak and crying. One by one their eyes turned to Vista; she seemed to be their only hope now.

Iggy took a deep breath and rolled his shoulders, his frustration at the constant interruptions reaching a new level. 'Now, if everyone is done *whimpering*, there's something I'd like to show you all. I came a very long way to get here, and I'd like to get started if you don't mind.' He reached inside his bag and the room stopped. Everyone fell silent.

With a closed fist, he pulled out his hand and slowly uncurled his fingers to reveal a small vial containing a deep red substance. As delicately as he could, Iggy opened the vial and began to smother the ghastly liquid all over his hands, much to the revulsion of the onlooking fairies. Once they were sufficiently covered, he rubbed his palms together, fingers interlocking, and closed his eyes. A smile stretched across his face and his eyes narrowed into slits. He looked as though all his wishes were about to come true.

To Vista's horror, along with every other fairy in the room, Iggy's fingers began to glow. The light in the room appeared to be sucked away as everyone's attention turned to his hands. They glowed a deep crimson and carried with them a stench unlike anything they had ever smelt before. It was the kind of stench that filled your nostrils and caused you to feel woozy and nauseous all at the same time, unable to focus on anything but the smell and the glow. There was no question now that it had turned darker, Iggy's hands radiated before them, giving everything a reddish glow as an eerie silence fell amongst them.

'Now, this is the part that I like.' Iggy spoke through the hush and opened his eyes, glaring at Vista over his hands. As the glowing light between Iggy's fingers grew larger, Iggy's eyes turned darker until, eventually, they were completely black.

Cries and panic refilled the room, every fairy attempting to run but finding it was no use - Iggy's magic was holding them all in place, forcing them to watch as the magic he held grew bigger and brighter.

'So, here's what's going to happen,' Iggy spoke, 'this little beauty in my hands that I'm sure you can all see - and no doubt smell - is just a little something I've been working on. It's going to do me and every other creature in this forest a huge favour. *Today, I'll finally be able to rid Letherea of all you snivelling little bugs for good.*' He grinned and licked his lips as the sound of cries and shrieks erupted louder than ever. 'It's beautiful isn't it? You see, its sole purpose is to *destroy* – that's all I taught it how to do. Its ingredients represented strength, hope, trust and loyalty...' His eyes drifted over to Vista with that last ingredient, 'What they represent have become the very things it detests most – the very qualities the Home Tree and its fairies *claim* to have! See how it grows bigger?' he asked the fairies, savouring the moment, 'Eventually, it will swell so large that it will consume the entire Home Tree with all of you in it.' Screams escaped the fairies as they looked upon the magical ball in fear, they trembled before it, shaking their heads and crying as Iggy laughed. In truth, Iggy still didn't know for sure if he would survive his own spell, but either way, the sight before him was worth it. It was a worthy price to pay for his revenge.

'Now, don't take this personally...' Iggy paused, laughing cruelly, 'actually, you should all take this *very* personally. The truth is I hate you all, each and every one of you. Especially *you!*' he turned to look directly at Lilleth who had joined the other fairies, crumpling to her knees and staring at the growing magic before them in fear. 'You see, all you had to do was choose me, but you didn't.' Iggy's voice was rising. His face had twisted with hatred as he looked down on her, 'YOU DIDN'T CHOOSE ME AND NOW YOU'LL BE SORRY!'

Lilleth couldn't speak, but her eyes pleaded with Iggy. It was amazing that this was the same fairy they had all looked up to and admired. Watching her now, kneeling on the floor crying and terrified, she looked no different than any of the others.

'Stop it!' Vista stood helpless, her eyes moving over every inch of the room, her mind desperately seeking a way out of this horrifying situation.

Iggy raised his eyebrows, as though startled by her outburst and giggled, 'Why would I stop when I'm winning, hmm?' They were both practically shouting to be heard above the shrieks.

Vista gritted her teeth. Her fists were clenched so tightly she could feel her fingernails digging into her palms. The pain seemed to fuel her, it was like tiny pin pricks against her skin and she focused on the sharpness of it – it seemed to be keeping her in the moment, forcing her to stay present and not let her thoughts distract her.

She glared at Iggy. He was still standing before the growing magic, it looked almost like a ball in its shape, but viciously sparking, sending flickers of deep red spitting into the air. It was as dark and putrid as ever, now so large that Iggy hardly needed to support it anymore. The fairies cowered before it and Iggy chuckled as he admired what he'd made. Slowly, he turned his face to meet Vista's. His expression was twisted in glee and his black eyes studied her. Every time he heard a whimper, his smile tweaked a little.

'You can't win, you know,' Vista yelled. She watched as Iggy spun the putrid magical ball, only half listening to her. The ball was still growing, 'The Home Tree's been here for as long as Letherea and fairies are important – we were the bringers of beauty once, before the forest made the wisps.'

The only thing louder than Iggy's cackle were the confused echoes carried by the fairies as they questioned what Vista was talking about. Lilleth kept silent, her gaze resting on Vista with a look of confusion – *did she think I wouldn't find out?*

'Well, aren't you a clever one?' Iggy mused. He glanced at the magical ball and quickly seemed satisfied that it was now large enough and strong enough to support itself. Taking a step away from it, he smirked at Vista, 'or rather, your *friend* is a clever one... where is he anyway?'

Vista froze. The noise around her continued but Vista fell deaf to it for a moment. *How did he know about Grecko?*

'You know who I'm talking about. The big, ugly gnome you're always hanging about with.' Iggy turned to look at the weeping fairies surrounding them, 'He's the reason you're all in this mess actually -

she was trying to help him. How does it feel, Vista, knowing that without your wings, none of this would have been possible?'

'It's not my fault that you tricked me!' Vista's voice rose, she could feel her calm slipping, 'what about the other ingredients you needed? WHAT ABOUT GRECKO'S DAD?' She was screaming now and instantly regretted it, again worrying how it must sound to poor Grecko down below.

Iggy clicked his fingers and stomped his feet, a look of delight spreading across his face, 'that's it, THAT'S IT! Grecko... That's been driving me *crazy* for the longest time, trying to place that ugly gnome's face. I knew I'd seen him before!'

Vista couldn't believe it, Iggy was smiling – he was actually smiling.

Had he really forgotten Grecko?

'How can you be so happy? You *killed* his Dad!'

'Yes I know, but in my opinion, it's not all that bad.' he reasoned, his gaze turning to Lilleth's tear drenched face, 'There are worse things than dying you know? Like being turned away by the only family you'd ever known. Made to feel like a *freak* because you were different. I think I deserve a little bit of revenge, all things considered, don't you?'

Vista recoiled. 'There's no excuse for the things you've d-'

'OH YES THERE IS!' he screamed, cutting her off. Iggy's temper was rising and, to Vista's horror, the magical ball seemed to be reacting to his mood. The moment Iggy screamed, the ball swelled and its smell grew stronger, like the smell of burnt rubber. It spun in mid-air, gaining speed as Iggy began to derail. The fairies watched on in horror, none daring to blink, but for once Vista didn't need to worry about the sound. They had stopped their screaming, every mouth hung open in silence, their fingers white as they held each other's hands tightly. Iggy took a small step away from Vista, shaking his head as though trying to re-focus, 'My dear Vista, you seem to have sent me off track, where was I?' Iggy clicked his fingers, sparks shooting out of them as the fairies cowered and trembled, finding their cries once more, 'Oh yes, I remember...'

Iggy pointed his fingers towards the branch and bile rose in Vista's throat as she heard the confused shouts of Grecko coming from the ground below. *What's happening?*

Grecko's shouts grew louder as he found himself being lifted into the air and floating up towards the Home Tree.

'Obviously that big ugly thing out there won't be able to fit inside, but everyone can see the gnome hovering nicely by the branch, can't they?' Iggy pointed to Grecko, who looked in hopelessly from outside the Home Tree. Every fairy gawped, and Iggy waved tauntingly at him, wearing an impish grin, 'Hi Grecko, how's life?' he teased.

'IGGY,' Grecko cried, swiping at the air, 'don't yer dare hurt Miss Vista!'

Grecko focused his eyes on Iggy and before anyone could speak he pulled his arm back and launched something into the Home Tree, straight in Iggy's direction. Vista leapt back in shock and everyone else ducked, still frozen to their spots, as something small and black hurtled through the air. With no time to react, Iggy found himself struck right in the temple. Stumbling backwards, he brought his hand to his head, a look of fury on his face. The magical ball raged and spun as Iggy glowered at Grecko.

'A *ROCK*? I won't forget that when this is over!'

He spun his hand, and the magic that was holding Grecko up twisted him so that he now hung upside down, but he was undeterred. 'If yer hurt Miss Vista, I'll make sure yer pay fer it. Don't forget the forest'll always be on my side.'

For the briefest moment Iggy paused, appearing to grow slightly troubled by Grecko's words. Vista noticed him subconsciously raise a hand and scratch at his face, the way she'd seen do in the forest when those buzzing critters had hovered around him. He pulled himself upright and pursed his lips, waving a hand in Grecko's direction. Opening his mouth to speak again, Grecko's eyes scrunched up in anger as no sound came out. Iggy had turned him mute.

'He's right you know, the forest won't ever let you live well again! If you think getting to the Home Tree was hard then just imagine getting out of it after this...' It was a long shot, but if the forest made him nervous then Vista had to use it.

'SHUT UP!' The magical ball swelled, glowing a deeper red and the fairies shuddered, many closing their eyes at the sight of it. Vista pretended not to notice as she went on, avoiding Grecko's fearful eyes watching her. They'd clearly hit a nerve.

Feeling her confidence rising, Vista continued to push, 'You're not welcome in the forest, Iggy. You took your magic and made it dark. I've seen magic and it's good – it's *you* that's evil, it's *you* that's wrong!' Vista stepped forward, breaking the gap between them. Being so close to Iggy repulsed Vista, but as she felt Iggy's unease, her heart skipped a beat. Her feet edged a little further forward and she tried to avoid the magical ball as it spat out crimson sparks.

I can do this.

'You think I'm the evil one? What about them?' he yelled, pointing at the trembling fairies, 'What about *her?*' His manic eyes turned to Lilleth, spit flying from the corners of his mouth as he screamed, 'SHE LEFT ME... SHE CHOSE THEM OVER ME!'

Iggy spun around and marched towards Lilleth, clenching his fists as he moved. Lilleth continued to stare at the floor, unable to face him and Iggy shot a look back at Vista, daring her to try and stop him. As he glared, the magical ball reflected in Iggy's dark eyes, making him look more insane than ever before. It continued to hover as sparks of wretched stench spewed out, making it hard to think.

Every eye was upon Vista, every face waiting for her next move. Without warning, Layla's words popped into her head. *How had I forgotten?*

Closing her eyes, she willed the noise and panicked pleas to fade away. Vista envisioned herself back in Layla's home and Layla whispering in her ear, *'There will be a sacrifice that you must make.'*

A sacrifice!

Aware of everyone still watching her, Vista tried to focus, avoiding Iggy's stare as he hovered over Lilleth. She risked a quick glance back at Grecko, forcing a smile through her watery eyes and mouthing the words, 'Thank you.'

Turning back to the ball, it amused her slightly that Iggy hadn't thought to freeze her – what kind of threat was a wingless fairy after all?

Taking one last look towards Iggy, she saw he had started towards her again, possibly sensing her change.

The room slowed. Time itself appeared to be stalling, allowing her an extra moment or so to process. Vista gazed at the fairies - her family - all crouching fearfully on the floor, held down by Iggy's magic. She thought of Grecko - her new family - hovering outside the Home Tree, forced to watch with no way of helping. She thought of Mila perhaps still hiding near the entrance. The room was full and yet so empty, Vista feeling completely alone in what she was about to do.

Her mind made up, Vista winked at Iggy. For the first time in her life she felt she was making the right decision. Iggy's face creased, her wink throwing him off guard.

Not wanting to give him a single moment to stop her, Vista took a deep breath, screwed her eyes tightly shut and threw herself into the magical ball.

23

The Way Things Were

As Vista entered the glowing ball, many sounds followed her. She heard the screams of the fairies, Iggy's shrieks of panic, and perhaps most painfully, Grecko's cry of pain.

Then she heard nothing. Everything went silent in a way that reminded her of her oldest memory; the moment just before Lilleth had collected her from her water flower. Vista could still remember the deep silence and the feeling of weightlessness that encompassed her within those blue petals.

Slowly, her body felt as though it was being encircled by magic; covering her and filling her entirely. Her body spun as the magic flowed through her, her limbs tingling – giving the sensation she was coming alive for the very first time.

She gasped and slowly opened her eyes, easing into her surroundings. Everything was white everywhere – no shapes, no shadows, just a white eternity spread out like the wings of a dove. Floating in this sort of stillness made her dizzy. Her body was weightless, creating the illusion of flying. She looked down at each of her arms and spread them all around her - nothing. The sheer emptiness was disorientating, but there was no pain like she had been expecting.

Is this death?

Before she could think anymore on it, she felt herself falling. Perhaps falling was the wrong word, it was more likely she was floating. She shut her eyes and floated down until she felt herself land, surprised to meet with a solid surface.

Where am I? She struggled to tell how long she'd been floating, it could have been anywhere between moments and an eternity.

Nervously, she opened her eyes as her blurry vision eased and she blinked rapidly, trying to focus. Colours swam before her – greens and reds and browns, it all seemed familiar. Her body felt stable again, rather than the floaty sensation she'd had before, and Vista was grateful for that. Using her fingers, she scratched at the floor beneath her, rubbing her hands over the familiar grooves. Hesitantly, Vista pushed herself upright and rubbed heavily on her eyes. It was like waking from a deep sleep. Blinking again, her vision softly returned. She was in the Home Tree – sitting just inches away from the spot in which she'd sacrificed herself just moments before.

Standing motionless in front of Vista were the fairies, their shocked faces all focused on her. Self-consciously, Vista tried to stand, but had barely made it to her knees before being engulfed by them all, burying her in hugs of gratitude and applause.

'What happened?' she asked, her voice muffled beneath fairy hair.

'You saved us all.' Lilleth stepped forward, her eyes were puffy and swollen and she dabbed at them self-consciously with her wrist. 'You sacrificed yourself to save us.'

'But... I don't understand. How am I still alive?' Vista didn't want to be dead, of course - it was more that she had *expected* to be dead.

'I'm afraid I can't answer that. But it seems you have been rewarded...' Lilleth gestured towards Vista's back and Vista followed her gaze.

Jumping up in shock, she saw two beautiful wings jutting out between her shoulder blades, identical to her originals. If Vista hadn't known any better she'd have guessed they'd never left.

'Wings? I have wings?' she questioned as joy spread across her face. Watching them for a moment, she felt herself jump as they began to flutter. *So that's what it feels like!* Her hands trembled with shock as she asked, 'But how? Does that make me a real fairy now?'

'I can't answer how, Vista, but you have always been a real fairy. Being different doesn't make you any less a part of our family. It simply shows how brave you are. It seems we fairies have forgotten how brave we used to be. Regardless of wings, you're one of us. I just wish you'd known that sooner.' Lilleth smiled, blinking away her tears.

Vista smiled back, enjoying this approachable side of her mother.

'Grecko!' His name hit her like a bolt of lightning, 'Where's Grecko?'

'It's okay, Miss Vista, I'm out 'ere.'

Vista turned to the branch to find Grecko hanging onto it awkwardly. 'Hold on, we'll come and get you down!'

'No need,' he huffed, heaving himself onto the branch. Clearly, it was much stronger than it looked. 'View's quite nice up 'ere, yer jus' take yer time in there...'

Smiling, she was almost knocked sideways by Mila, bounding over and embracing her.

'Welcome back!'

Welcome back... Vista hadn't considered that this might mean she was back. She smiled at Mila before absentmindedly making her way towards the branch and Grecko. He watched her approach, his face a mixture of pride and sadness.

'Glad ter see yer got yer wings back, Miss Vista,' he said, smiling sadly, 'That was a real risky thing yer did in there. I would 'av bin a mess if I'd lost yer.'

'I'm sorry... I just couldn't let anyone die.'

Grecko stared out at the view and puffed out his cheeks, 'Yeah, I know... what a day eh?'

Vista chuckled. Without warning she felt every emotion she'd been suppressing bubble to the surface, causing her to laugh and cry all at the same time.

Grecko cocked his head to the side and watched Vista, the sight of her weak with laughter rubbing off on him. Soon they were both helpless, the fairies inside peeking oddly at them. Vista thought they must have looked like the maddest creatures in all of Letherea, but she simply didn't care. Perhaps it was the shock.

'So...' Grecko wiped his eyes and fidgeted on the branch, 'I guess yer'll be staying 'ere now then?'

Vista turned on the branch and looked back at the Home Tree's entrance, fondly stroking her wings.

She thought of the fairies inside, of their community and love for each other, and found herself smiling. Her heart warmed with visions of flying with her family and soaring through the skies. Then, gazing out over the forest, Vista breathed in the cool air and pictured Grecko's hut. She realised, with amusement, that she truly did love their home; every dirty bit of it.

Everything she had learned about living in the forest was thanks to Grecko.

Looking towards him, she smiled. *I can have both.*

Vista couldn't think of a single good reason why she couldn't stay with Grecko and still be a fairy after this day – after all, Lilleth had just told her how brave she was. *Things could be different now.*

'Actually, I was hoping maybe I could stay with you?' she asked.

Grecko cocked his head and stared at Vista, afraid he might have misheard her. When she smiled and continued to nod her head, his face broke into a grin that threatened to split his cheeks in two.

'Oh, Miss Vista, I'd like that very much!' he said and reached out a hand. Vista climbed aboard, cuddling his thumb affectionately. 'Jus' gotta get me down from this tree first.' Grecko chuckled – he did look a bit ridiculous.

Vista made her way inside, with the intentions of saying goodbye. As she entered the Home Tree, the fairies gathered - it reminded Vista of the reception Lilleth used to receive whenever she entered a room. Awkwardly, she fidgeted with her dress, unsure of where to look, 'I just wanted to say...' she fumbled, twiddling her fingers, 'I wanted to say how important you all are to me. I was so afraid that Iggy would hurt you and destroy our home but he didn't and...' Nothing she could say felt like enough, 'I wanted so badly to keep you safe and I feel like I have...' Vista looked around at the faces before her, each one hanging on her every word, 'You will always be my family but I want to explore everything that Letherea has to offer. I'm going to be leaving with Grecko and go back into the forest. I would really love it if you would all come and visit me sometime?'

The fairies murmured amongst themselves, each one unsure of what to say. Then, from the back of the group came a small voice, it belonged to a fairy youngling whom Vista did not know the name of. 'What did you mean about fairies being the bringers of beauty?'

Vista was taken aback, in truth she'd forgotten she'd even mentioned that during her altercation with Iggy, 'Oh... well-'

'I think I can explain this one,' Lilleth stepped forward, composing herself. Her hair was still out of place but her face was slightly less puffy than before. She looked at Vista and smiled before facing the crowd, 'it's true that fairies were indeed the bringers of beauty - a long time ago. Vista has proven today that fairies are capable of much more than we give credit for and I-'

A noise outside made Lilleth pause, it sounded like the muffled cries of a newborn infant. Lilleth moved quickly to the window and listened, her face creased with concern - she appeared to know this cry. Without another word she flew out of the tree and down to the ground, Mila instinctively grabbed Vista and the rest of the fairies followed suit.

24

Saying Goodbye

Grecko, who had already awkwardly shuffled his way down the tree trunk, was crouching down by a nearby bush, his back to Lilleth and the others. A hush fell over them as Grecko turned around, holding in his hands a small infant. In fact, it was just one hand as this infant was only about half the size of Grecko's thumb.

'What is it?' Mila asked, looking directly at Vista as though she now held the answers to everything in Letherea.

Vista shook her head, *who would abandon an infant like this?* She searched around her but saw no-one, other than themselves. *The bushes are big, maybe they're hiding?* she considered.

Vista was just about to call Grecko and ask him to search the bushes with her when she caught sight of Lilleth.

Lilleth was barely blinking as she stared at the infant, a look of recognition on her face. Her eyes filled with tears, and she stifled a cry as she answered Mila's question, 'It's Iggy.'

Iggy?

Nobody said a word as Lilleth approached Grecko and held out her arms for the baby.

It was bizarre to look upon an infant whom you knew would one day grow to be so cruel, Vista wasn't sure how to feel about it. It felt wrong to look at a baby with such disdain and yet, after what Iggy had done, she struggled to look at him in any other way.

Grecko handed over Iggy but appeared to be just as conflicted, 'will he grow up ter be the same?' he asked, staring at the infant.

'No, Grecko, I'm sure he won't,' Lilleth reassured him, 'Iggy was a symptom of his surroundings – he learned about his magic surrounded by fear and anxiety towards it. I see now that trying to prevent him using his magic did more harm to him than good. He never learnt how to control it – he never had the chance to be an imp.' Lilleth looked down at the baby in her arms and then turned her attention to Vista, 'I made a mistake keeping him the first time. The love you displayed for everyone must have reversed Iggy's potion. The qualities Iggy taught it to detest – strength, hope, trust and loyalty – were all qualities that he believed the Home Tree and the fairies had lied about possessing.' Lilleth blinked away tears, the sight still jarring to Vista, 'By sacrificing yourself, you displayed them in their purest, strongest form and Iggy hadn't prepared for that. It forced it to transform from a potion to destroy, into a potion to rectify, to set things back the way they were. It gave you back your wings, and it gave Iggy his second chance.'

'So, imps ain't all as bad as Iggy was?' Grecko interrupted.

'In truth, I've never met another imp but I don't believe they are.' Lilleth pulled Iggy closer before eyeing Grecko with an apologetic look, 'Many have suffered because of Iggy's hate, but I think you have suffered more than most. I want you to know that magic may revert potions but it can never go away completely – it always leaves a mark. Iggy will likely remember what he did to you and your family some-how. He won't understand his memories, of course, but they will plague him throughout his life – showing up as nightmares, most likely. They'll be his burden to bear.'

Sighing, Grecko looked at the baby, his face showing the slightest bit of pity. It seemed harsh that an innocent baby would have to suffer for his past self's crimes.

Lilleth called for the attention of all the fairies, 'Iggy is innocent now, and deserves to be with his own kind. I'm going to take him to them,' she paused before continuing, 'We will continue our discussion when I return, I feel it may be time to make some changes.'

Lilleth stood for a moment, looking at everyone. Imps hadn't been seen in the magical forest for quite some time, so it would likely be a while before she located Iggy's kind.

With a nurturing hold and a flap of her wings, Lilleth and Iggy were away. Lilleth's figure glistened as the morning sun kissed her wings. Birds flew around her but she did not look up – her eyes remained downwards, carefully watching the infant that she cradled so lovingly. The forest grew quiet as they flew away. The birds that went to Lilleth returned to their treetops as she drifted out of sight, not even the breeze blew.

Vista thought over how tightly Lilleth held Iggy in her arms, and awed at how strong a mother's love could be.

A buzz started circulating over the changes that were to come, but Vista decided to broach the subject of the fairies' safety within the forest another time. *There's been enough drama for one day.*

Once Vista had been hugged more times that she could ever recall and watched Grecko awkwardly shake fingers with some very grateful fairies, she knew it was time to leave. The Home Tree was safe again, but she knew this wouldn't be the last time she'd see it. Things felt different this time.

When she hugged Mila, it lasted a little longer than the others. Mila held on extra tight, and Vista was sure she'd heard a slight whimper as Mila pulled away. Affectionately, Vista patted her on the arm and smiled.

'I'll see you again soon, okay?'

'Miss Vista, yer ready ter go?' Grecko sat cross-legged in front of her.

'I'm ready.' Vista smiled and went to climb into his hand.

'Uh... I reckon yer forgetting 'bout summit?' he chuckled, motioning to her back.

For a moment Vista had forgotten, she'd grown so used to being carried – she'd even allowed Mila to carry her down from the Home Tree during all the commotion over the infant's cry.

'I-I'm not sure Grecko-' she was interrupted by a chorus of fairy voices, all urging her to give her wings a chance. Vista looked around at them nervously. Despite feeling her wings flutter this time - as natural as wiggling her fingers - there was still that knot in her stomach at the thought of trusting them again.

'Yer be fine,' Grecko said encouragingly, 'Trust me.' He wore a relaxed, knowing smile and Vista knew she didn't really have a choice. *I can't expect him to carry me forever.*

'Alright... I'll try,' she swallowed hard, a lump in her throat the size of her fist.

The fairies behind her cheered as she focused on Grecko. Vista felt a pair of arms wrap around her waist and turned to see Mila gripping her tightly. 'You'll be brilliant!' she announced, closing her eyes and squealing with excitement.

In truth, the enthusiasm and confidence surrounding Vista only made her more nervous. It almost seemed worse to fall when everyone felt so confident.

'If yer want, yer can jump from me hand, Miss Vista,' Grecko said quietly to her, 'I reckon the branch might be sorta scary ter jump from after the first time.'

Vista looked at him with relief. *He understands.*

She gave a small nod and Grecko placed his hand out for her to climb onto. Obligingly, Mila stepped backwards, joining the other fairies as they all huddled together on the ground, excitedly looking up at Grecko and Vista.

Vista could feel her body shaking, her lips quivered as she reached back to touch her wings, feeling them flutter beneath her touch.

I can do this, she told herself.

'Now don't forget, yer one o' the fairies. Yer a family. It ain't jus' yerself – never 'as bin.' Grecko reminded her, 'I'll always catch yer!' he added, winking as he did so.

Vista smiled anxiously towards him, 'Thanks, Grecko.'

She felt his arm extend outwards, and the sound of fairies cheering her name rose up from the ground below. *I can do this, I can do this, I can do this.*

Glancing briefly at the ground, she paused and looked back at Grecko – still wearing his encouraging smile. 'I got yer an' yer got all of us...' he reminded her again.

Giving his thumb a squeeze, she teetered a foot slowly off the edge of his hand and paused.

With her eyes closed, she could feel the coolness of the air on her cheeks and tried to imagine how it would feel to have the wind brush against her face whilst flying. Her breathing quickened as she tried hard not to think of her first fall, and she rubbed her palms against her dress in an attempt to wipe the sweat from them.

Just do it!

Fluttering her wings, Vista jumped.

That's when she felt it – a jolt through her spine as her wings burst open and sprang into life. The wind made a whistling noise as it glided past them and Vista shrieked with delight. Her breath caught in her chest and the fairies below exploded into applause, each one of them flapping their own wings and taking to the air to join her. Grecko laughed and cheered, swinging his arms ecstatically as he watched from the ground.

She'd never seen the world from this angle before – it was breath-taking. Tears stung her eyes and her heart fluttered in her chest, so fast it seemed to be humming. Vista flew to the tops of the trees, and grinning wildly, launched herself down, the wind pushing her hair back and flushing her cheeks. Her fellow fairies followed, all laughing and applauding as they went. She spun in mid-air, allowing her wings to carry her in every direction as she spread her arms out and closed her eyes, feeling free. Tilting forwards, Vista dove into the flowers, flying through the petals and rising engulfed in their flowery scents. The fairies around her ducked and dove, flying around to admire her new wings.

'You did it Vista!'

'How does it feel?'

'You can fly!'

Vista felt so free, the most free she had ever felt in her life. She was finally who she was meant to be.

Her wings carried her back down towards Grecko, and he beamed at her proudly.

She flew towards his face and kissed him lovingly on the forehead, 'Thank you Grecko!' she said.

The fairies flew down to join them, each one congratulating her once again. There was no doubt in her mind that she would no longer feel alone.

'Yer ready now, Miss Vista?' Grecko asked, after flying for a while longer.

'Yes, let's go,' she said, hugging each fairy goodbye for the hundredth time.

Turning to go, Grecko walking and Vista flying beside him, she thought over how leaving the Home Tree didn't feel quite so frantic as it had done the last time.

'Grecko?' Vista said, slightly breathless.

Grecko peeked at her out of the corner of his eye and chuckled. Without saying a word, he held out his hand and Vista floated down onto his palm, relaxing into the familiarity of it.

'Thank you! My wings will strengthen soon, I'm sure,' Vista giggled, curling up comfortably and resting against his thumb.

Grecko smiled in return, 'I'm sure they will.' He didn't seem to mind one bit.

Out of nowhere, a flash of rainbow colours appeared and rested upon Grecko's shoulder.

Vista gasped in amazement, 'Grecko, look, it's a wishing bird!' Her tiredness forgotten, she bounced ecstatically in his palm, jumping up and down before immediately trying to contain her excitement, not wanting to scare it away.

'I've heard all about these birds, but I've never actually seen one. You've got to make a wish, Grecko, they're the rules!'

Grecko smiled broadly at Vista. Slowly, he tilted his head to one side and looked at the bird.

What more could he possibly wish for?

THE END.

ACKNOWLEDGMENTS

None of this would have been possible without the incredible support of everyone at Smashbear Publishing. Thank you so much to the entire team for taking a chance on this story and helping send it out into the world.

A special thank you to Loredana Carini, for all her patience and encouragement throughout this process and a huge thanks to Zola, Marija, Molly and Belinda for their hard work and perseverance in making this book as polished as it could possibly be. I sincerely hope we can all work together again one day.

To my partner Layla (I know you get embarrassed with compliments) but you have been so supportive throughout this entire process. You've shared in my excitement and stayed up late with me when I couldn't stop writing, letting me bounce ideas off you whenever needed. I couldn't have done this without you!

To my Dad – you're the reason I felt confident enough to keep writing. You encouraged me when I didn't have the confidence to keep going and without your support, my dream would never have become a reality.

To my Mum – you've always been there for me, always so certain I could accomplish my dreams and I'll always be grateful to you.

To Jo and Alex – you guys have gone above and beyond in getting the word out for The Wing Thief, always there to help with social media when I found it too confusing! Who knows how many more people will have seen this book thanks to you two. Thank you both so much!

To Dan and Kirsty – I'll never forget your help towards getting The Wing Thief published. Without you both, I would have been stuck. You stepped in when you knew I needed help and I'll never forget it. I'm so thankful to you both.

Thank you so much to everyone. I love you all and can't believe how lucky I am to be able to share this incredible experience with you.

ABOUT THE AUTHOR

Samantha Atkins launches her debut novel with '*The Wing Thief*'. She currently lives in Wales with her partner, their two children and two dogs; Stella and Lexi.

Printed in Great Britain
by Amazon